SPIDER-MAN®

THE
LIZARD
SANCTION

SPIDER-MAN®

THE LIZARD SANCTION

DIANE DUANE

ILLUSTRATIONS BY
DARICH ROBERTSON & SCOTT HOBLISH

BYRON PREISS MULTIMEDIA COMPANY, INC.
NEW YORK

BOULEVARD BOOKS, NEW YORK

Special thanks to Lou Aronica, Ginjer Buchanan, Lucia Raatma, Eileen Veith, Julia Molino, Ken Grobe, and the gang at Marvel Creative Services

SPIDER-MAN: THE LIZARD SANCTION

A Boulevard Book
A Byron Preiss Multimedia Company, Inc. Book

PRINTING HISTORY
Putnam hardcover edition/October 1995
Boulevard edition/August 1996

The Putnam Berkley World Wide Web site address is
http://www.berkley.com

Check out the Byron Preiss Multimedia Company
World Wide Web site address:
http://www.byronpreiss.com

ISBN 1-57297-148-7

BOULEVARD
Boulevard Books are published by The Berkley Publishing Group,
200 Madison Avenue, New York, NY 10016.
BOULEVARD and its logo are trademarks
belonging to Berkley Publishing Corporation.

PRINTED IN THE UNITED STATES OF AMERICA

10   9   8   7   6   5   4   3   2   1

ACKNOWLEDGMENTS

Many thanks to Jim Dumoulin of Kennedy Space Center, maintainer of the Center's home pages on the World Wide Web, for much useful information.

Thanks also to Paul McGrath for technical assistance, and to Peter Morwood for advice on militaria, and for secretarial and catering services.

For Joe Motes, Ruthanne Devlin,
and the many other nice people associated
with SeaTrek '89:
with thanks for a happy trip to Miami and southward,
not forgotten yet—not by a long shot . . .

Now, just take a look at that," said a voice out of the predawn darkness. "Did you ever see a bug that big in your life?"

It was a fair question. Southern Florida was famous for a lot of things, but one that didn't get as much attention as the tourist attractions and the balmy climate was the insect life. There in the near-darkness, Airman Ron Moore stood gazing down at his feet and shook his head. He shifted the machine gun he was carrying from the crook of one arm to the other, eyeing the glossy brown-black palmetto bug that wandered past his shoes, waving its antennae in apparent nonchalance as it went about its business. It must have been at least four inches long from its head to the ends of its wing-cases.

"I don't know," Ron said as his friend Lyle came up from behind him. "I would have thought something this big would violate the square-cube law, huh, Lyle?"

"From the size of it," Lyle said, "I bet it could violate any law it liked, as far as bug laws go."

"No, I mean the law about how big critters can get without having backbones."

"Oh." Lyle breathed out, a small laughing sound in the night as the palmetto bug wandered off. "I'd say this one ought to get at least a ticket, then. A moving violation—walking while invertebrated." He peered at it as it trundled past him. "Or exceeding the federally mandated number of legs. Would that be a misdemeanor or a felony?"

"Bug misdemeanors," Ron said, sighing. "You need a reality transplant, you know that, Lyle?" He turned to look behind them at the one source of light besides the setting moon, a few days short of being full. The moonlight glistened rough on the marshland all around them and the water close by, but the next best source of illumination was Launch Complex 39, a mile and a half east of them.

It was not lit up like a Christmas tree, as it would be in eleven days' time when STS-83 went up. With the budget as tight as it was these days, there was no point in leaving the lights on all night. Anyway, it upset the migrating birds, not to mention the local bats. With the Shuttle still just behind them in the Vehicle Assembly Building, pad 39-A itself was quiet, though not quite all in the dark: two of the forty big Xenon spots were on, trained down low on the Fixed Service Structure near ground level, and giving light to the people running final inspections on the huge north-side LOX tanks before they were filled in the next couple of days. That was not a job that Ron would have wanted, himself. Being that close to high explosives made him twitch.

Not that tonight's job was exactly the equivalent of being rocked to sleep, either. He glanced over at Lyle, who had turned away from his examination of the palmetto bug and was giving other matters his attention again.

"No sign of it yet," he said, shifting his gun again.

"Nope," Ron said. "I thought we would have seen it by now."

Lyle shook his head, scuffed his boots on the concrete a little, and whistled a few notes' brief imitation of the little peeper-frogs whose tiny voices filled the night. Ron had wondered whether Lyle knew something more about this cargo than he was letting on. That wouldn't have been out of the ordinary. Ron was Air Force; Lyle was NASA Security, and though in the strictly military pecking order he didn't count, Lyle could sometimes be counted on to know things that the military side wasn't told.

"Transport came in at two," Ron said. "Or so I was told."

Lyle nodded. Canaveral Air Force Base saw a fair amount of freight traffic, but little cargo came in so late unless it was somehow sensitive. Night flights attracted notice just by their relative scarcity. This one had come in with a jet escort: a pair of Phantoms, with all the hard points occupied and the safeties off the fighters' guns. The big C-130 transport had touched down on 12 Left, its escort sweeping by on either side as it decelerated, and then both jets had circled overhead, keeping watch until the Herc got onto the taxiway and down to the apron, where the security detachment in their jeeps and trucks were waiting for it.

"Not late," Lyle said, "I don't think. They just wanted to make sure that everything was in order before they started moving things around."

"Things," Ron said softly. Lyle laughed again, and looked down the canal.

The big concrete apron on which they stood was somewhat better lit than 39-A, though, again, not overly bright, for the sake of the birds and bats, and so as not to attract attention in other ways. Right behind them, the VAB towered up, the flag and Bicentennial star on its upper reaches showing in pale and dark grays in the moonlight, its lower walls much brighter in the mercury lights shining down on the parking and haulage aprons. The apron on which Ron and Lyle stood was part of the main haulage and access area, right between the pool at the end of the barge canal and the VAB proper, and just in front of its east door. Ron and Lyle were only two of about forty USAF and NASA security people scattered around to secure the VAB perimeter, and the barge docking and loading area on the west side of the canal's terminal pool. There were other people there too, not uniformed—mission supervisors and scientists, mostly from Johnson, consulting various kinds of instruments, or else just standing, waiting, empty-handed, gazing out toward the water, down to where the other end of the canal met the Banana River.

Ron looked out too. Lyle said, "See that? On the left."

Very faint, far out on the dark water of the river that splits the Cape in two the long way, a little light moved like a red star. Shortly thereafter, a green one showed to its left. A breath or so later, a loud annoyed sound came floating up from the eastern end of the canal, like an aging comedienne going "Haaah, haaah, haaah" at someone's bad joke.

"Ducks," Lyle said. "There's a bunch of them nesting down there."

Ron raised his eyebrows. The wildlife around here had

never paid much attention to the act of Congress that turned this scrubby, marshy coastline into Cape Canaveral. NASA, seeing no reason to be a bad neighbor, especially to endangered species, let them be most of the time—though at launch times most of the birds were encouraged by Air Force falconers to clear out for a day or so. They always came back without much fuss, though, and complained at passing traffic in the air and on the water as if they thought they owned it.

Now the barge coasted silently past the nesting sites in the reeds at the canal's far end, and the ducks got quiet again.

"There were a lot of guys sent out to do far-perimeter work earlier," Ron said. "Out by the public road."

Lyle nodded. "I heard about that. Guess the trouble they were expecting didn't materialize."

"Just as well," said Ron. "I guess the hour helped."

Lyle laughed softly. "More likely telling people that the thing wasn't coming in until next week helped, too."

They walked a few steps together, keeping one eye on the canal as they examined the flat bare area of concrete they had been told to police. Past them went a couple of NASA specialists, one in a lab coat with a radiometer, one in a T-shirt that said "The Dream is Alive," both wearing the proper new ID badges: Ron and Lyle nodded to them as they went.

"Interesting," Lyle said, "the way they changed the badges all of a sudden last week."

Ron nodded. Such things happened often enough, but rarely without a few weeks' warning, bureaucracy being what it was. This change, though—new badge format, new photos, holographic fingerprints embossed into the badges, new scanners with which to read both them and the wearer's hand—had been imposed on both sides, USAF and NASA, with no warning at all. "You get the feeling," Ron said, "that someone Upstairs was worried about—?" He wouldn't name any names, just pointed with his chin at the barge lights coming toward them from down the canal.

Lyle scuffed again, paused, looked up: they both turned and

slowly started to pace back the way they had come. "Hard to tell," he said. "You hear a lot of scuttlebutt, you don't know what to make of half of it. Most of it's bull. All the same . . ." Lyle frowned. He was a big, heavy-featured man; in the dim reflected light from the VAB, his eyebrows and his cheekbones had more shadows than they usually did, making him look slightly sinister. "You've heard the news lately. I don't think it's the public protest that's bothering the higher-ups, so much—the people who've been marching out there aren't violent—"

"With this much explosive stuff around," Ron muttered, glancing back toward 39-A, "I wouldn't want to get violent, either."

"Well, no. But I think there may be more to it. We've been seeing a lot of the Coast Guard people lately—"

"So have we," Ron said. It was something he had been wondering about. "Normally they're busy further south."

Lyle nodded. "Something's up. Nothing really major, to judge by the signs, but all the same, cutters are popping up like mushrooms after a rainstorm, and people are acting pretty nervous. Were you told particularly not to listen to any excuses from people not wearing the proper ID?"

"Just run 'em in, the Boss told me," Ron said. They came down to the barge-landing dock again, and stood there, with several other USAF and NASA security people, now, watching the barge drift slowly down the canal toward them. Ron could hear the faintest *putt-putt-putt* noise emitting from it.

"And if trouble started, shoot first, ask questions later?"

Ron looked at Lyle just a little sidelong. These were not matters one normally discussed "in the clear." Their different services usually had slightly different approaches to such problems. But Ron nodded slowly. "Unusual," he said, very softly. "Normally they would want to wring someone out pretty conclusively, rather than. . . ."

There was a small silence. "It suggests," Lyle said in as low a voice, "that the people who might be, shall we say, breaching security wouldn't be expected to know anything worth wringing out of them. Or, if they did, then whatever they're up to is likely to be so dangerous, the Folks Upstairs would rather they were shot out of hand—even at the cost of intelligence about what they were after."

Ron nodded. "Not nice," he said. "But you're right. There's an atmosphere as if people think someone is taking an unhealthy interest in things down here. Unusual." He shivered a little, an odd response on a warm night.

The *putt-putt-putt* was loud now, threatening to drown out, however briefly, the noise of the peepers. The barge was almost out of the canal and into the docking pool, its ghostly reflection preceding it in the water. Another brief ruffle of duck squawks, then quiet again as it passed the reed beds at the near end where the canal and the pool met.

The barge was one of the typical long, low ones that usually carried the Shuttle's pairs of reusable solid-fuel boosters to the VAB for mating. The boosters were flown into Canaveral Air Force Base from the contractor in Utah, then boated over and up, this being considered safer than subjecting them to the shocks of even brief overland travel. One side of the pool was flattened to take the barge side-on, and the dock there was reinforced to take the heavy unloading cranes necessary to lift the boosters off and truck them into the VAB.

The usual long cargo was missing from the barge's upper deck this time, but the barge still rode very low in the water. There were a couple of men on deck—one in a NASA windbreaker, another in USAF uniform. Dim red lights showed in the ship's cabin, and very dim white ones from the below-decks hatchway.

There was no rush forward to warp the barge in. The guys with the instruments stepped forward and moved toward the barge as cautiously as if they expected it to blow up at any moment. Ron cocked an eye at Lyle. "I thought they said that this cargo was fairly routine."

Lyle looked at him. "Compared to what? I think these

things can get awfully relative. And it strikes me that Upstairs has no problem giving us a little disinformation. They've done it before."

They watched the science team holding out their various instruments: things that might have been Geiger counters, one that looked more like a prop from a science fiction movie than anything else, and another one that looked like a fly-fishing pole. Lyle chuckled a little under his breath. "What're they gonna do," he muttered, "check it for trout?"

Ron smiled slightly. "Well, at least we've got past the bug jokes. Think we'll make it any further up the evolutionary ladder before our coffee break?"

One of the scientists looked up then. "Hey, Maddy," he said, "come take a look at this, would you?" Another of the team, one of the windbreaker-wearers, came over and put his head over the railings, looked in slight alarm at the barge.

There was a splash. All around the dock, heads snapped toward the water. Ron lifted his gun a bit higher.

On the barge, a figure came out of the wheelhouse, looked around. From behind the boat came the much louder and closer "Haaah, haaah, haaah" of another duck. The officer on the barge—its captain, Ron judged from the stripes on his windbreaker's sleeves—looked over at the ripples spreading in the water, then over at the people on the dock, and said, "One of you guys drop something?"

People on the dock muttered, peered, denied anything to do with the splash. The duck went on with its noisy protests for perhaps a minute or so; the barge's second officer came out of the wheelhouse as well, and the two of them looked around the boat, seeing nothing which might have caused the noise. The two scientists who had been conferring now looked over at the barge's officers.

"You about ready?" said the captain.

"In a moment, Cap'n," said the man with the "fishing pole." "Not quite sure why you should be spilling so much beta."

The duck started quacking again, a louder and more insistent noise. People on the dock laughed. "Sounds like you forgot to pay toll on the way up," one of them said.

The suggestion was greeted with chuckles from the barge crew. "Heaven forbid anybody on this run should be denied their proper overtime," the captain said. "Mike's got a sandwich—we'll take care of them on the way out."

More splashing ensued—and then a single much larger splash. The captain turned, looking out toward the pool.

The problem was not there. Something vaguely human-shaped, but much bigger, with an odd, slick sheen to its skin, was clambering up out of the water onto the dock. Ron, gazing at this, first thought that someone from the barge or the dock had fallen in—but that wasn't the case. Anyway, no one on the security team looked like that. No uniform—was that some kind of diving suit? It looked almost scaled. But since when did diving suits have tails?

That tail whipped fiercely from side to side as the creature clambered up onto the dock, glared around it. It braced itself then with its forelimbs, and with its hind legs and tail gave the barge a great push and sent it almost staggering back into the water, away from the dock. The barge wallowed and rocked, and big backwash ripples came rushing and splashing up onto the dock. The creature leapt off the dock then, splashed down into the water, and in two strokes and a leap, was clambering up onto the side of the barge.

Ron glanced at Lyle, who stood there understandably slack-jawed, and then at the others. All around, weapons were being leveled at the barge, but all the other security people were exchanging the same shocked, horrified looks. Their instructions had been clear enough. Use weapons as they must, but under no circumstances must the cargo be shot at: it was too delicate, or too dangerous, to risk a bullet. People had drawn their own conclusions from those instructions, some of them probably erroneous, but in any case no one wanted to be the first to fire—and certainly not without a clear target.

The barge captain had one, though, if no one else did. As

the creature jumped back into the water after pushing the barge away, he was already drawing his gun. By the time the thing had climbed up the side of the barge and was putting its head up over the gunwale, the captain already had the gun leveled and took aim right between the thing's eyes. As calmly as anyone could have under such circumstances, the captain said, "Hold it right there, mister!"

The scaly creature paid no attention, but went straight for him—and the gun might as well not even have been there. A great inhuman noise, halfway between a roar and a snarl, was the only answer the captain got. He managed to get just one shot off. Where it went, there was no telling: judging by the whine of the ricochet, it missed. Barely a moment later, the creature was on him. Ron had one shocked sight of the captain's face, frozen in astonishment and horror, as he went down. The second officer came at the thing, but the great green scaled shape backhanded him to one side as if he was a rag doll.

Behind Ron, Lyle was indulging himself in a splendid flow of language which Ron really wished he'd heard while still in grade school, and lifted his gun to sight as the second officer went down.

"In this light?" Ron said softly. Lyle squinted down the length of the barrel, then let it drop, and let out one helpless breath that was more of a curse than anything he'd said out loud. Things were moving too fast: in this light, it would be too easy to hit one of their own by accident, never mind the cargo they weren't supposed to hit. Closer to the dock, two of the security men slung their guns over their shoulders, kicked their shoes off, and dove, two clean, fast splashes.

Over the quick, short, economical sounds of their strokes, came other sounds. The creature on the barge went thundering and thumping down the stairs from the deck into the barge's below-decks cargo space. A crash, as a door was burst open: a breath's space, and then semiautomatic fire—several short bursts. Lyle cursed again at the sound of an immense crash—

then a moment's stillness. The people on the dock looked at each other in horrified surprise.

Then sound again: thrashing, bumping, shouts—"No, what are you—!" "Get away from that!" "No!!" Another crash. Another silence, longer. The men in the water swarmed up over the side of its barge by the access ladders at the bow and amidships.

From belowdecks came one last immense crack of sound, a splintering, breaking noise. The barge swayed, listed to its port, away from the dock. The security men began to unsling their weapons but had no time to do anything more. With dreadful speed, that big, lithe bipedal figure came swarming up out of the barge's cargo hold again. The first of the security men went at the thing, catching one outflung arm and pulling it back behind the creature, not bent, but straight—the first part of the old elbow-breaking move, usually a surefire crippler and guaranteed to give an assailant so much pain to deal with that there wouldn't be time or inclination for resistance. This creature, though, simply jerked its arm forward again. All the security man's strength couldn't stop it, and the creature flung him forward and right into the bulkhead, to lie beside the captain and second officer.

The second security man launched himself in a splendid front snap kick at the thing's knee that should have brought the creature crashing down. But the blow had no more effect than if he'd kicked a tree, and the creature merely grabbed him by the scruff in one huge clawed paw or hand, shook him, and threw him overboard.

Abruptly, from behind the creature, a third security guard, whom Ron hadn't seen, came up over the gunwales behind the creature. He leapt and took it right around the throat with one forearm and pulled back hard. Ron gulped, waiting to hear the crack. But there wasn't any. The creature bent itself convulsively forward, threw the hapless security guard over its back, and as he hit the deck and rolled, and even then tried to bring his gun to bear, it grabbed the gun from him and bludgeoned the man away with it—then threw the gun overboard after the last man.

The barge was listing further and further to port. The creature paused there, threw a look over its shoulder at the crowd on the dock. A clear shape, briefly isolated, everyone else down: it was the moment. Ron cocked his rifle and fired, then cocked and fired again. All around him, shots winged and whined through the air. There was the occasional shower of sparks, a ricochet from a bulkhead—someone's marksmanship going very awry: their bosses would have words with them later. That roar went up again. Then the creature leapt into the water. A mighty splash, and it was gone.

A hubbub and brangle of angry voices broke out in the dock area: orders were shouted, and more people jumped into the water, swam out with lines. The barge was reefed in, tied up. The scientists standing around with their "fishing poles" and Geiger counters put them down or dropped them, and hurried over to help.

Ron was one of the first aboard, Lyle close behind him. Others were already trying to help the captain and his second officer. Someone else was on the honker, calling for assistance. Away back on the dock, in the direction of the VAB, the stuttering red lights of the emergency vehicles could be seen approaching.

Ron and Lyle and others moved among the hurt men, helping them up where possible, making them comfortable when it wasn't. Others got down in the water and helped fish out the man who had been chucked overboard. He had come up for air, spluttering, not much the worse for wear, except for some nips from outraged ducks. The question everyone was asking him, and the captain and the first officer, was simply, "What was that?"

The captain sat against the bulkhead, still rather stunned, but clear enough that he knew what he'd seen. "I thought the dinosaurs were all extinct," he said. "That thing—it had big jaws, like a Gila monster's. Mean little eyes. It looked at me before it hit me. Something in it enjoyed what it was doing." He shook his head, moaned a little as one of the security men tried to straighten out his arm. "No, don't—it's busted. Wait for the EMTs."

Ron noticed again the way the boat was leaning in the water. Downstairs, other people were checking the cargo. One of them, a NASA security man named George, came up the stairs, and Ron said to him, "How is it down there?"

George shook his head. "Got a big hole in the side—she's taking water pretty quick. We need to get her unloaded and then up onto the ramp, before she swamps and sinks."

"I thought these couldn't sink," Ron said.

"They're not supposed to get holes punched in 'em like that, either," George said. He gestured with his head down the stairway. "Looks like our boy lost his temper pretty good down there."

One of the scientists down in the hold stuck his head up into the stairwell. "Milissa, you want to come down here and check me on something?"

A small handsome brunette woman came down the deck and went downstairs to join him. A few minutes of bumping, grunting, and shifting noises ensued. Then Milissa could be heard saying, not loudly, but with great feeling, "Mist!"

Ron looked over at Lyle. " 'Mist'?"

"Computer game of some kind, isn't it?" Lyle said.

"Not the way she said it."

Ron went over to where a couple of the other security people were still working with the captain. Milissa and George both came upstairs, then, and they both looked as grim as a month of rainy Sundays. "Harry," Milissa said to another of the scientists, "you'd better get on the horn to Ops *right* now. We have a big problem."

"Why? What? Didn't—" His eyes widened. "Oh, no—"

"The cargo manifest," Milissa said. "We went through it twice . . . and we're short one object down there. Just one."

"Not—"

"Item fourteen eighteen."

Harry went ashen, even in this light. "I'll call the front office," he said, and jumped off the barge, hit the dock, and kept on running.

The ambulance had pulled up now. Kurt, one of the night-shift EMTs, slipped past and knelt down beside the captain, and seemingly from nowhere, without asking questions, produced an inflatable splint for his arm. The captain, who had been following Milissa and George's conversation, looked paler than a broken arm alone would suggest—so much so that Kurt stopped to check his pulse a second time, halfway through the splinting. Ron looked at the captain and said, "Fourteen eighteen?"

"If we don't find it," the captain said, again too calmly for the circumstances, "we are all in for a very difficult . . . uh, rest of our lives, I would say." He sighed. "And here I was two months off retirement . . ."

"The minor payloads are all in place," a voice was saying to another figure coming rapidly up the dock. "However—"

"What's missing?"

"Fourteen eighteen."

Backlit by the yellow flashing light of the car that had brought him in, a lean tall dark-haired man stepped from the dock onto the deck, and took in everything in one long sweeping glance: the injured men, the pale, sweating scientists, the list of the barge.

"Evening, Dan," said the barge captain.

Dan looked down at him. The expression was cool, and not one Ron ever wanted turned on him. This man was the Cape's night Ops supervisor, widely believed to be capable of roasting even four-star USAF generals with a look and a choice word when they got in the way of the smooth running of what he considered his operation. "You look awful, Rick," he said. "Get your butt over to the hospital right now. Then I want a debrief. You, you, you—" he pointed at Milissa and George and the head of the USAF security team "—I want a debrief in five minutes. Mike—" this to another of the NASA security people "—get onto the CG and have them get a cutter and the Harbor Patrol out. I want divers down, and I want the Banana River exit sealed and netted. Where did whoever that was go?"

"Down . . . but it didn't come up, sir."

"Diving gear?"

"No evidence of any."

"Doesn't prove a thing. If they move fast, they may still have time to catch it. Go."

The security man to whom Dan had been speaking went off in a hurry. Another one whispered, not meaning to be heard, "And what if we can't find it?"

Dan turned slowly and looked at him—a look that could have been sliced, curled, and dropped into the bottom of a martini. "I hear Outer Mongolia is very nice this time of year," he said.

As if on cue, several people jumped into the water behind him. Ron hefted his gun. "Boss," he said to Lieutenant Rice, the senior USAF security officer who had just climbed onto the barge, "I got a clean shot at that thing. I *know* I hit it. It wasn't just some guy in a Kevlar bodysuit."

"No," the lieutenant said. "That much at least is plain. Not that it's going to make any difference to our careers." He sighed. "Come on—let's help them shift that cargo out of there before this boat goes down. Then—" He flicked a glance back at Pad 39-A.

"Will it go anyway?"

"Oh, it'll go," Lieutenant Rice said. "Question is . . . will we."

Ron gulped and went below to help move cargo.

pider-Man swung across the rooftops of Manhattan. The summer sun shone down on New York City, reflecting off the buildings like rows of skyscraping jewelry. Today, he barely noticed. Web-swinging, which was often a release and a joy for him, one of the things that made being Spider-Man so much fun, held no allure even on this bright, sunny day. Ever since Mary Jane went away, he frankly hadn't had much taste for anything.

He stopped that train of thought and chucked it out, pretending to drop it to the pavement dozens of yards below. It wasn't like she was going to be gone forever.

She had turned to him one morning a couple of weeks ago, after the business with Venom and the Hobgoblin had had ten days or so to settle, and she'd said cheerfully, and in the kindest possible way, "Sweetie, I need a rest from your life."

"Excuse me?" Peter had said.

She'd touched his cheek, then. "I didn't mean to make it sound that permanent. Look, Tiger . . . I just need a break. I got a card from Aunt Anna last week. She said, 'Why don't you come down and see me next week?' And, well, why don't I? I've been telling her for the past three years that I would come down to Miami as soon as work permitted. And things have gotten busy . . ."

"Yeah," Peter said, "I know, I've been meaning to find a way for us to get down there."

"So, look," MJ said, "the time for this trip isn't going to just happen. That doesn't even happen in normal people's lives, let alone ours. I think I need to make the time. I think I need to go see her . . . if only to get her off my case. The tone of that last card was edging just a little bit toward sharp. So I'm going to head on down. I'm not going to hurry. I'll take the train. I haven't taken the train for a long time—it's a lot better now, they say, than it used to be."

"I don't know, MJ," Peter said. "Trains get derailed. They get delayed. And besides, the plane's cheaper . . ."

"It's cheaper because they get rid of you in two hours," MJ said. "Whereas this takes you overnight."

"But people get killed on trains—"

"Only in novels," MJ said firmly. "And only on classy trains. I am sure no one ever got assassinated on an Amtrak train. The atmosphere'd be completely wrong. You," she said, winding her arms around his neck, "just don't want me to go anywhere without you."

"That's absolutely right," Peter admitted, shamefaced, and hugged her. "Am I that transparent?"

She smiled at him gently. "You'd make a great window," she said. "You missed your calling. Except that somebody has to be Spider-Man."

He chuckled.

"You just don't want me to leave."

Several minutes later, when he came up for air, Peter said, "No, I don't. Ever."

She looked at him sidewise. "It's going to get crowded in the bathroom."

"You know what I mean."

"Yes," she said, "but do you know what I mean? Peter—" She hugged him again. "To let the other person breathe, sometimes you have to let go just a little. I know it's an act of faith. But do you seriously think that if you let go just a little, I wouldn't come back?"

"Well, no—but—"

"Then relax." She smiled at him. "I'll miss you too. A lot. I just need—" She shrugged. "Call it a vacation in the normal world. Where superheroes and super-villains are something you hear about on the news but don't see much of."

"You're sure it's just two weeks?" Peter said, pulling MJ close again.

She smiled, and hugged him. "For a hero," she said, "you can be such a weenie sometimes. Anyway, there's something else that needs doing. I've got to see about scaring up some work. There simply doesn't seem to be any film or TV work for me in this town lately."

"I noticed," Peter said. She was being a lot kinder about this statement than she had to be. MJ had had to walk out on her last near-commitment on discovering that New York was apparently about to be blown up, and Spider-Man was apparently going to be stuck in the middle of it. It still astounded Peter, in those dark moments he sometimes experienced in the middle of the night, that MJ had not taken the offer which the producers of that show had made her, and immediately flown out to Los Angeles with them. He wouldn't have blamed her. In retrospect, on that particular night—with Hobgoblin preparing to nuke Manhattan if he wasn't paid a staggering ransom—Peter actually would have preferred knowing MJ was on her way to somewhere relatively safe. But she had her own priorities. Since then, though, either because word of her bolting from a successful audition had gotten around, or just from good old-fashioned bad luck, there had been no more TV work for her anywhere.

"Seriously though, hon," MJ said. "We've got enough money to last us a little while, but not that long. Right now I don't see anything happening at the *Bugle* that'll allow you to raise your prices significantly. Do you?"

"Well," Peter said, "no. There are only about thirty other people jockeying for the same work I'm trying to get. Some of them are better photographers than I am . . ."

"You have something marketable," MJ said. "You have a gift for getting good shots of superheroes . . . and supervillains. No one else seems to have quite the knack for it that you have." Her eyes glinted at him. "But there's only so far you can make that stretch. Listen—I've been taking a look to see where the modeling market has been moving lately. And all of a sudden there's a lot of action in the Miami area. A lot of modeling agencies, PR agencies, and so forth are beginning to concentrate down there. They like the tropical ambiance: the weather's dependable, and it's a good place to shoot. And they like the fact that all those other agencies are gathering down there: everybody's scratching everybody else's back, and they can all do a lot of business. I think it might be very smart if I saw about scaring up some modeling work. It won't be expensive: Aunt Anna will put me up as long as I want to stay."

Peter nodded. "Just two weeks?"

"Well, it takes time to get known in an area, check out all the possibilities. And what if I find work?"

"Stay there," Peter said, immediately and with energy. "Work. Make millions of dollars. Be that way. I'll come down there and be your kept man."

MJ smiled at him. "And they say chivalry is dead. Now, you know I'd rather stay here with you! But if someone has to go out and bring home the bacon . . ." She shrugged. "No point in me sitting around here with my feet up waiting for something to happen."

"It's disgusting," Peter said. "When I win the lottery, I will keep you for the rest of your life in sinful luxury. You will lie in bed on silk sheets all day and eat chocolates."

"None of this Godiva junk, either," MJ said. "Teuscher or nothing."

"And you'll never have to lift another finger—"

"Boooring!" she said. "But anyway, I know the agency can find someone to place me with down there—just enough to keep me going while I case the joint. And if I hit something larger—say, a steady contract—it'll pay back more than the costs of the trip."

Peter sat down and sighed. "I guess we have to, don't we?"

MJ sat down by him. "Yes. That's life at the moment, Tiger. But it'll sort itself out eventually. You wait and see. Meanwhile . . . Florida."

And so it had come to pass. He had put her on the train, Amtrak indeed, though from Penn Station rather than Grand Central. MJ had been disgusted at that. "Romance is dead," she said. "There is no romance in going anywhere from Penn!" But she had climbed on readily enough, ensconcing

herself in the unassigned seat on which she had insisted when
Peter started making noises about the price of the train ticket.
She had waved good-bye as the train pulled out, and dabbed at
one eye expressively as she went, making a sad-happy mouth
as the train pulled off down the track.

For the first couple of days, there was no mistaking it: he
moped around. He went out and had a pizza, and it tasted like
paste. Life just wasn't the same without her there—or, rather,
without her available to be there; knowing that even if she
wasn't across the table at the moment, she would be later that
evening. The next day was about the same. He couldn't bring
himself to go out: he puttered around the apartment develop-
ing some contact sheets, reveling (however briefly) in the
knowledge that he could use the bathroom as a darkroom
without having to clear curlers off the counter, and knowing
that MJ wouldn't come barging in despite the fact that he had
put the Red Light sign up outside. But none of the contacts
looked any good when he processed them.

This is silly, he had thought. *I was a bachelor for years. Did
just fine on my own. Why is this so difficult?*

The next day, though, at seven-thirty in the morning, the
phone rang. He wasn't able to get to it before the machine
went off. By the time he came staggering out of the bedroom,
rubbing his eyes and lurching into the living room, all he
heard was a few words in Kate Cushing's voice: ". . . here
pronto. Bye."

His editor at the *Daily Bugle* rarely called him herself: usually her assistant did it. Peter hurriedly wound the message
back and replayed it.

The machine beeped, then said: "Parker, Kate Cushing. I've
got a work opportunity for you up here today. I'd appreciate it
if you'd present yourself about nine, or if you can't make it
here by then, just get up here pronto. Bye."

After wrestling with the shower and clambering into his
Spidey suit, he leaped across the rooftops and swung along
weblines at about eight-thirty, wondering what was quite so

urgent. Kate had told him that it would be all right for him to have a couple of weeks off, after that stupendous set of pictures he had brought her of Venom and the Hobgoblin.

He sighed. It seemed about five minutes ago, some ways. He had had an interesting couple of days last month when first Venom and then Hobby had shown up in New York, with (literally) explosive results. It hadn't actually been Venom, at first, but someone who looked like him . . . and killed, not what Venom would have considered the deserving guilty, but the uninvolved innocent. Venom himself had turned up on the scene fairly quickly, certain that someone was impersonating him, and determined to stop it. It still amused Peter, in a crooked way, that Venom had been concerned about having his reputation ruined. As Spider-Man, Peter naturally had to try to deal with Venom when he showed up: the man/symbiote team was a criminal by everybody else's lights, if not by Venom's own. And then, on top of that, Hobgoblin had shown up, first getting involved in a few odd thefts, and finally presenting the city with a nasty *fait accompli* hidden under its streets: a small nuclear weapon, but plenty big enough to leave a glass-lined crater where Manhattan had been. He had attempted to hold the city hostage, and a most peculiar set of circumstances had stopped it: a not-very-holy alliance between Spider-Man and Venom, and the intervention of a bizarre extraterrestrial creature—the very same being that had been misidentified as Venom—that had gotten loose in New York and considered radioactives, even a nuclear bomb, to be tasty dinner fare.

When that dust settled, Peter had presented himself at the *Bugle*—rather sore and the worse for wear—with a spectacular set of photos of the final battle royal involving Spider-Man, Hobby, Venom, and the eater of fissionables. Kate had been very impressed and had noticed Peter's very worn-out condition and told him to get lost for a little while. *I wonder why she wants me found so soon?* he thought. *But I'll find out soon enough. . . .*

He came to a graceful landing on the roof of the Bugle building, right behind the huge sign that declared the identity of both edifice and newspaper to the city at large. A quick, long-practiced change of clothes, a trip down the stairs from the roof access, and he was in the City Room.

That room was in its usual stir and roil of activity, heading for the deadline for the midafternoon edition. Peter made his way through the many lined-up desks of editorial. The air was full of the earnest miniature-machine-gun sound of many people all pounding frantically at their keyboards. Only a few heads looked up, and only a person or two waved, as Peter went by.

He made for the rear wall, where the glassed-in offices were, Kate's among them. Coming to her door, Peter checked his watch: just nine-oh-five. *Not too bad,* he thought.

From inside the office, a hand reached into the venetian blinds covering the window, pulled them down: eyes peered out at him, and then the hand let the blinds spring up again. The door opened, and a voice from inside said, "On time for a change. Come in, sit down."

Peter did so, perching himself on her sofa in an alert edge-of-the-cushion position: one good way to get yelled at in Kate's office was to sprawl, especially as there was nowhere much to sprawl in—the sofa, along with every other flat surface, tended to be covered with books and papers and photos and all other kinds of whatnot. Kate went back to her desk, and started (or, Peter thought, resumed) pacing back and forth behind it as she talked. This mannerism Peter knew well: almost everybody associated with J. Jonah Jameson seemed to pick it up sooner or later, so that an editorial meeting at the *Bugle* looked very much like feeding time in the lion cage (and with JJJ there, it tended to sound like one as well).

"I can't do it, Jim," she said to the speakerphone. "You know I can't. Certain Parties will have my head on a plate."

"Not my problem," said Jim, whoever he was, on the other end of the conversation. "You're just going to have to cope."

Kate muttered something incomprehensible, chewed her lip for a moment. "All right. On your head be it. But unless you get the goods, I am *not* going to reimburse. And until you get the goods, I'm going to assume this is some sleazy scam to get more time on the beach at La Croisette."

"Aww, Kate . . ."

"Don't aww-Kate me. Get out there and ask him when he's running for President. And get an answer, you hear me?" She punched the hang-up button on the speakerphone forcefully, then sat down behind her desk and started rummaging for something. "This is a nuisance," she said. "That's the man I was going to send to Florida with you."

"What?"

"You *are* free to go to Florida?"

"Uhh," Peter said, flabbergasted. "For how long?"

"Till the story breaks," Kate said. "Knowing you, it shouldn't take forever: I'm sending you partly as a good-luck charm this time."

"What's the story?"

She came up with her address book, started paging through it. "The Space Shuttle *Endeavour* goes up week after next," she said.

"That's good news," Peter said—he had forgotten about the semi-impending launch in his post-MJ malaise—"but why send a reporter to cover it? Or a photographer, for that matter? The local stringers have been good enough in the past. And the NASA publicity staff have some of the best photographers around—"

She waved at him in annoyance. "I don't want pretty pillar-of-fire pictures, Peter. Do you know Vreni Byrne?"

"No."

"She's a stringer who came over from the *Chicago Tribune* a few weeks back," Kate said. "She was doing overseas work, mostly . . . wants to do some at home now. Investigative, by preference. She's good, doesn't need her hand held. Now—" Kate chewed her lip, that nervous mannerism again. "Some of the local press down in the Miami area, down near the Space Coast, have been reporting some odd things going on around Canaveral. Nothing huge, nothing obvious or definite, but all the same . . . Security down there has been a *lot* tighter than usual. The press officers at KSC haven't been as forthcoming as they usually are. There've been these funny reports of sudden changes of ID, people being ferried in and out of Canaveral AFB, all very hush-hush. And at the same time, there've been some disappearances down that way. Not the usual missing-persons stuff, but people who are characterized as being otherwise very stable, very dependable—just gone. And some odd thefts and attempted thefts, all in the same general area, about a hundred miles across." She shrugged. "I don't know that there's a connection, but when things like this start happening in a physical location so close to each other, it just makes me wonder. Anyway, the sudden boost in security down there is reason enough to be interested, especially since no one's even attempting any explanations. Usually they tell you flat out that something classified is going on: NASA does enough missions for the military, after all, putting up spy satellites and so forth. This mission is innocent enough, at least on paper: they're putting up some new power equipment for the space station, doing some experiments on bees . . ." She shook her head. "It's all sort of odd. I want it looked into."

Peter raised his eyebrows. "Are they letting people in as usual? Tours and so forth?"

"Yes. Naturally I'll want some fresh pictures. No, I don't expect you to try to get into any place that's restricted—I don't want the paper's credentials pulled just on a hunch. But I do want you to get out and about with Vreni—mooch around the rest of the Space Coast area that's being affected by these thefts and disappearances. You're good at catching the unexpected stuff, the slightly cockeyed angle . . ."

"So we're going to be staying in the Miami area?"

Kate nodded.

Peter's heart leaped then. "Uh, well, yeah! And until the story breaks . . ."

"This one may take some rooting around," Kate said. "Vreni is not a fast worker, but she's thorough, and I'm reluctant to hurry her. She will drag you all over the countryside, though: be ready for that. We'll give you a travel stipend before you go, and you'll pull company credit cards for this run. Don't go overboard, either," she said, looking sharply at Peter. "I've been catching merry hell from Himself over abuse of cards." Peter smiled at the reference to JJJ. The publisher had always considered company credit cards to be little more than an excuse for reporters to take money right out of his pocket. "And why shouldn't I," Kate continued, "with Jim suddenly announcing that he's the only one Arnie wants to talk to at Cannes? So I have to put up with his shenanigans, and the damned hyperinflated hotel bills—" She caught herself, and sighed. "Never mind. I'll put up with yours as well, to a point."

Peter grinned.

"Oh, I neglected to mention," Kate said then, with a small smile. "An old friend of yours has been spotted down that way . . ."

"Yeah, I know," Peter said, grinning sheepishly. "She's visiting her aunt—"

Kate looked at him cockeyed. " 'She'? He's had a sex change?"

"Sorry? Who'd you mean?"

"The Lizard."

Peter's mouth dropped open. He closed it again.

"Since you've consistently gotten the best pictures of him," Kate said, "it occurred to me that you would be good for this job. To Robbie, too, for that matter—in fact, he specifically recommended you."

Peter smiled. A recommendation from Joe "Robbie" Robertson, the editor in chief, was always welcome.

"And of course for the other reasons as well," Kate said with a lopsided grin.

Peter blinked and started running over the conversation in his mind, wondering which reasons she meant, exactly.

"The sex change is just a rumor, then?"

"Oh! Yeah, it is, sorry," Peter said hurriedly.

"You and MJ haven't had some kind of falling-out, have you?"

"No! No, it's just a family visit. She planned to be down there for just a couple of weeks."

Kate looked at him for a moment. "If necessary," she said, "when your card bill comes in, I will overlook a few nights' worth of extra meals and, shall we say, double accommodation."

Peter actually blushed. "Kate—thanks."

She waved him away. "I was young once, too, but it was hard to get any work done then with the damn dinosaurs all over the place. Just make sure you bring back the goods. Meanwhile, Vreni'll be along in an hour or so. Come back here around quarter of eleven and I should have finished talking to her."

"Right. Thanks, Kate!"

Peter went out, wondering.

He headed across the street to the little Stadium Deli across the way, got himself a coffee and a cheese Danish, and sat down at one of the Formica-topped tables in the back, half listening to Julio, the deli's owner, singing something low and mournful in Spanish. The rest of his thoughts were elsewhere, well back in the past.

How many years had it been, now, since that trip to Florida with JJJ? It was only a little while after he became Spider-Man. He shook his head, sipping the coffee and grimacing. It seemed like forever since the tragic saurian shape of the Lizard had first burst across the path of his life, and Spider-Man's. It had unfolded into yet another of those stories which seemed all too common in the world these days. A scientist named Dr. Curtis Connors, hardworking, dedicated, brilliant—maybe too brilliant for his own good—wandered down an avenue of research that would soon enough prove deadly for him. Having lost an arm during a tour in the Armed Forces, he had experimented with a method of regenerating the arm in much the same way a reptile could grow a new limb.

But this particular experiment, which might have been innocuous enough, went terribly wrong. It had left Connors saddled with a new kind of glandular dysfunction that the world had never seen before, one which, at unpredictable intervals, twisted his body backward down the evolutionary scale into a dreadful and untoward mixture of reptile and man, a bipedal saurian of astonishing strength, speed, and size, locked into a mental state of uncontrollable rage. The change came and went with little warning and could not be put off or cut short, turning a brilliant man into a crazed monster. What this did to his family life . . . Peter shuddered.

Sometimes he liked to complain to himself or to MJ about their problems. Their life together wasn't always easy: being a superhero's wife was no picnic, Peter knew. He rubbed his ribs absently; they were just now reknit after the last time Venom had cracked them. But whatever other problems they had, MJ did not have to worry that Peter would turn into a giant lizard without warning and tear up everything in sight.

Curt Connors's wife and children did, though. His wife Martha had been married to an intelligent and sensitive man, a leader in his field of biology in a quiet sort of way. Now she found herself having to try to hold the family together when Curt quit his day job, couldn't hold or find another, and tended to vanish for prolonged periods, driven by his curse, or his attempts to find ways to cure it. Peter knew, too, Curt's own fear that in one of his rages he might hurt the family he loved. Connors had taken to vanishing for longer and longer periods, driven as much by that fear as by the monster.

Both as himself and as Spider-Man, Peter had met the family on various occasions, and had forged a kind of friendship with them. It wasn't entirely pity. He knew that Curt Connors was no evildoer, no criminal by choice: he knew that the things the Lizard did weren't Curt's fault, that the Lizard was manipulable, terribly vulnerable for all his rage and strength. True criminals and villains were all too willing to make use of so blunt but effective a tool, if it should chance to fall into their hands. Curt's shame at being so used was one of the things that kept him away from his family and drove him so relentlessly to find a cure . . . not that the problem itself wasn't reason enough.

Peter kept in touch with the family every now and then to see how things were, checking to see whether they had heard from Curt, and how they were doing in general. It was about all he could do for them. Curt's wife was too proud to accept any other kind of help, even from the most well-meaning of their friends.

He checked his watch and sighed. It was pushing ten-thirty. Surprising how fast time could go when you were musing over something like this, but Peter felt very sorry for Curt. His own bizarre accident with the radioactive spider, so long ago, had at least left him with abilities he could control and master. Curt had not been so fortunate, and Peter was determined to do anything he could to help him.

"Hey, Mister Peter, you look sad today! Whatsamatter, is the coffee no good?"

Peter looked up. It was Julio, who ran the place: a big, friendly, florid, dark-skinned, mustached man, making his way down the Formica tables and wiping them off as he went along.

"Nah, just thinking, Julio," Peter said.

"Aah, too much of that's bad for you," Julio said. "Sours your stomach."

Peter smiled and kept to himself the thought that Julio's coffee was more likely to take care of that job. It wasn't very good as a rule, and it was amazing that he sold so much of it in a city full of coffee freaks; but at the same time there was so much caffeine in it that it could practically raise the dead, and the hacks at the *Bugle* prized it above gold when they were fighting a deadline. "Yeah," Peter said, "I'll watch out for that. Hey, Julio, I'm going to Florida."

"That's great, Pete! You go down there, you make sure you get some of that Cuban food. Better than up here; you can't get the good plantain here. You get yourself a nice fried steak, and some Cuban sandwiches, and . . ."

"Julio, if I start eating all this stuff, they're going to need a forklift to move me when I get back."

"If you don't eat good food when you get a chance," Julio said severely, "God will be mad at you."

"If I don't get back to the *Bugle*," Peter said, checking his watch and getting up, "Kate will be mad at me. Almost as bad. See you later, Julio!"

On the sixth floor, there was noise coming out of Kate's office when he paused outside it. A female voice, very pleasant but raised in what sounded like extreme annoyance, said something he couldn't make out, and was answered much more quietly. He knew that tone: Kate's "no nonsense" voice. Peter lifted his hand to knock: the door was pulled open, so that the knock never fell. "There you are," Kate said. "What kept you? Come on in."

He stepped in and Kate said, "Vreni Byrne—Peter Parker. Peter—Vreni."

The woman who got up from Kate's couch to shake his hand was a petite blonde in jeans and a silk shirt, no makeup, no jewelry . . . and possibly one of the most stunning women he had ever seen. It was difficult not to gape at her. "Uh, hi!" Peter said, trying to get his thought processes back in order. "You were with the *Chicago Trib*, weren't you?"

She nodded, pleased. "That's right. And I've seen your stuff here and there. Not bad at all. We should do all right together."

There was something about the way she said this that suddenly made it plain to Peter that Vreni thought his work was bad—or at least fairly substandard—but she wasn't going to start out by alienating a photographer with whom she was being sent out on a story that didn't particularly interest her. Peter instantly suspected that she was going to do as little work as possible on this, and intended Peter to carry it with his pictures. He'd run across this type of attitude before; it was one of many reasons why he was grateful that he was usually able to work alone. Not to mention the awkwardness of having to leave your partner to go off and change to Spider-Man. *Come to think of it,* he thought, *that may cause problems.*

Deciding to cross that particular bridge when he came to it, Peter set his face into a smile and sat down at the other end of the couch. Vreni and Kate sat back down as well. "I've explained to Vreni," Kate said, "what I was telling you earlier about the situation down at Canaveral. Since you may be away for a while, you ought to take today to get things in order for being away for a prolonged period. If you need to draw any equipment from Stores to take with you," she said to Peter, "take care of that this afternoon—have them call my office if there are any questions."

"There are some long lenses that might come in handy," Peter said, trying very hard not to let a grin of total equipment-lust show on his face. He had never had an excuse before to get his hands on such things. JJJ didn't authorize their use that often.

"Fine. Just take good care of them . . . those things are expensive." She looked at Vreni. "Have you got a laptop with the *Bugle* composition software in it?"

"Got it last week."

"Good, then you're all set. Today's Wednesday . . . I would like to have a report from you two on initial indications of what you've found by next Tuesday. Ideally, I want to put something in the Sunday supplement, the day before the Shuttle goes up. Supplement deadline is Thursday . . . that's for final copy. Anything newer you find that warrants followup will go in the Sunday daily edition. Anything else?"

They both shook their heads.

"Okay, then get on with it. Go see Travel and get your flights or whatever sorted out, and draw a company card each from Accounting. If at all possible, I want you two in Miami and starting work by Friday. Is that doable?"

Peter looked at Vreni: she nodded. So did he.

"Right. Now get out of here so I can get some work done."

Out they went, and Kate's door closed behind them with the air of someone who had solved a very annoying problem. Peter resolved privately to ask around and see if there was something about Vreni and Kate that she should know about: some old disagreement or piece of unfinished business. One or another of the office gossips would have the info, he was sure.

As they walked away from Kate's office, Peter said, "Ms. Byrne—"

"Call me Vreni. If I can call you Peter?"

"Right. Vreni, I get the feeling that you're not entirely overjoyed at being sent on this story—"

She breathed in and out, then chuckled a little, almost against her will. "No, I was supposed to be going to Cannes. Miami was not exactly in my plans. But when life hands you lemons, you make lemonade . . ." She smiled slightly. "There are good aspects to it, I suppose. I've never seen a live Shuttle launch: this will be my chance. Have you?"

"No," Peter said, though in his career as Spider-Man, he'd traveled to space once or twice, and flown in space-faring vehicles more impressive than anything NASA had yet built.

He also did not mention, right now, that there was one reason for going to Miami that outweighed any number of Shuttles, as far as he was concerned. "I'm looking forward to it."

"Right. So we'll get ourselves down there and see what we can discover about this security problem they're having. Those long lenses you were mentioning," she added, "those can be good for getting quiet photos of things a couple of miles away, can't they?"

"They sure can," Peter said. "Considering the size of Kennedy, and the fact that at least some of the things we'll want pictures of will be off-limits . . ." He shrugged, and then caught her smiling at him.

"I never yet saw a photographer," she said, "who didn't want to get his or her hands on one of those lenses just to play with. Nice that we're actually going to need one."

Peter laughed. "Vreni," he said, "you haven't seen one now, either. But you're right, I'll need it." He paused. "Did Kate mention the Lizard to you?"

Vreni waved a hand. "She did, but . . . I don't know—I find it kind of hard to take seriously. Crazed human super-villains, yes: heaven knows there are enough of those running around. But I don't understand what kind of damage a big crazed lizard can do. Why doesn't someone just shoot it?"

Peter raised his eyebrows. "It's been tried," he said.

"Then somebody's not trying hard enough."

"Maybe not," Peter said, restraining himself from further comment. This was no time to get into a discussion of how the creature she was calmly suggesting should be shot was a friend of his. "But if we're lucky, we won't run into him. It sounds like there's going to be enough other things about this story to keep us busy."

"Yeah," Vreni said. "Let's go down to Travel and get those tickets organized."

That business took about an hour, while they fought with the folks down in Travel—some of the wiliest-brained cheapskates Peter had ever met; no doubt hand-trained by Jameson—to keep from being put on a flight at three in the morning for the sake of a cheap fare. They finally settled on a noon flight out of Newark on Thursday, and Peter and Vreni were left free to go off to Accounting to get their credit cards.

Vreni then went off to take care of personal business, and Peter went down to Stores and had Mike the equipment manager bring out every long lens that was presently available. One of them, a beautiful 2000-millimeter f8 lens, Peter was strongly tempted to simply grab and run away with, never to be seen again, but then he saw the scratch on the lens's achromatic coating, and shook his head and pushed the lens back at Mike with the greatest possible regret. "How the heck did that happen?" he said.

Mike, a tall handsome young black man, grinned slightly. "Jets game," he said. "A tackle went right through the sidelines, apparently. Hit Joel Rhodes—he was covering that game—knocked him on his butt and broke his leg. Knocked the lens into a bench."

"What a shame," Peter said, more for the lens than for Joel, another photographer he had met and didn't much care for; a rude and abrasive type. "Oh well. How about the fifteen, there?"

Mike handed Peter the 1500-mm lens. It was two and a half feet long and nearly a foot wide at the lens end. "Hmm . . ." Peter sat there briefly doing math in his head to determine the thing's range.

"Pete," Mike said, "got a little something here you should see." He turned away, went rummaging back among the steel shelves.

"What? I thought you said this was all the big lenses."

Mike came back with a box about the size of a standard personal computer case, opened it up. Peter looked inside.

"That's a telescope," he said, bemused.

Mike lifted the small cylindrical object out of its nested packing in the case. It was black, eight inches in diameter, and only about eighteen inches long.

"Questar," Mike said. "Yup, it's a telescope, but look there. See the camera fitting?" He pointed at the barrel of the telescope, where there was a standard bayonet mount. "You put your 35 right there, at the Cassegrain focus. This thing can produce virtual close-ups at five miles."

"Wow," Peter breathed. Even the 2000 wouldn't have been able to do that.

"This has been out doing nature work," Mike said. "Something to do with those owls up in timber country. You can't get close enough to them for photos, usually. You can with this, though."

"Where do I sign?" Peter said, looking over his shoulder in terror lest someone else should come in here and want it too.

"Right here." Mike shoved the usual equipment-requisition voucher at him. Peter scribbled hastily, while Mike put the Questar back in its case and snapped all the catches shut.

"Manual's inside," Mike said. "Take good care of it. Jonah finds out I gave this to a freelancer, he'll freak."

Peter seized the box and grinned at Mike. "No problem there. The question is, will you ever see me again?"

Mike chuckled as Peter hurried off.

The rest of the day was a whirl of preparation. Peter had to let the building super and the alarm company know that he was going to be away for a while, put a bigger tape in the answering machine, get rid of all the perishable food in the refrigerator, give MJ's modeling agency the phone number for the Hilton in Miami, in case they couldn't reach her themselves, and about fifty other things. When the dust finally settled, it was nearly ten o'clock at night, and he hadn't even begun packing yet. He hadn't had any dinner, and he was dead tired. However, there were a couple of phone calls he had to make: one which would be delightful, one not so.

He dialed the good one first. The phone rang about eighteen times. MJ had warned him to expect this. "It's down in the front hall," she said: "Aunt Anna doesn't like extension phones. And we're usually outside in the sun, so give us some time if you call." *It's a little late in the day for sun,* Peter thought, but all the same, he let it ring. Finally someone picked up. "Hello?"

It was Anna Watson. "Hi, Aunt Anna, it's Peter!" he said.

"Oh, hello, Peter! How are things? MJ's just out of the tub; I'll get her for you." The phone was put down, and footsteps went off out of earshot. Faintly, voices could be heard chatting in the background, and a giggle. Peter smiled; he knew that giggle. Then more footsteps, hurried, and the phone being picked up.

"Hi, Tiger! Oh, I miss you!"

"I miss you, too," Peter said. "But not for long."

"What?"

"I'm being sent to Florida."

"Really? Where?"

"Miami."

"Oh, Peter!"

He filled her in quickly on the Space Coast story, what he knew of it. Then, more quietly, he said, "They think they've seen the Lizard as well."

"Oh, no," MJ said softly.

Peter tried to sound lighthearted. "I don't know that we'll necessarily run into him. The odds—"

"Don't quote me odds," his wife said, sounding resigned, but also just slightly amused. "They're sending you down here because you're good at getting pictures of super-villains. You'll run into him." She sighed. "But at least you're going to be here!"

"We should be able to see each other most nights," Peter said softly.

"Ohhh . . . !" Her voice clearly implied what she intended for at least some of those nights. Peter shivered, just once, with anticipation: it was amazing what a little separation could do for a relationship.

"Absolutely. But never mind that for the moment," Peter said. "How are you getting along down there?"

She chuckled. "Hon, this was actually a pretty good move. Remember I told you about North Beach?"

"Uh-huh."

"Well, it's even worse than I thought. You couldn't spit on Beach Boulevard and not hit someone toting a portfolio. A lot of them are wanna-bes, but a lot are genuine talent. There's plenty of work here, if you can make the right connections.

And if you can cut through the talent that's already been hired. . . ."

"How's the competition?"

Her voice sounded rueful. "Very polished. Some of these people have big careers elsewhere and are just sort of slumming for the season. Anyway, I've left my bio and CV and representative stills at about eighteen different agencies."

"There are that many of them down there?"

"I haven't hit all of them yet, by any means, just the biggest ones. 'Start at the top and work down' seems to be the best approach if I'm going to make any kind of impression with all the other talent around here."

"All those people ought to get out," said Peter righteously, "and leave the field to people like you who need the money."

She laughed. "You tell 'em, Tiger."

After that there wasn't a great deal of content to the phone call: it devolved rapidly into smoochy noises, which Peter reluctantly brought to an early conclusion. "I'll tell you everything else tomorrow," he said, "when we get in. I'm booked in at the Miami Hilton. But meanwhile I've got one more phone call to make."

"I think I know who," she said, that resigned sound again. "Well, tell them I sent my best."

"I will. I'm just hoping he's not in trouble of some kind."

MJ sounded rueful again. "I would more or less define being the Lizard as being in trouble," she said.

"Yeah. Listen, honey—gotta go."

After another five minutes of kissyface noises, Peter hung up and checked his address book for the second phone number and slowly dialed it.

Several rings, and the phone was picked up. "Hello?"

A boy's voice. "William," Peter said mock severely, "isn't it past your bedtime?"

"Peter! How are you?"

"I'm fine. Is your mom around?"

"No, she ran down to the 7-Eleven for some milk—we ran out. She'll be back in a little while."

Peter thought for a moment. "Okay. I just wanted to let her know that I'm going to be coming down your way."

"Super!" There was a pause, and William's voice dropped a little. "Dad's not here," he said sadly.

"No, huh?"

"He hasn't been here for—" A pause. "Four months. Just a little more."

"Do you have any idea where he is?"

"Not really. We knew he was getting ready to go away for a while—he packed a lot of stuff, and sent it away in boxes. He wouldn't tell us what it was, or why he was sending it, or where. I got worried, Peter . . . I thought maybe he wasn't going to come back at all."

"But he didn't take everything, did he?"

"No, he left a lot. But we're not sure what that means, either. He doesn't talk to us like he used to, Pete. Anyway, he went away. Then the last we heard from him was about two months ago. He sent a postcard from somewhere down by the Everglades." William stopped. "It wouldn't be so bad," he said then, "if he would write more. Sometimes I wonder if he really just wishes we weren't here."

He *may*, Peter thought sadly, *but not for the reasons you think*. He felt so sorry for William: he knew what it was like to desperately want a father. His own parents had died when he was very small, leaving him to be raised by his aunt May and uncle Ben. Ben died shortly after Peter gained his spider-powers—a death Peter could have prevented. The guilt associated with that act haunted him to this day.

But Peter had no idea how he would have reacted if he'd had a father who had Curt Connors's problem. Aloud he said, "I doubt it. Anyway, as I said, I'm coming down. It's partly about him, and partly about the Space Shuttle."

"What? The next launch? The one with the bees?"

"Yup."

"Cool!" And for several minutes William babbled happily, for apparently he and his science class, along with science classes in several hundred other schools around the country, were involved in this bee experiment—something about finding out whether bees' swarming and directional abilities were affected by microgravity, and how much. There was also something about honey-supported hydroponics which William carried on about so excitedly that Peter could barely follow him. If there was anything William had inherited from his father, it was his love of the sciences, and biology in particular; Curt had been as good a teacher as he had been a researcher.

After a while, though, William trailed off, paused. "You know, though," he said, "if it's partly about the Lizard—you be careful, Pete. You know . . ."

"I know. He's dangerous sometimes. But I'll have backup on this one. Spider-Man told me recently that he's going to be heading down this way himself."

"Oh, great!" William said, sounding relieved. "That's okay, then. You think we might see him?"

"I haven't seen his appointments calendar," Peter said. "No telling. But if I run across him, I'll tell him you were asking after him."

"Thanks, Pete! It'd be cool to see him—and he might know something about how Dad is."

"I hope so. Listen, William, I'm running up the phone bill. Let your mom know about what I've been telling you, okay?"

"I will. Where are you going to be?"

"The Miami Hilton, for the first few days at least. But I'll give her a call when we get in."

"Okay. Thanks, Peter!"

"Right. You take care."

Peter hung up and sighed and went off to pack.

TWO

T he trip down was uneventful. After locking up, setting the alarm, and dropping the spare key with the super, Peter caught a cab for Newark and met Vreni at check-in, where they got onto one of the most crowded commuter flights he had ever been on in his life. It took Peter a good five minutes to wrestle the Questar into the overhead baggage compartment, which was already so full that he thought he might have to spend the trip with it in his lap.

Not the best way to begin a working relationship, Peter thought, as he and Vreni wedged themselves into seats so tightly pitched and close together that they might just as well have just given up and tried to sit in each other's laps.

"They've mistaken us for sardines, these people," Vreni muttered under her breath as the plane taxied away from the gate.

"Yeah. The *Bugle* paid peanuts for the fare," Peter said, eyeing the tray that one of the flight attendants carried past, "and it looks like that's all we're going to get to eat, too."

She laughed then. "Wait till we're up," she said. For once, it didn't take long; once the plane was in the air, she reached for the tote bag she had shoved under the seat ahead of them.

Peter watched as she produced from it a package of crackers, several good cheeses from Zabar's, a couple of small bottles of San Pellegrino mineral water, and plastic cups and knives. "Self-preservation," she said to Peter, pulling down her tray. "I stopped trusting airline food, or even expecting it, a long time ago. Pellegrino?"

"Thanks," he said, delighted. She handed him one of the bottles. A short time later they were working their way through an early lunch, and getting annoyed, envious, or just plain hungry looks from all the other passengers in sight.

As they chatted over the next couple of hours, Peter started revising his original opinion of Vreni, although a little reluctantly. Vreni Byrne was quick on the uptake, and very opinionated. Occasionally she could be abrasive. But these traits made a good investigative reporter, and that was how she had gotten her start in journalism. Her talent had taken her a long way. She had been in Rwanda, and in South Africa during the worst of its troubles; she had been in Moscow for the coup that brought down the Soviet Union, in Berlin when the Wall fell, and in Latveria when Victor von Doom was deposed. She had been in the Kurile Islands when Japan and Russia almost went to war over them—a carefully covered-up business, that, and Peter shuddered as she told him more about it, and how close the world had been, once more, to its first real nuclear war. She had investigated Chinese piracy off the Philippines, pollution in Antarctica, and Atlantean attacks of offshore oil rigs. Vreni had been a busy woman.

"After a while, though," she said, "you get tired of running around foreign places. You want to rake some muck on your own doorstep." Vreni smiled a little. "The problem is, even a reporter can get typecast. My editors at the *Trib* liked the work I was doing overseas—liked it too much to let me work at home. So, I gave 'em the slip."

"What do you make of *this* story so far?" Peter said.

She shrugged. "Not sure there is one, frankly. It all seems pretty disconnected. Oh, I respect Kate's judgment, don't get me wrong. Unquestionably she has an instinct for these things. Nonetheless—" Vreni stretched as well as she could in the cramped space "—we'll see how fast the story runs away from us when we get down there."

"From us? Or with us?" Peter said, slightly bewildered.

Vreni shook her head. "From us. I've learned this over time: the faster the story runs away from you, the more it avoids you and tries not to be told, the better it is. If we start getting avoidance reactions right away—" there was a slightly feral edge to her smile "—we'll know we're onto something hot."

She laid out her plans briefly for him: "I'll go down some of the usual channels first. I should be able to make some connections in the Miami police department via my old contacts in Chicago—maybe even over the weekend, if things work out right. Then there's the initial prelaunch press conference at

Kennedy on Monday. We should hear then whether there have been any changes in the Shuttle's mission to account for these sudden changes in security. You should be there for that; see if you can get some other pictures, too, background Cape stuff. Test out that widget of yours."

"Definitely," Peter said. "I'm going to see if I can get some practice with it over the weekend—it's a little idiosyncratic to work with, but it should produce some terrific results once I can figure out how to use it best."

"Right. After KSC, we should go out on Tuesday, assuming nothing else comes up, and interview some of the people who're associated with these weird disappearances and so forth. They're scattered around the northern part of the Everglades, mostly. We'll take two days over it, I would imagine, while I start assembling the first draft of the article for Kate. Second draft in on Thursday . . . and the launch is the Monday after."

"And then pictures of the launch."

"Of course. Make sure you pick up the launch passes on Monday—no point in leaving it till the last minute."

"No question," Peter said. Whatever else happened, he was excited about the prospect of being at the Shuttle launch; being at it with the Questar as well was the chance of a lifetime. *I should be able to show the NASA photographers a thing or three,* he thought, *if I can get enough use of the 'scope over the week to get used to it. And what practice I don't get, Spider-Man will.*

"And then there's the Lizard," Vreni said. "I'll grant Kate this: his appearances are in the same general area as these weird thefts and disappearances. But there's no proof that he's directly involved . . ." She trailed off, thinking, then shook her head. "We'll see what happens. If he, like the story, runs away from us . . ." That smile curved her lips again.

Peter privately considered that it wasn't the Lizard running away from him that he had in mind, especially when he had his Spider-Man suit on. *But as she says, we'll see what happens.*

Two hours later they touched down at Miami International Airport. As Peter and Vreni came out the ramp into the gate area, Peter turned to say something to Vreni, just behind him, and was tackled sideways by something that hit him like a ground-to-air missile—if ground-to-air missiles had flowing red hair. The kiss went on . . . well, Peter wasn't actually sure *how* long it went on. He was faintly aware of the sound of Vreni's amused chuckle behind him. When he broke the clinch and smiled into MJ's eyes, she raised her eyebrows at him, a teasing look, and said, "No better than eight point eight, I make that. You're out of practice already."

"Hmf."

"Do you have a lady in every port, Peter," Vreni said, politely enough, "or is this someone to whom I should be introduced more formally?"

Peter chuckled. "Mary Jane Watson-Parker," he said, taking a moment to admire MJ's miniskirt, "Vreni Byrne."

"Delighted," Vreni said, as she and MJ shook hands, and certainly she seemed to mean it. "The people at the *Bugle* all say how lucky Peter is to have caught you."

"Luck had nothing to do with it," said MJ. " 'A guy chases a girl until she catches him,' as the song says. It was pretty much that way with us. But—Byrne as in the *Chicago Tribune*?"

"Why, yes."

"I thought so. I saw you on their magazine show on cable—"

They all headed down toward the baggage-claim area, chatting all the way. Peter was bemused to discover that Vreni was a fan of *Secret Hospital*, knew MJ's acting from her all-too-brief stint on that soap opera, and liked her style. After recovering their bags, the three of them caught a cab to the Hilton, and by the time they got there, MJ and Vreni were gossiping like mad over the antics of some of the other actors in the series. *What a relief*, Peter thought as they got out. He had been slightly concerned that MJ would be annoyed with him for being in the company of such a good-looking woman. *But she's above that kind of thing . . .*

"Are you staying here too?" Vreni said to MJ, as she and Peter went in with their bags.

"Not while he's on a job," MJ said. "I'm with relatives. We'll be visiting, though."

"Well, I hope to see more of you! I'm going to go up and get settled," Vreni said to Peter, "and then I'm going to start setting up some of our first interviews. I'll see you tomorrow morning. Breakfast?"

"You're on," Peter said.

Vreni headed off, and MJ watched her go. Then, when she was safely in the elevator and its doors shut, she turned to Peter, fisted him lightly in the ribs, and said, "Where did you find *her*?"

"Oh, MJ, come on—"

She burst out laughing at him. "I'm teasing. I'm in too good a mood to be jealous about anything, even if I didn't know Kate wished her on you. Come on."

They walked off through the lobby together, heading for the coffee shop. Peter hugged her to him as they went. "Why the good mood, then? Any luck?" he said.

They went in, waited to be seated. "A nibble," MJ said, as the waitress led them to a quiet table in the corner.

"A modeling job?"

"No. Television."

"Here? That's weird."

MJ nodded, stretched a little, and smiled. "One of the local afternoon talk shows apparently has a little modeling spot three times a week. Local couture, that kind of thing. They've just lost the model who was working for them, and now they need a replacement."

"You think you can get this job?"

"I have no idea. I think half the people in town must be trying to get it. A lot of competition . . ." She shrugged. "Can't do anything but try. And what about you? Where are you going to have to be?"

Peter shook his head. "Up and down the coast—depends on what arrangements Vreni makes. There's going to be a lot of driving, though, between here and the north Everglades. But I'd say we'll be here for at least a week, until just after the shuttle launch, and then maybe a little afterwards. Meantime . . ."

The waitress came. After they both ordered drinks, MJ said, leaning over the table and taking Peter's hand, "A lot of driving there may be, but none for you just now—or later, either."

"What exactly do you have in mind?"

"Tiger," she said softly. The smile spread to a grin. "How long has it been since we last saw each other?"

"Eleven days," he said. And added, "Fourteen hours . . . and twenty-three minutes. Mark." Then he eyed the key card for his room, which he'd dropped to the table. "Never mind the drinks," he said. "Never mind lunch. Come on."

"No way!" MJ said. "We have to keep up your strength. But, afterwards . . ."

Peter grinned back, resigning himself to the delightfully inevitable.

He did go out, though, around six that evening. Peter stopped down at the hotel's car rental desk and took possession of a neat little compact, then drove MJ to Aunt Anna's. He spent an hour or so there with them, sharing gossip and catching up on family business. Then he left, for there was one visit he needed to make before he and Vreni got started on business the next day.

He drove most of the way. One thing he had learned was that, while Spider-Man had little trouble web-slinging his way around in his home turf in Manhattan, it was sometimes more difficult to make good speed out in open country. For long distances, a car really did work better sometimes, and he was glad enough to have one at his disposal now. Besides, with his spider-sense warning him of any kind of danger, he was probably the safest driver on the road.

He headed up and out of Miami on I-95, not desiring to get caught in the tangle of interchanges around Hialeah and Fort Lauderdale, and soon realized that being the safest driver on the road wasn't all that much of an accomplishment on the Florida highways. Once he got out of the city limits, though, the driving was a bit more sane; he went straight north along the eastern coast until he hit Route 98 near Palm Beach. There he turned west, heading inland for about thirty miles, toward the southern shores of Lake Okeechobee.

South Bay was a small city at the very southernmost point of the lake, where the North New River Canal flowed into it. The place was very much in the Floridian style of "middle America": white-shingled houses, neat front yards, palm trees, swimming pools here and there, a busy little complex of main streets in town, and a quiet, flourishing suburb surrounding it all and running up against the lake. Rough spaces of wetland were dotted here and there—a token of the presence of the northernmost part of the Everglades very nearby. Long, quiet, rural roads ran into the city from several sides, and it seemed like every other house Peter passed along these roads had a boat in the driveway—even if it was only a rowboat or an inflatable dinghy.

Around dusk, he left the car in a parking lot near a Kmart several miles outside town, and strolled off into an empty lot nearby, a tangle of undergrowth-height live oak and slash pine. It was surprisingly quiet, except for a mockingbird which sat high on a crooked palm and sang skilled and insistent imitations of every bird he knew and many he didn't.

It squawked, though, a few minutes later, and flew away hurriedly as a jet of webbing shot up into the palm tree's crown. A moment later Spider-Man swung up into the tree, crouched there among the fronds, and glanced around him, while the mockingbird settled two trees over and sang scandal and outrage at him, flirting its tail and rousing its feathers at him.

"Hey," Spidey said, "take it easy, Caruso. I'll be out of your way in a moment." He looked around and got his bearings. While still driving, earlier that evening, he had picked up a street map of the area, along with several other maps that he needed for research purposes. Now with its help, he picked out a couple of landmarks—a water tower, a radio mast—made sure of the direction in which he was headed—north, toward the lake—and set out.

It was a little less easy not to be seen in this mostly flat landscape than it would have been in Manhattan, but he made the best of his environment, enjoying it as he went. There were still some surprisingly big, surprisingly old cypresses here-abouts, a few of them big enough to be several hundred years old, and there were high-tension towers to use for anchorage (if you were careful about where you put the webbing) and plenty of other masts and poles. Spider-Man webbed his way northward, not rushing it too much, enjoying the balmy evening air, until he found the little suburban development he was after.

It was only a couple of blocks from the lakeshore: a little semicircle of shingled tract houses, one of several nearly iden-tical cul-de-sacs radiating out from a central access road. Spidey perched on a power line tower behind the cul-de-sac and checked out the one house he was interested in. It had a neat woven-wood plank fence surrounding its backyard, which contained a small patio, numerous rosebushes, and a very beat-up lawn surrounding a pole with a basketball hoop. Off to one side was a brick barbecue, with embers still glowing in it. The house had a much-used but serviceable-looking Buick sit-ting in front of it, and the lawn was slightly overgrown. Off to one side, on a small trailer, sat an aluminum canoe.

Spidey smiled inside his mask—more a sad smile than any-thing else—looked around him to make sure he could see no one watching, and swung down into the house's backyard.

There were sliding glass and screen doors opening out onto the small patio. The curtains inside them were open. Through them, Spider-Man could see a living room, and a pair of jeans-wearing legs sticking out in front of a chair. The owner of the legs was slumped or slid so far down in the chair that there was no seeing the rest of him.

Spidey slipped quietly up to the screen door. "William," he said softly, "you're going to ruin your back sitting that way, you know that?"

A frozen moment of silence, and then a blond boy leaped out of the chair and came tearing back to the screen door, staring to see out into the fast-falling darkness. "Spider-M—!"

"Sssh," Spidey said. "Can I come in?"

William slid the screen door aside, beckoned him. "Come on in," he said, and as Spidey stepped through the door, William pulled the curtain behind him, then went hurriedly to the front of the living room and shut those drapes too.

"Nosy neighbors?" Spidey said, approving.

"Yeah. Wait a minute, I'll get Mom—" William hurried off, leaving Spidey there for a moment to look around him. The inside of the house matched the outside: small, tidy, understated. Everything looked a little worn, though, a little old. The arms on some of the chairs and the sofa were rubbed almost bare, the upholstery looked slightly faded. But everything was clean. Pictures hung on the walls, some of them Martha's watercolors—she had a way with the brush. There was a particularly beautiful one of Manhattan at dusk that Spidey had always admired.

"Spider-Man—"

He turned, saw her come in through the kitchen door, drying her hands on a towel. Martha Connors had been always been an extremely attractive woman: red-gold hair, a determined face. Now she was becoming merely striking, but more formidable. Her face showed ample evidence of the pain she had lived through, but there was no surrender in it, and those cool eyes looked at Spider-Man fully expecting that there might be more pain in the offing, and not shying away from it.

"How are you, Martha?" he said.

"Not too bad," she said, and it was a lie, but a social one. "Sit yourself down. I would assume that this isn't strictly a social call."

"Not entirely. But you know I worry about you two."

"We're fine," William said. This too, was clearly a lie, but his accomplishment didn't yet match his mother's. Still, Spidey had to give him marks for effort.

"It's not too bad," Martha said, "really. It's true the work for Farrar Chemical that I was doing dried up, after Curt—left. But we're doing all right. I'm doing temp work now: tele-working, for IBM over in Boca."

"Mom's a professional Web surfer," William said with some excitement. "She gets paid to hang out on the Internet and send people questionnaires, and look at Web sites."

Spidey laughed softly. "Sounds pretty good."

"It's a steady paycheck," Martha said, "if nothing else. Some people still need clothes and food and books for school, after all."

"How is school?" Spider-Man said.

"It's a total bore," William said, sitting back in the chair in the backbreaking posture again.

Martha looked wry. "I'm afraid he's not exaggerating," she said. "One of our main problems is that the local school district has run out of room in its fast-track program. Curt always did insist on making sure that William read a year or two, or three, ahead of his classmates; and he picked up so much science and math from his dad that he's pretty, well, overqualified at the moment."

"I want to take my JSATs this year," William said, "and they won't let me. They're drainheads. I did a JSAT dry run last year and I got seven ninety. If they would—"

"William," his mother said dryly, "don't push it. We've been over this ground before. You're just going to have to put up with the situation for another year. And anyway, you need more work on your social studies."

"No, I don't. It's boring. I'm going to be a scientist like Dad; you don't need social studies for that."

"William," his mother said, in a sigh. Spider-Man smiled again, but they couldn't see it. He cleared his throat instead.

"Martha," he said, "I see you have your work cut out for you. One thing, though. Have you heard anything from Curt?"

She shook her head. "Did Peter tell you about the postcard?" Spidey nodded. "There's been nothing since then, unfortunately. He's actually been here very little the last year or so. Whether that means he thinks he's getting near some kind of solution to his problem, or he just thinks it's too dangerous for him to be around us right now—I don't know."

Spidey sighed. "All right," he said. "Will you do me a favor? Let me know if you do hear anything?"

"How?"

Spider-Man produced a small spider-tracer. "I know," he said, to William this time, "that the last time I offered you one of these, you told me you didn't need it, since you were going to be taking care of your mother. And you've plainly done a good job of it. Now, though, it's a question of taking care of other people, who might get hurt if I don't have all the information I need to work with. There are some things going on down here that I'd like to rule the Lizard out of, if I could, and I can't do that without your help."

William looked at the tracer for a moment, then stretched out his hand to take it. "This works the same as my other tracers. But there's something added. See the little indentation on the top?" Spider-Man said. "Just enough to take a fingernail. Press a nail in there, then talk to it. I've got it hooked to— well, consider it a very small and stupid voicemail system. It's good for about fifteen seconds of sound. When you activate it, I'll be alerted, and I'll get the message shortly." He did not say that the tiny mobile-cell connector in it would dump the message to Peter Parker's answering machine.

William glanced at the little thing, then pocketed it. "Okay."

"He's not in trouble," Martha said, "is he?"

Spider-Man shook his head. "Truly, I don't know. If I hear any report that I think can be depended upon, I'll see that it gets back to you—if you want to hear it."

She looked at him steadfastly enough for a moment, then turned her eyes away. "I very much want my husband back," she said. "William's father . . . we need him. A great deal. Lizard or no Lizard. But I understand what he's doing. Please tell him—" she lifted her eyes to Spider-Man's mask again "—if you see him, tell him that we love him anyway. And we miss him . . . and want him home again, as soon as he can come. Meanwhile . . . we're all right."

Spider-Man nodded, and swallowed, to try to dislodge the lump from his throat. "I'll tell him. And if there's anything I can do for you—"

"You've already done more than enough," Martha Connors said. "But take care of yourself, as well, Spider-Man. We worry about our friends, too."

He got up. "William—"

"If anything happens," William said somberly, "I'll let you know."

Spider-Man turned toward the screen door. "And get to work on that social studies," he said.

William gave him a dry look. "Puh-leeze," he said, "not you too. . . ."

Spidey chuckled and slipped out into the night.

Peter met Vreni on Friday morning for breakfast, as planned. She had had little luck getting her police connections in order, as yet. "I'm going to make some calls today to some of the people down in the Everglades who claim to have seen the Lizard," Vreni said. "I don't think I'll need you until Monday at the press conference, and after that we can drive down to the 'Glades and take care of whatever appointments I've managed to set up."

"That's fine," Peter said. "I want to get out today and work with the Questar." *And here,* he thought, *I was worried about having to ditch her.*

"Have fun with the new toy," Vreni said, signaling the waiter for the bill.

He was loading up the rental car in the hotel's underground parking garage, and putting the Questar into the trunk with visions of a delightful afternoon of shooting lots and lots of film on expense account, when he heard a voice yell from way across the garage, "Peter!"

He turned, surprised. Vreni was practically running toward him. "What? What's the matter?"

"I'm so glad I caught you," she said as she came up to him, panting. "The hotel thought you'd left already. They've changed the day for the press conference."

"When is it?"

"Today! At noon. I didn't get the message from the hotel until just now."

"Good thing we're both early eaters," he said. "If we drive like crazy people, we can get there just before it starts."

"Let's do it," she said, and jumped into his car.

They drove up I-95 as fast as Peter dared. Vreni wanted to drive, but Peter was fortunately able to refuse. "You're not on this car's insurance," he said, and Vreni could grumble as she liked; it was true. He had other reasons, though, besides the inherent safety his spider-sense gave him. One of his newsroom cronies had told him a story about Vreni trashing a UN armored personnel carrier in Bosnia. *If she can do that to an APC,* he thought, *no way I'm going to let her do it to this poor little Chevette. Especially since the car's in my name, and I'd wind up paying for it.*

They hit the Cocoa Beach extension to the Bee Line Expressway at about twenty of twelve. A few minutes later they were at the main gate to the Kennedy Space Center, twentieth in a line of cars which seemed to be taking a long while to get in. Armed Air Force personnel, Peter saw, were looking closely at each car as it passed the gates: NASA security people were chatting with each driver.

They slowly crept up to the checkpoint, and the young NASA security man there peered in at Peter's car, while his Air Force buddy walked around it, examining it. "Can I see your driver's license, sir?" the security man said.

Peter handed it over, along with his *Daily Bugle* ID card. "We're down from New York for the press conference," he said.

"Thank you. Ma'am, may I see yours, please?"

Vreni handed her license and *Bugle* ID to the man, throwing Peter a wordless look that said, *Do you believe this security? Something's up.* Peter raised his eyebrows at her, said nothing.

The ID was handed back after a moment. "Thank you, sir, ma'am," the security guard said. "Straight ahead, turn right at the sign for Spaceport USA, and park in the Public Affairs Office lot toward the back."

They drove in and parked. Peter got the Questar out of the back of the car—he was not going to leave that piece of equipment out of his sight if he could help it—and they walked hurriedly to the main building. Spaceport USA was the Center's main public facility, a long low building housing a museum, the Astronauts' Memorial, and various free exhibits about satellites and space travel. Out behind it, dwarfing everything else, the "Rocket Garden" stood, with various old Mercury and other boosters, and the slightly sad shell of a Saturn lying on its side. "I want some pictures of those later," Peter said as they headed in through the front door.

"Tourist," Vreni said under her breath. Peter grinned. Indeed the place was full of tourists, people in T-shirts and shorts, and sticky children eating ice cream and shouting with excitement at the sight of the Space Man, some probably underpaid employee walking around in a space suit in this heat, and providing photo opportunities for the visitors.

To one side was a corrugated sign with plastic letters stuck to it, saying "STS-73 Press Conference." An arrow pointed off to the left, toward a meeting room down past one of the two IMAX theaters. A crowd of people, some with tape recorders and cameras, were heading that way. Peter and Vreni followed them.

Inside the room was the usual briefing-room kind of seating, plain folding chairs and a long blue-draped table, with the NASA curved-chevron logo behind it. To one side, in back, was a table with press packs piled up on it. Vreni edged over there to pick up a couple of them, while Peter placed himself fairly well forward on the right side, in position to take pictures of the presenters.

The room was half full, no more, when the people running the press conference came in from a side door. One of them, Peter guessed immediately, was an astronaut: his hair was shorter than anyone else's there, and Peter had noticed early on that there didn't seem to be many long-haired male astronauts, at least not so close to a launch date. The other three, two men and a woman, were civil servants, NASA people. *No military*, Peter thought, *at least not openly*.

Vreni plopped herself into the chair next to Peter's and tossed his copy of the press pack down onto the floor where he could get at it, then started leafing hastily through her own as the oldest of the men sitting up at the table, a gray-haired sort with a lined and kindly face, started testing his microphone.

"Good morning," he said. "Or good afternoon. This is the press conference for STS-73, and we want to apologize to you for the sudden change in schedule. Unfortunately we discovered at the last moment that we had a schedule conflict with other launch-related activities on Monday which would have made this conference impossible then, and it seemed more logical to relocate the event earlier rather than later, since toward launch date, staff schedules become very harried . . ."

Peter thought the man, a Mr. Buckingham, who was involved with "Launch Processing" according to the kit, looked harried enough at the moment. He had the expression of a man with problems on his mind which he had put aside for the moment. Buckingham began discussing the upcoming Shuttle launch, detailing launch time and crew information. The Shuttle in question would be *Endeavour*; her commander this time out would be the man sitting next to Buckingham, whom Peter had spotted earlier, Commander Ronald Luks.

Peter got a few pictures of Luks, a big, tanned, good-looking man, while he spoke. Beside him, Vreni was paying little attention to this, perhaps understandably, for almost everything being discussed here was also in the press pack. She was flipping through the pack as if looking for something in particular, and not finding it. Her scowl grew deeper by the moment. Then, quite suddenly, Vreni's eyebrows went up, and she pulled out a pen and began to scribble on the press pack in messy shorthand.

Commander Luks was now talking in an easygoing way about the mission, which would be his first as mission commander, and his third flight on the Shuttle. Peter got a couple more shots of him, and then caught a look on Buckingham's face, a sudden flicker of concern as Luks mentioned the partially built space station, *Freedom*. He managed to get at least one shot of it before the expression vanished as if it hadn't been there. Peter had little time to consider what might have caused it, for Vreni nudged him and pointed at a paragraph under the one she had been making notes on.

MPAPPS, said one of the equipment descriptions: "the Mission-Peculiar Ambient Power Production System." Peter looked at Vreni, shook his head: *what's it mean?* But she flashed him a sudden smile, that feral look she had worn when speaking of the story "running away from you."

Another mission specialist, one of the ground scientists involved with project design, Dr. Brewer, was speaking now: a startlingly redheaded man in his early forties with more freckles than Peter had ever seen on a human being. Brewer chatted briefly about the birds and the bees—literally. Besides the school-science experiment with bees, some other livestock was being brought along: a pair of hummingbirds, to see how weightlessness affected their sense of balance (if at all) and their flight habits. These would be relocated to *Freedom* for long-term evaluation by the team in residence there, and would later be moved to the new space station annex, *Heinlein*, when it was ready to be assembled in orbit late next year or early the year after. When the description of these and other experiments ended, Buckingham finally asked for questions.

Vreni sat looking at her notes for a few minutes, while other reporters made inquiries about the change of schedule in the press conference, the health of one payload specialist who had had to drop out of the flight because of a broken leg, and other such queries. Finally there was a moment's pause, and Vreni put her hand up.

Buckingham nodded to her. She smiled at him and said, "Vreni Byrne, *Daily Bugle*. Mr. Buckingham, there has been a lot of discussion by various environmental groups lately of a Shuttle payload which was originally scheduled for this flight, the CHERM or Compact High-Energy Reactor Module. A lot of people were complaining about it, saying that they didn't want something which turned out to be a small, fast 'breeder' reactor containing half a kilogram of plutonium, shot off over their heads where something untoward might, God forbid, happen to it . . . say, a mission abort which would leave the stuff at the bottom of the Atlantic, or an explosion which would powder it all over the Southern Tier and cause deaths by cancer and mutations in the thousands. Leaving aside the thorny question of nuclear nonproliferation in space—are we to understand that the disappearance of this module from the schedule for STS-73 is a reaction to public opinion? Or has the thing malfunctioned somehow?"

A slight stir of interest went around the room. Buckingham looked completely unconcerned, an expression which Peter noted, and took a shot of. "The protests about the CHERM," Buckingham said, casually enough, "have been a matter of public record for some months now. NASA understands the public's concern in this matter, and everybody will understand that our concern for the safety of our neighbors on the Space Coast and elsewhere on the planet is a daily matter and something we take very seriously. It was decided that the CHERM equipment package, especially its security capsule, needed more study and a reevaluation before sending it aloft, in light of various issues mentioned not only in the press but in Congress and elsewhere in government. However, we are also investigating other venues for the CHERM equipment's launch, since it, or something like it, is going to be needed aboard *Freedom* eventually."

"I know people like to say that we should make do with solar power," Commander Luks said genially, "but in space, with the extremes of heat and cold we experience, and the amount of power needed to manage the backups which keep our crews safe, solar just isn't enough. The only space-sufficient power source which can safely be lifted from Earth into LEO with our present technology is atomic. We can't burn coal up there, unfortunately."

A little ripple of laughter went around the room. "Yes," Vreni said, smiling too, "Senator Lysander's line has been quoted a lot lately. The CHERM package, then, is not going up on STS-73?"

"The CHERM package is not going up," Buckingham said.

"Thank you, sir. One more thing, then. I note in the press pack the presence of the MPAPPS or 'Mission-Peculiar Ambient Power Production System.' Would you elaborate a little on the function of this, since it's listed in the cargo bay payload manifest up front of the pack, but not in the developmental test objectives supplement?"

Buckingham looked slightly bemused at that. "Isn't it? It ought to be. Briefly, the MPAPPS is an ancillary power generation system containing old-style fuel-cell technology. It's being attached to *Freedom* as a redundant backup for other energy management systems, specifically to the computer systems which handle life support for the station. With the second wing being brought on-line after STS-72/74, and new personnel coming aboard from Russia and ESA, extra planned redundancy has to be added."

"I see," Vreni said, and that smile was still very much in place, the look of a woman watching a story run away from her at full speed. "The MPAPPS isn't atomic in nature, then?"

Buckingham chuckled. "Miss Byrne, if I said that I wouldn't be very accurate, since we are all atomic in nature—"

"Please, sir, I don't think you mean to sound so disingenuous. I'm asking whether this new piece of equipment is indeed an atomic reactor—in fact, the same reactor originally scheduled to go up, but under another name."

"It is not," Buckingham said.

"Thank you, sir," Vreni said, and sat down. Another reporter jumped up and started asking questions about the Agency's possible cruelty to animals, but Vreni scribbled on her press pack again, looking profoundly satisfied.

A few minutes later, still another reporter, from the *Los Angeles Times,* stood up and began inquiring about security breaches on the KSC grounds over the past couple of weeks. "Nothing has happened," Buckingham said, "which in any way affects or threatens the launch of STS-73, if that's what you're concerned about. We are indeed breaking in a new facility-wide security system, which always means a certain number of false alarms and hiccups—as any of you know who've installed or tuned an alarm system lately. But no one's stolen the silver."

More chuckling went around the room, and the press conference turned to other topics, while Vreni turned and winked at the *LA Times* reporter, a little man with shaggy hair and wicked eyes. Finally, about an hour after it started, the conference ended, and the people up at the head table posed briefly for a photo opportunity, then left.

Peter took the opportunity, even though he didn't have to, then went off after Vreni, who was chatting with the guy from the *Times.* "Bobby," she said as Peter joined them, "Peter

Parker. He strings for the *Bugle*. Peter, this is Bobby London, *LA Times*, as you heard. I owe you one, Bob."

"My pleasure," Bobby said softly. "I got wind of some craziness down this way last week. No one seems to want to talk about it: either outright denials, like this, or a lot of muttering, but no details."

"If I hear something," Vreni said, "I'll pay you back that much."

"No more?" Bobby said.

"One favor at a time," said Vreni, "and every reporter for herself. Peter? We should probably get back to Miami—there are some things I want to look into."

"Right."

They said good-byes to London and headed off to their car. "So?" Peter said.

Vreni laughed out loud as they got in and stowed their various gear. "They're running scared about something, that's for sure, and probably the reactor is at the heart of it. Usually they can't throw enough information at you at these press conferences. But I've never heard of one this short before."

"So is this the reactor that Greenpeace and everybody was protesting about?" Peter said as he started the car.

"Good question. I didn't believe Buckingham, just then . . . that's all I'm sure of. And here's the question—"

Peter drove out the entrance, where security people were still checking the people coming in. Vreni said nothing until they were back on the freeway again. "Look," she said, "if they wanted to send something up secretly, why didn't they just do that? They've done it before."

"Maybe," Peter said, "they thought that no one would be interested in the reactor—a mistake, granted—and now they're trying to cover up the fact that they're putting it up anyway."

"Yes, but why mention this MPAPPS thing, then? Which sounds so much like some kind of clandestine power source—a reactor by any other name? Why not just put the thing up there, hush hush, and be done with it?"

Peter shook his head. "It's beyond me."

Vreni sighed. "Well, at least I have something to run with now. I'm going to get started on those interview schedulings today, and see if I can get hold of my police buddies. Meanwhile, if I can get some interviews scheduled for tomorrow . . ."

"You're on," Peter said. "After I drop you, I'll be out with the camera and the Questar. I've got to get the hang of this thing. Breakfast tomorrow?"

Vreni nodded. "The Breakfast Club, that's us. Let's make it early, though. The Hilton holds these big brunch buffets on weekends, and if I see all that food, I'm going to try to eat it. Not a good thing."

Peter chuckled. "For either of us. Early it is."

Several hours later, Peter was standing in a swamp, being bitten all over by hungry mosquitoes, and was happier than he'd been in months.

After dropping Vreni off, he had called Aunt Anna's to check in with MJ. She wasn't home: Aunt Anna told him that MJ wasn't expected back until late—something about a gallery-opening party being run by one of the people with whom she had left her CV, a gathering at which it was smart for MJ to put in an appearance.

Oh, well, Peter thought, and set himself up for a day out, and an evening as well, doing work of different kinds. He packed the Questar, and one other piece of useful equipment: his police-radio scanner. He also brought an extra camera—one which he had been using, as Spider-Man, quite effectively of late. It had a motion-actuated mount, with a little circuit board, a whole PC's worth of intelligence, to drive it. A couple of weeks ago, after finishing the business with Venom, he had added one more useful piece of hardware to it—a simple vise-style C-clamp. The camera had shown a tendency to fall over, occasionally, when he left it to its own devices on a tripod. (His usual method of webbing the camera in place had the drawback of not allowing the motion sensor to move freely.)

The C-clamp, though, would leave it freer to move and less likely to do a dive from a wall or other unstable situation. Peter could even clamp it onto a pole or a tree limb, now, and be fairly certain of finding it where he left it when he got back, rather than lying on its lens in a puddle, or smashed to bits.

An hour's drive out of Miami on Route 41 brought him into the Big Cypress National Preserve. It was in the Everglades, though not part of the Everglades National Park as such. Twenty-four hundred square miles of hardwood tree islands, scattered slash pine, dry prairies, marsh, and mangrove forest. Here and there he would pass a little knot of houses, maybe with a tiny store nearby, and nothing else for miles except the huge boles of cypress and beds of waving reeds. Birdsong was everywhere: once, when Peter stopped to give himself a break from driving and listen to the wind, he heard a low coughing cry repeated several times, and it took him some minutes to realize that the sound was that of a Florida panther, somewhere out there among the tangled islands of marl and knotted tree-roots, going about its business.

He stopped several times to work with the Questar and do some wildlife photography that was as good a practice for the next couple of weeks' work as he was likely to get. The Questar's range was indeed ridiculous, and it took him a while to get used to it. He could sight a rock half a mile away and get a close-up of a cottonmouth sunning on it which suggested he was more like ten feet from the stone—though he much preferred the real distance. A flock of flamingos a mile off, an alligator a quarter-mile away, rolling lazily in a drainage canal—they seemed close enough to walk up to and touch. Peter began to wish desperately that some money would drop from the heavens so he could afford a Questar of his own. *I might as well wish for that Hasselblad they left on the moon,* he thought, and then wondered whether one of his fellow super heroes might be passing that way anytime soon. If they were. . . .

Peter chuckled to himself and straightened up. It was getting near dusk again. He had pulled off to the side of the road to catch the moon coming up, for the Questar was after all primarily a telescope, and it would be stupid, he thought, not to experiment with that aspect of its function as well. Big and round, the moon slid up. Peter fussed over the camera's f-stops, looking for the best setting to catch that apparently huge disk without the diminution of its apparent size that was every photographer's bane. He blew nearly a roll of film on that alone. Behind him, in the car, the police scanner muttered softly to itself, mostly about speeders and domestic disturbances.

The moon was an hour or so up the sky when Peter stopped at last. *Vreni's not going to want to hear excuses in the morning,* he thought, *and we'll have a lot of driving to do tomorrow, I would imagine. Better pack up and go.* And he was doing just that, and had just slid into the driver's seat of the Chevette, when the scanner started talking to itself again. It had been quiet for a while; the new urgency in the dispatcher's voice caught Peter by surprise.

"Okee four one eight—"

"Four one eight, go."

"Got a report of a large reptile walking around near Deep Lake." That was one of the small towns in the area, in the heart of Big Cypress, near Route 29.

"That's the fourth 'gator today," said four one eight wearily.

"Not a 'gator," said the dispatcher, somewhat anxiously. Peter blinked.

"What?"

"No 'gator, four one eight. The report was of a reptile. Also from Deep Lake, report of a large man in distress, seen heading out of town in a hurry. And a silent alarm. The general store in Deep Lake."

Peter grabbed his road map, shook it open, and checked his position. Deep Lake was no more than two miles away.

"Okay, dispatch. ETA ten minutes. We're over by Ochopee at the moment—that break-in."

"Ten-four, four one eight."

Peter leaped out of the car, seized the Questar and his camera bag, locked the car up, and hotfooted it into a clump of cypress near the roadside. A half a minute later, Spider-Man swung down out of the trees—having first webbed the Questar, the camera bag, and his car keys tightly to the cypress's innermost trunk, about fifty feet up, just in case anyone should stop to have a look at his car with less than friendly intent. His own camera, the small C-clamped one, was tucked away in his costume should he need it.

He took off cross-country at his best speed. Here the going was better than in the suburbs: the biggest trees, the most ancient of the great bald cypresses, stood up like towers dotted across the landscape, their huge thick branches outstretched and ready to catch a slung web. Where the bald cypresses didn't grow, the lesser ones grew in plenty. Spider-Man might not get a lot of height, but he made good speed. With little chance of anyone seeing him, out here in the middle of almost nowhere, the two-minute mile was no problem.

Deep Lake was a very small town indeed: a gas station, a diner, a post office, a little general store, and a scatter of small houses on a side road behind it. The blue strobe light of the general store's alarm was flashing, and lights were on inside. Spidey swung past and glanced in the window, saw no one hurt, only some shelves knocked over and an old man looking at them, shaking his head. He would have stopped and looked in, but his spider-sense twinged hard, and he looked down past the faint aura of radiance thrown by the town's three streetlights. He thought he heard, in the vast country silence, someone or something crashing through the undergrowth.

Swiftly he went after the noise, out of town and on down Route 29, then eastward into the swamp. Swamp was probably the wrong name for it; it was wet prairie, really, mixed with dry-footed reed beds alive with the singing and peeping of frogs. Louder than the frogs, he could hear heavy footsteps thudding on soft ground, splashing through the wet, and a low, almost singsong growl. The footsteps went in a two-footed rhythm. *Definitely* not *a 'gator,* Spidey thought.

Here there were fewer trees to work with. Spider-Man leapt again and again, and finally, ahead of him, caught sight of what he pursued—or, rather, whom. The moon was higher, and glinted off wet, scaly hide. Color was washed out of everything in this light, but Spider-Man knew that that hide would be green by daylight. He saw the lash of the tail. The growl got louder.

One big leap brought him down right in front of it. Shocked, the creature started, then planted its huge hind claws, grounded the powerful tail behind it for balance.

"Curt," Spider-Man said. "Curt, we've only got a couple of minutes to talk. The police are coming—"

The Lizard flung his arms wide, and roared, flexing his claws. A glint in the air—*did something fly off to one side?* Or was it a bat, or some night-flying bird, flickering briefly bright in the moonlight? Spidey didn't dare take his eyes off the Lizard to see—a moment's error with this creature could leave you very dead.

"Curt, listen," he said. "Martha—"

Another roar. The Lizard shook his head wildly from side to side as if even the mention of her name caused him pain. *Maybe it does,* Spidey thought, wrenched with pity. He wanted not to have to try this tack again, but anything that might get through to Curt Connors, to the man trapped inside, was worth trying. "Martha and William—"

Half roaring, half screaming, the Lizard rushed him. Spider-Man leapt sideways and felt the wind of the Lizard's plunge brush by him, felt the claws go whiffing past his face, just missing. *Sometimes I really miss the good old days when the Lizard was semi-intelligent, and not a mindless, rampaging beast,* he thought.

He heard cars, two of them, pull up by the roadside. That

was followed by car doors being thrown open and slammed shut. Flashlights came on, and people headed out into the darkness toward them.

"This is the police," said an amplified voice. "We're armed, and we'll shoot if we have to. Come out and give yourself up."

Spidey leapt up and out of the way to get a look at where the police were. He was astonished when his spider-sense warned him that one of those huge clawed hands was reaching toward him. Unable to twist out of the way in midair, the Lizard plucked him out of the air and dashed him to the ground. Stunned, he lay there just long enough to gasp and roll sideways as the Lizard's razor-sharp claws came down and slashed the ground where he had been. Spider-Man shot a web at the Lizard, but as fast as he shot it, the creature clawed it aside.

"Hold it right there!" yelled a man's voice. Enraged, the Lizard spun, took a fraction of a second to sight on the intruder—then leapt. Spidey barely had time to shoot out one last strand of web, aiming for the Lizard's legs. He caught him. The Lizard slammed down hard on the ground. "It's the Lizard!" Spider-Man shouted. "Get out of here! Get back in your cars!"

A second's silence—then gunfire. There was no way to tell in what direction the bullets were traveling. All Spidey could see were muzzle flashes, and all he could hear were ricochets. The Lizard tore the web off his legs, reared up again and made for the officers. Spidey staggered to his feet, picked the one decent-sized cypress in the area, and shot a line of web at its top. It held. *This works for Tarzan and Luke Skywalker,* he thought, *let's see if it works for me.*

The Lizard charged, claws outstretched. Right in front of his face, Spidey came swinging by, caught the first cop out of the Lizard's path, grabbed the second between his legs, and swung them both up and out of the Lizard's reach, into the cypress. The three of them thudded into the trunk, and the cops had the sense to cling on tight, while the Lizard rushed the bottom of the tree and hit it almost head-on. The crash shook the whole tree, but it held fast: three hundred years' worth of hurricanes had taught it a trick or two.

The Lizard roared rage and defiance, shook the tree, but the tree still held. Then came what Spidey had feared: the Lizard sank his talons into the trunk and started to climb it. Hurriedly Spider-Man looked around him, sighted another treetop that he thought he could hit with a web.

Out on the road, a third cop car arrived, sirens blaring and lights flashing, then a fourth. The Lizard let the tree go, roared in fury, and loped off into the swamp. Spidey tried to tell where he was going, but in the uncertain moonlight, it was hopeless—in less than a few seconds, the Lizard might as well have been invisible. And, encumbered as he was with a pair of cops, there was no opportunity to hit him with a spider tracer.

"You guys all right?" he said to his two fellow travelers.

One of them answered unprintably. The second said, "And who the hell are you, buster?"

He slid down the webline with both of them and saw them safely onto the ground before answering, "Just your friendly neighborhood Spider-Man, officer."

"Not mine," said the first policeman, and spat expressively.

The second dusted himself off, eyed Spider-Man with an expression that looked thoughtful, if not entirely friendly. "You on vacation?"

Spidey had to laugh. "No," he said. "This is a business trip."

"And was that your business?" the second cop said, gesturing after the Lizard with his chin.

"Partly," Spidey said. "I heard he'd been seen down here."

"More than seen," said another of the policemen, one of the group who had just arrived. They were carrying shotguns, and one of them had leveled his at Spidey. "They took Saunders's store apart, back there. Money missing. And, Harry? Your gun's gone from your car. So's Ed's."

"Your friend there," said the second policeman to Spider-Man, "seems to have had a friend with him."

71

"Not my friend," Spider-Man said. "An accomplice?" That was a new one on him. The Lizard was a loner by nature. *This puts an entirely new spin on things. . . .*

"Never mind that," said the first policeman. "What're we gonna do with you, now, Mister Friendly Neighborhood?"

"He's a crook like the others," said one of the newly arrived cops. "Arrest 'im."

Spider-Man sighed inside the mask, and looked toward the second policeman, who looked back with that thoughtful expression again. "I think we might have trouble with that," he said. "Anyway, you did us a good turn just now, son. That thing would've fileted us. But this is *our* neighborhood, so I think it would be best if you let us handle matters around here, and took yourself on back wherever you came from."

"I understand you perfectly, Officer," Spidey said. "My pleasure to have been of service."

He shot a webline up into the tree and swung away, heading northward toward Route 41. When he got back to the spot where he had parked his car, he got in, started it up, and moved it several hundred yards farther along the road and out of sight, on a small service road running parallel with a canal by the road. *If they noticed it*, he thought, *I don't want them coming back and tracing it . . . it could cause uncomfortable questions.*

Once the car was seen to, and he double-checked that the Questar was still lodged in the tree, he webslung his way back to within a few hundred yards of where he and the Lizard had clashed. The police were still going over the area, so Spidey perched in one of the bald cypresses, waiting for them to leave. They took an hour or two about it, going very thoroughly over the ground where the fight with the Lizard had taken place. Finally, though, they realized there wasn't much more they could do until morning, on such varied and uneven ground, and they left.

Spider-Man came down from his tree then, slightly stiff, but no less intrigued than he had been earlier. That memory of something, faint but definitely there—flying off the Lizard? or being thrown?—was nagging him.

He went over the ground with spider-senses alert. Even so, the terrain was so variable, such a crazy unpredictable mixture of wet and dry, of bog, dirt, mud, reeds, and prickly undergrowth, and the light was so poor, that it wasn't until the false dawn began that he found it. "It" was a little can, about a foot long and matte-silvery, like a very upmarket thermos bottle.

Now then, he thought, and worked on getting the top unscrewed. It took a certain exertion of his super-strength to loosen the thing—a normal person probably wouldn't have been able to get it open without mechanical help. Finally, though, he got it off, and peered into the "thermos."

Nothing.

He shook the bottle. The faintest sound of impact inside: something, not rattling, just thumping gently against the sides of the bottle. There was something in there.

Then why couldn't he see it?

He upended the bottle over one hand. Something slid out, into his palm. Impact—but without weight.

Spider-Man peered at the object in his hand, if "object" was the word he was looking for. *It's a piece of smoke,* he thought, completely mystified, for that was what it looked like. If you had a smoke-filled room, and took a knife and cut a rectangular slice of the air, sort of the shape of a slender brick—and then took it outside into clean air to examine it, it would look just like this. The edges of the substance seemed to fade away into the air itself. The body of it was semitransparent, and grayish, just like smoke. It was lighter than an object of equivalent size made of paper or hollow plastic.

What on Earth is this? Spider-Man wondered. *Is it even from Earth? And what the heck was the Lizard doing with it?*

Spider-Man put the "smoke" back in its bottle and closed it tight, webbed it to him, and started back to the car as dawn's early light started to come up over the wetlands, and the first birds of morning started to test their voices. He was going to have to find out what this was, and what the Lizard was doing with it. But it was going to have to wait a little. In a couple of hours, Vreni would be waiting for Peter Parker, downstairs at the Hilton.

As he swung off toward the road, he yawned. *If I'd known the superhero business kept calling for these all-nighters,* he thought, *I doubt I'd ever have gotten into it.*

But this was at least partly a fib. Spider-Man swung off into the new morning, the proud possessor of a piece of smoke, and a whole new batch of unanswered questions.

THREE

When Peter got back to the hotel, it was nearly seven. He'd agreed to meet Vreni for breakfast at about eight. There would be just time to get himself up to the room and run a lot of cold water over himself very quickly in an attempt to wake up.

Not that the evening's events weren't interesting enough, but Peter was having a reaction that happened sometimes after a night's excitement: the adrenaline would run out, and he would find himself totally wrecked. There was no time for that now, though. He had a long day of driving and shooting ahead of him.

Peter took the elevator up to the twelfth floor in the hotel and walked down the long hall to his room. As he slid the key card into the door, he saw to his surprise that the little light on the doorplate, which usually flashed green when the door was ready to open, was now coming up red. He tried the knob, and found the door bolted from the inside. "Hello?" he said.

"Ung," said a weary voice from inside. He heard the closet door slide aside, someone feeling among the clothes there: then the sound of the door unbolting, the chain coming off. MJ opened the door, blinked blearily at him. "If you're going to have such late nights while you're down here," she said, "I wish you'd let me know."

"What're you doing here?" he said, coming in and shutting the door behind him.

"Well, since you did slip me that spare key," MJ said, "I thought I might as well make use of it. I couldn't get back to Aunt Anna's from that party last night. It was too late, I didn't want to disturb her; and the cab would've cost a fortune." She shrugged. "So I thought I'd just crash here."

"Well," Peter said, hugging her, "I'm glad somebody got to use the room last night, because I sure didn't."

"I noticed," she said, sitting down on the bed. "Business, I take it."

He nodded. "Take a look at this," Peter said.

He rummaged among his bags and things and came up with

77

the thermos bottle, unscrewed it, and went over to sit at the table by the window. MJ got up and looked over his shoulder as he tapped the contents of the bottle onto the table's surface. There lay, in the morning sunlight, the piece of smoke. Where the sun struck it, it seemed even less there—just a pale misty oblong, a little brick of fog. MJ looked at it, her eyes wide. "What is it?"

"You tell me."

She reached out a hand toward it, then pulled the hand back. "It's not radioactive or anything, is it?"

Peter shook his head. "Couldn't tell for sure," he said, "but if it were hot enough to be dangerous, I'd get a twinge from my spider-sense. I don't get anything like that at all, so . . ."

"And you found this where?"

Quickly Peter told her about the Lizard, and his encounter with him. MJ shook her head. "Strange," she said. "I thought that these days he was sort of mindless when he was the Lizard. I mean, as Curt Connors he might make plans, or do intelligent things, but—as the Lizard?"

"I don't know, MJ." And then Peter checked his watch. "Oh, jeez, look at the time. I've got to get into the shower, honey."

He headed for the bathroom, shedding clothes in all directions. MJ wandered after him. "You're gonna like that shower," MJ said. "It's so strong, it nearly rips your hair off."

"Good," Peter said. He turned it on, producing a violent stream of water and a satisfying cloud of steam. He climbed in and started to scrub.

"You'd better shave too," MJ said. "Your seven-o'clock shadow is showing."

"I just bet. How did you do last night?"

"Ohh," she said, sitting down on the sink, "not great."

"Why? Wasn't it a good party?"

"Oh, it was good. There were all these network TV people there. Lots of nice food." She sounded morose.

"Doesn't sound like you enjoyed yourself much."

"I didn't. They were all better-looking than I was."

"Oh, come on! I think that's statistically impossible."

"No, I'm serious. And in the middle of the party, they introduced the model who's going to get that part on the talk show."

"Oh, really." Now he understood where the moroseness was coming from. Peter sighed. He thought he knew what MJ was thinking: that they needed the money, but also that being passed over for a job was a personal blow to her, no matter how casually she acted about such things.

"And she," MJ said, "was gorgeous. *Gorgeous*." She pouted slightly. "It's just not fair."

"No," Peter said, "I guess it's not. What're you going to do now?"

"I don't know. I was talking to some of the people at the party last night. Some of them were from agencies I'd applied to." She shook her head. "It's funny, but they see acting as a step down from modeling. They think that if you've gone into acting in TV, you've essentially written yourself off as a model. I don't understand it. I would have thought it'd give you more credence, not less. But that doesn't seem to be the way it works, not down here." She laughed, a somewhat bitter sound. "All of them were interested in talking to me about my TV work, but if I talked to them about modeling, they looked at me as if they thought I just wanted to come back and . . . slum. And it's not like that! You know that."

"You wouldn't know how to slum," Peter said, groping around for the shampoo bottle. "It's insulting for them to even think that way."

"Oh, I know, but they don't see that. A lot of these people are really kind of wrapped up in themselves."

Peter smiled slightly. This was a complaint he had heard from her before, and it was, he supposed, understandable. When your work and your livelihood depended on how good you could make yourself look to other people, the temptation to become very self-centered, it seemed to Peter, would be tough to resist. He had kept to himself, some time back, the suspicion that one reason MJ's modeling career was a little up-and-down was because she did not have that self-centeredness. But that was one of the things he loved about her, and he wasn't sure he'd trade it for any amount of success.

"Anyway," MJ said, "I had a couple of offers."

"Anything serious?"

MJ laughed again, pulled a Kleenex out of the box, and began shredding it methodically. "They weren't much better than wage slavery, really, and the travel allowances—" She shook her head. "I'd be crazy to take them. I *do* have my pride." She glanced up at him. He could just see her out the shower curtain, and the look in her eyes was an almost stern expression that he had seen before. "You start working cheap, here or anywhere, and word gets around. Pretty soon no one will have you anymore. So . . ." She trailed off. "Are you angry with me?"

"What? For not taking bad job offers? You have to be the judge of these things, babe. This isn't my area of expertise." He put his head out the shower curtain and smiled at her. "You want advice on how to climb up the sides of apartment buildings, or where to sock Venom to make him yell—"

"Please," MJ said. "I'd just spent a few days without even thinking of him. But I see your point."

"Well," Peter said, "I'll be guided by your opinion. If you think a job's bad, you shouldn't be taking it."

She sighed. Peter got out of the shower and hastily rubbed himself down: it was almost seven-thirty. "You know," she said, looking up at him, "you're really good to me."

"Well, I should be! You're my wife!"

"Yeah, well, you put up with a lot, you know that? Me and my insecurities."

"And you don't put up with a lot?" He hung up the towel, drew her close. "With a husband who swings around on webs and gets himself in trouble? I think you have a fairly high tolerance level, actually. I'm a pretty lucky guy."

She pulled his face down to hers. For a long minute or so, there were no words. Then MJ said, "You want me to rinse out your uniform for you?"

Peter chuckled. "It doesn't need it yet. Besides, if one of the hotel staff came in and found it hanging over the tub—"

MJ dimpled. "I see your point. Well, never mind." She stepped out and started rummaging in the closet for her clothes. "I should go back to Aunt Anna's. I left a message for her, but you know how she is. Until she sees me with her own eyes and hears everything that happened, she won't be satisfied. And she won't have anything to tell the neighbors." She chuckled. "'My Niece The TV Star.'"

"Well, give her my best."

Peter started dressing hurriedly. When he turned away from checking himself out in the mirrored sliding doors, he saw MJ staring thoughtfully at the little piece of smoke on the table. "It's so strange," she said. "It looks—" she shrugged "—illegal somehow."

"Illegal as in drugs?"

"No . . . just as in, it shouldn't be there. It looks wrong."

She reached out a hand, prodded it hesitantly. Then MJ put up her eyebrows. "It's a little springy. Did you feel that?"

"No." He came over to MJ and reached out a finger, poked the stuff. There was indeed a response as if he were pushing on very resistant foam rubber. But when he pushed it and let it spring back, he couldn't see any change in the object, no evidence of what he could physically feel it doing. It was very strange.

"I've got to find somebody who can tell me what the heck this is," Peter said. "But it's going to have to wait. Vreni's going to have a lot of interview appointments today, I think."

"What're you going to do with this?" MJ asked.

"Oh, I'll take it with me . . . there's room in the camera bag."

"Why would the Lizard have it?" she continued, as Peter shrugged into a light jacket and started packing his work bags up. "Where would he have been taking it? Where did it come from?"

"I hope I can find out," Peter said.

In San Francisco that morning, the mist hung low, as it often did: sometimes until noon, nearly, before burning off. Many people in San Francisco paid no particular attention to this, being used to it. Others paid no attention to the weather because they couldn't see it.

Down in the darkness, below the city streets, the doings of the open sky were no concern of theirs, except on rainy days when the water made its way down through the drains and trickled into the city's underheart. Down there in the darkness, under the great buildings, under the old city, a newer one had been born. A place of tunnels and warrens, lit here and there by lamps illumined with stolen power, maintained with materials brought down quietly from the surface by night. It was a city of the disenfranchised, the homeless, the victimized, of people who had turned their backs on the mist and the sunshine both, and sought a different kind of life, private, silent, remote.

In one such quiet warren, a man sat on someone's castaway chair, and thought. It was not strictly accurate to call him a man—not anymore. The core of him was human, but things had been added. He was not a single being any longer . . . and had almost forgotten what it was like to be one.

He was part of a symbiosis, one that some people found deadly, others found reassuring. In a long-forgotten tunnel between two buildings, in a little makeshift "living room" containing a table and chairs, and the remains of a takeout meal, Eddie Brock, known to his friends and his enemies as Venom, sat going over some paperwork and considering his options.

The decay and destruction of something he loved was on his mind. The past month or so had been a busy one for him. San Francisco was his home, but he left it willingly enough when business called. Business, for him, meant defending the innocent, the helpless, from those who would prey upon them; defending them violently, if need be. He had gone to New York to do that, for he had gotten word that someone there was masquerading as Venom and attacking innocent people. If there was any kind of behavior he could not allow to happen in his name, it was that. Making his way to New York, he had dealt with the problem—had helped to deal with the creature which, as it turned out, had unwittingly been impersonating him by night in the streets of New York.

There had also been other satisfactions. Going to New York had also meant dealing with Spider-Man. Venom had dealt with the wall-crawler, at least to his temporary satisfaction, giving him one or two extremely conclusive drubbings and reminding him once again of the error which Spider-Man had made in rejecting the symbiote/"costume" which was now part of Venom. Venom had been slightly surprised, as well, during their brief and peculiar alliance, to find that Spider-Man was perhaps slightly less a hopeless case than Venom had thought. Not that this would make any difference in the long run: Venom would destroy him eventually. The symbiote's emotions regarding Spider-Man, and Peter Parker, were too clear for Venom to ignore. Sooner or later the moment would be right, and this particular aspect of his history with the symbiote would become a closed chapter.

For the meantime, though, Venom had parted from Spider-Man, content to let him live a while longer in return for his aid against the bizarre extraterrestrial creature which had been killing people in Venom's apparent likeness, and also for his action against Hobgoblin—unquestionably a factor in keeping all of Manhattan from being blown halfway to the moon.

Other aspects of the month's work, though, were still niggling at Venom. The extraterrestrial monster had mostly killed in search of radioactive materials, its food. And there turned out to be far too much material of that kind in the city for Venom's taste . . . courtesy of a strange import-export firm called Consolidated Chemical Research Corporation. This firm had stored radioactive materials in odd places around Manhattan, places too accessible to normal human beings who could (and did) come to harm by them. Barrels of waste, caches of fissionable material, things that had no business being in a city full of the innocent—Venom and Spider-Man had recovered a number of caches. The New York City government, alerted to this problem, had been cleaning up the sites as best it could: as far as Venom could tell from the news, and his more clandestine sources of information, they were doing a fairly good job.

But his own concerns didn't stop there. A firm like CCRC, which had been so careless once in the middle of one of the most heavily populated areas on the planet, would likely be just as careless elsewhere. Any big company which became so cavalier with the lives of human beings was a concern to Venom, and he intended to keep working at this problem until it was solved.

He looked at one of the pieces of paper which lay on the chipped Formica table on which he sat. He didn't have to reach for it: the symbiote, which was presently masquerading as his shirt and jeans, put out a slim graceful pseudopod and flipped the page over so that Eddie could see the next one, a long list of names and addresses. Venom had continued to look into the corporate structure of CCRC.

Through his investigation of state and county documents, Eddie had found that CCRC's New York branch had been having dealings with numerous companies of varying types in various states. Some of these had been shut down abruptly over the last month: corporations were sold or otherwise divested, registrations were shifted around. Now there were only a few active links to CCRC left. Venom had found it very interesting that all of them were in Florida.

One of these was a large foreign merchant bank called Regners Wilhelm, a German-based firm, outwardly very respectable. One was a chemical supply firm called Haller Chemical. And yet another—and this one Venom found a matter for some concern—was the United States Government. CCRC seemed to be supplying something—the details were presently fuzzy—to Kennedy Space Center.

All of this gave Eddie Brock a lot to think about. He was disturbed by the government connection. He was even more disturbed by the presence of any CCRC operation in Florida. The great aquifer which underlay the state was one of its greatest assets, and was tremendously vulnerable. Already the water system there had been much damaged by the thoughtless misuse of the past century. And the flatness of the state made that aquifer very susceptible to contamination: such contamination would take months, maybe years, to purge itself completely from the ecosystem, doing who knew what damage both to animal life and the humans living there—the innocents who had no other source of water, and would shortly find themselves being poisoned if radioactive by-products were to be stored as carelessly in Florida as they had been in Manhattan.

Until a day or so ago, Eddie Brock had been content to turn all these things over in his mind, and plan, trying to figure out what was the best way in which to proceed. But then a piece of news had been brought to him that gave him much more concern.

The Lizard had been seen in Florida. All around him, Eddie could feel the symbiote twitching against his skin in the beginnings of rage. The Lizard was a thoughtless, mindless monster, one that needed to be killed: it had done enough harm to the innocent in its own time. Occasionally Spider-Man had served to contain the thing. But now, to this already dangerous cocktail of CCRC carelessness and involvement in Florida, the Lizard had been added.

Venom knew that the Lizard had been used in the past by another super-villain, a woman named Calypso. At least Hobgoblin, who would love such a tool, was safely out of the picture, and put away in the Vault for the moment. But there were others who were free, and wouldn't scruple. And Curt Connors, the Lizard's human alter ego, was a scientist, one with expertise in biochemistry—but chemistry first and foremost.

It all made Venom slightly suspicious. Eddie Brock was a journalist before Spider-Man conspired to ruin his good name. And now those old instincts kicked in: he smelled something, something suspicious. Something that needed his attention in Florida.

In addition, if the Lizard was in Florida, it wouldn't be surprising if Spider-Man showed up. Venom couldn't bring himself to object to that.

Eddie smiled a little, to himself and his other, put the paperwork back in its neat pile, and stood up.

Florida is supposed to be very nice this time of year, he thought. *It's time for us to go.*

Peter met Vreni for breakfast. She looked at him with some concern. "Had a bad night?" she said. "You've got big circles under your eyes."

Peter nodded. "A late one."

"Will you be all right for today?"

"Sure, as soon as I get some coffee in me."

"All right. I've made a couple of appointments for us down in Ochopee—and a couple in the spot where the Lizard was actually seen last night. We're in good shape; we'll have fresh reports. I'll drive today, if you like—"

"No, it's okay," Peter said hastily, "I still have some work to do with the Questar—can we do it in two cars?"

"No problem."

After breakfast, they retraced the route that Peter had taken the night before. About an hour or so later, they were parking in front of Saunders's store, which Peter had passed while going after the Lizard. Vreni interviewed Mr. Saunders— "You just call me Dave now, honey"—a dear old, unreconstructed "old boy" with a halo of thin white hair, who either had never heard about women's liberation or didn't care about it. He repeatedly called Vreni "honey chile," and although

Peter saw her eyebrows go up the first time, plainly she wasn't going to make an issue of it as long as the information kept coming.

"That big green thing came right in here," he said, waving his arms around at the front door, now hanging pitifully off its hinges. "Went smashing around, broke half the glass in the place—" Mr. Saunders gestured helplessly at the windows. "Gonna take me days to get all this fixed. Have to go all the way down to Ochopee for it." He glowered.

"Did he take anything specific that you could see?" Vreni said.

"Nope. Just banged around like a bull in a china shop." Mr. Saunders looked unhappily around his shelves, some of which had indeed had china on them. Now it was all swept together in a jagged pile in the corner. "There's most of my stock gone. Don't know if my insurance is gonna cover it."

"Well, certainly," Vreni murmured, "you would think . . ."

"Honey chile," said Mr. Saunders, turning a sharp-eyed blue gaze on her, "if you know an insurance company that routinely has clauses in its policies about damage by super-villains, you let me know, okay? 'Cause I think I'm gonna have to change my coverage."

Vreni swallowed and nodded.

"He came in here, plunged around, bashed things—it was kinda funny," Saunders said, "in a horrible way. He'd bash something, and then stand still, and turn all stiff-like, and look around. Then bash something else. Then stop still again. He did that three or four times."

Peter, taking pictures of the wreckage, was bemused by that. *Doesn't match his normal behavior at all—if anything the Lizard does could be considered normal . . .*

"I didn't see if it took anything. I got down under the counter. So would you," Mr. Saunders said. "He was roaring. Those teeth of his—" He shook his head. "Then out he went again, out the window, crash!" He pointed with his chin. "Ran out in the wet prairie. Don't know what happened to him after that. Heard him roaring and yelling, but I wasn't gonna go out and see about it. I gave him both barrels when he came in—didn't bother him no more than spitballs would've."

Peter took a few shots of Mr. Saunders while he talked to Vreni. "Have there been any strangers in the area the last few days?" Vreni said. "Anybody you wouldn't recognize?"

Mr. Saunders shook his head. "Nope. That's half the problem with this place. No one stops. Even the gas station—" He gestured at the pumps outside. "I can't get a good price for gas out here. We're too far from the distributor. Everybody who drives up here tanks up down in Ochopee or over in Naples, places like that. They don't want to pay five cents more a gallon . . . . and why should they? Naah, we had three people stop for gas in the past two days, and they went straight on away again."

"And no one's stopped for longer than that—say, to sightsee?"

Saunders laughed. "Missy, anybody came hanging around here, the whole town, all four houses of it, would turn out to see. No one comes here to hang around. There's nothing here. And tell you the truth, we don't really want folks from outside hanging around here, either. This isn't no city. It's a town, our town—we like it private. We like it quiet. No crime, no one bothers us . . . until now." He frowned at Vreni in a way that suggested to Peter that Mr. Saunders considered them both a sign of the decadence and imminent downfall of civilization.

"Well, we won't be troubling you much longer, Mr. Saunders," Vreni said. "But thank you for your help." She turned to Peter. "You about ready?" she said.

"Yup. Let's go."

They made two other stops that day: another in Deep Lake, and then a third in Ochopee. The Deep Lake one was to Mrs. Bridger, a little old lady who lived in one of the houses built off the service road near Saunders's. The Ochopee stop was with the Melendez family, a young couple and their two baby girls who farmed about five miles from Ochopee proper.

Mrs. Bridger sat on the porch of her tumbledown little house—which would have been new in the 1950s, but hadn't been maintained or repaired since in the wake of who knew how many hurricanes—and told how she had seen the Lizard swimming down the canal, three nights before. "You're sure it wasn't a 'gator?" Vreni said, as Peter roamed around taking pictures.

The old lady, half blind as she was, knew what Vreni was actually asking. "Oh no, dear," she said. "The alligators were swimming away from him just as fast as they could. They no fools." She chuckled. "He would stop every now and then, and then go on again. But he didn't make no noise, or do anything bad."

The canal ran close to Saunders's. *Casing the joint?* Peter thought to himself. *I wonder . . .*

A little later, Mike and Carol Melendez took Vreni and Peter out in the back of their little farmhouse and gestured away across the fields to indicate where the Lizard had cut across their bottom thirty, frightening their cattle, until, as Carol said indignantly, "A couple of them won't even give milk now, they were so upset." Peter took pictures of everything—those dead flat, beautifully green sorghum fields that the Melendezes were farming looked bizarre compared to the wild variation of the rest of the landscape around the Ochopee area. Mostly, though, as at Mrs. Bridger's, he concentrated on their faces—the proud, private look of them, all profoundly distrustful, Peter thought, especially of strangers. There's no way, he thought as he snapped away, that the one-armed Curt Connors could ever hide here. He'd stick out like a sore thumb. All these people had such a reserve, a resistance to strangers, that if someone new were around, Peter felt sure they would talk about it immediately.

There was something else that Peter started to notice as they talked to the Melendezes: they were afraid. He thought about it more, as he drove back toward Miami (more or less behind Vreni, who was zooming along ahead of him and apparently practicing for Le Mans). He got a sense that normally they wouldn't happily have told him and Vreni even the little they did, but they were frightened at this intrusion into their life of something so completely beyond its boundaries. Maybe they were slightly flattered that a big-city reporter and a photographer came out all this way to see them. *But there was more to it*, Peter thought. His gut feeling said that they possibly had seen more than just the Lizard, or more often than just this once. The stress had simply become too much for them, severe enough to make them want to risk their privacy. But he couldn't get rid of the feeling that there was more these people could have said, and they just weren't saying it.

Once, while the Melendez husband had been talking to Vreni, Peter saw his wife look over northwards, past their fields, into the depths of Big Cypress. The look on her face was, for that moment, one of naked fear. But when she turned back to Vreni and her husband again, the expression was gone.

Peter thought of the expression on Buckingham's face at NASA the other day, and filed the two expressions away together, for reconsideration later.

He and Vreni stopped at a diner by the Everglades Parkway for a late lunch, and didn't discuss much of the interview material there, for they were both aware of the locals watching them closely, of ears stretched in their direction. As they were walking out to the cars, though, Vreni said to Peter, "I don't know, but I get a feeling these people are withholding something."

Peter nodded. "I don't know what else we could say to get them to be more forthcoming, though. They all seem so private—"

Vreni sighed as she went to stand by her car. "Well, I'm going to keep nosing around. I'm still trying to get that police connection sorted out. Not much I can do on a Sunday, though. Tomorrow may be better. You want to do some more camera work today?"

"I think so," Peter said.

"Well, see if you can be back this evening around sevenish. I want to touch base with you then, and we can talk about this material a little more after I've had time to transcribe the tapes and think everything over. Then tomorrow we'll start some serious digging. Particularly, I want to pull some companies' registers from Okechobee and Seminole counties, and see what kind of industry is working down here besides tourism."

"No problem," Peter said. "Sevenish it is."

She sighed, climbed into her car, and roared off.

Peter, meanwhile, stopped at a roadside pay phone and dialed the Connorses, got Martha. "I'm so glad to see you made it down here all right," she said, her voice warm. "We had a visitor last night—"

"Oh? Who?"

"I don't think we should talk about it on the phone. But come on over."

About two hours later, Peter was sitting in the Connorses' little kitchen, going over much the same ground with her that Spider-Man had the other night. William was out playing ball with some friends elsewhere in the neighborhood.

Martha apparently welcomed that. "It's hard enough," she said softly, "to be, effectively, a single parent. But to be one under these circumstances—an unofficial one—" She shook her head. "You can't share all the difficulties, all the trouble, with children: it's not fair to them. It makes them think they're more of a burden than they are."

"But he's not a burden," Peter said.

"No, not at all. All the time, it's 'I'll take care of you, Mom, I'll help us.' That willingness—if work alone were enough to make the difference, I'd be a rich woman off his efforts. As far as he's concerned, nothing's good enough for me." She paused. "Your cup's empty."

Peter pushed it toward her; she refilled it. "He has friends down here," he said. "Do you?"

She raised her eyebrows. "Maybe you're going to think this sounds snobbish of me, but I don't seem to have interests anything like most of the people here. Not much in common. A lot of my neighbors seem so . . . fixated on their family lives, their children. They don't seem to have much of a life outside it, and to them, to have a son and not have a husband, not have the wage-earner on site. . . . Some of them are very old-fashioned about it. They think, some of them, that I must have done something wrong, or that he must have." Martha looked at Peter helplessly. "And of course that's not the case."

"Of course not," Peter said.

"So I let them go their way, and I go mine. They're civil enough. We meet in the store, or down at the PTA . . ."

Peter nodded. She spoke very lightly, but the kind of life she was describing must have been appallingly lonely.

The front screen door jerked open with a shriek, and banged shut again. "Hey, Mom," William's voice yelled, "whose car is that? Oh! Pete!"

William ran over to Peter, a skateboard in hand. There was a moment's confusion as they tried to work out whether to shake hands or hug each other, and wound up doing both. "I could say something incredibly banal," Peter said, "like how you've grown."

William rolled his eyes. "Pete—"

"Well, I'm sorry, but you have! Where did you get a whole extra foot of height?"

"Sent out for it," William said, and grinned. "Never mind. I'm glad you're here. Mom, I had an idea."

Martha looked at him curiously. "What, honey?"

"Wait." He ran off into the next room. When he came back, he was carrying several yellow manila envelopes. "It's just a thought," he said, opening one of them and peering into it, going through the contents. "I thought of it while we were playing basketball, and ran right over, and now they're all mad at me." And he laughed with the pleasure of someone who has more important things to do. "But look—"

William took some sheets of paper out of the envelope and

showed them to his mother. On the backs of them, Peter could just make out a check-balancing form. Bank statements?

"I know these are private," William said, "but look. See the code numbers?"

Martha looked at the statement, then looked sideways at William. "Can I show him?" William said.

"It's not as if our bank statements have thousands of zeroes on them at the moment," Martha said, wry. "Go ahead."

William brought the pile of bank statements around to Peter. "Look. Here are checks—" He pointed. "Some more checks—then some cash machine withdrawals. But we do all our withdrawals here in town." ATM TRANSACTION FF0138, said the line William pointed at now.

"That's the machine up on Main Street. Look at this, though—" He pointed at another. ATM TRANSACTION FF0152. And another. ATM TRANSACTION FF0132. And another, ATM TRANSACTION FF0148.

"Those aren't our machine," William said to Peter. "Dad still has his card . . . so he must have done those. I'm not sure where they are, though."

His mother was going through the envelope now. "Now, I wonder," she was saying absently. "You open one of these accounts and you get so much junk, but I don't believe Curt would have thrown anything out. He was always—is always—so methodical about his bookkeeping." Then her expression changed. "Here!" she said triumphantly, and came up with a little credit-card-size booklet, which she opened and paged through. "Yup . . . I thought so." Martha handed William the booklet. "This is First Florida's list of all the machines in the state. It has the code numbers there, honey."

"Awright!" He started to page through it, went over to a table for a pen, brought it back and started to work more or less over Peter's shoulder. "This one—this is Marco. This one—it's Sunniland, and this one is Ochopee—"

"William," Peter said, "there's a career waiting for you in detection."

Martha looked thoughtful. "That's about a hundred miles southeast of here," she said. "That general area."

"I think if you drew a circle containing all those towns," Peter said, "it's a fair bet he would be there. Unless he was purposely using those machines to create a false impression that he was there—"

Martha shook her head. "I don't think so. Curt isn't the wily type . . . he's *too* direct, if anything. That may be what caused all this trouble, in the first place." She smiled, a rueful look that Peter was getting to know better than he liked, the expression of someone coping with her pain. "If he's using those machines regularly, it's because they're pretty nearby. He hates to drive more than he has to."

Peter looked at the most recent statement. "This is dated the week before last," he said. "Can you get anything more current?"

She thought. "You know," she said after a moment, "I think the machine will give you a mini-statement of the account activity for the last week, if you ask it. I'm not sure if that'll have the ATM code numbers on it, but we can try."

"Do you mind if I make a note of these numbers?" Peter said. "Then, when you get that statement—"

"Wait a minute." Martha went over to the kitchen counter, got her purse, and rummaged in it. A moment later she came up with a wallet and pulled a card out of it. "Here," she said, handing it to William. "He knows my PIN number. Go on up there and get a statement, honey, and get twenty dollars while you're there."

"You need anything else, Mom?"

"You," Martha said, viewing her son with a practiced eye, "just want an excuse to go to the 7-Eleven and buy motorcycle magazines. You can have *one*."

It was about a quarter-mile's walk into town. Peter and William strolled down together, chatting.

"So how did Spider-Man look?"

"Cool. He always looks cool," said William. "He was worried, though."

"About your dad?"

"Yeah. It's good to know."

"What? That he was worried?"

William nodded. "It's good to know that people care. You hear stuff about the Lizard on TV, and a lot of them think he should just be shot. I want to shout, sometimes—just yell— 'Let him alone! It's not his fault!'" The words came out in a whisper, but Peter was shaken by how much force underlay them. "So," William said, a little more normally, a few seconds later, "knowing that someone knows . . . and would say the same thing—It's good."

Peter nodded. "Someone cares," he said.

They made their way to the bank. William slipped the card into the machine, input his mother's PIN number, and punched the button asking for the mini-statement. The machine extruded it after a moment, and William took it, glanced at it, and deftly tore it in half, handing Peter the side that didn't have the amounts on it, but did have the code numbers of the ATM machines.

"A few more uses," William said. "He's not taking a lot, though. We're okay. Is that one Ochopee again?"

"I think so," Peter said. "Interesting." That one was dated the day before, when the Lizard had passed through Deep Lake.

The two of them walked back to the house. Peter sat down and had one more cup of tea, chatting with Martha about inconsequentialities—how MJ had been redecorating the apartment, what she was up to—and then made his good-byes, promising that he would let them know as soon as he found out anything worthwhile.

He got back onto the freeway and started to think hard. Peter tended to agree with Martha that Curt wouldn't bother with driving very far from where he was actually based. It would waste too much time from whatever he was working on—and Peter was sure he was working.

Most of these ATMs take pictures, Peter thought. *I wonder if we could get the bank to release the pictures of his usages to us?* But without help from law enforcement, Peter doubted it.

He headed back to the hotel, ready to meet with Vreni. But when he checked in at the desk to pick up his room key, he was given a note from her which said: "Delayed to check something out. Tonight is off. Breakfast club tomorrow? V." And another message as well, hastily scribbled: "Call Aunt Anna's immediately. MJ."

Oh my gosh, he thought, *what's happened? What's wrong?* Peter hurried up to the room, hunted around for Aunt Anna's phone number, and dialed it.

The phone rang. And rang, and rang, and rang. Peter sat there thinking, in increasing tension, *Are they gone? Did something bad happen? What, what—*

Someone picked up the phone. "Hello?"

"MJ! I got your message—"

She squealed. The sheer joy of the sound took Peter completely aback. "I got it! I got it!" she yelled.

"You got what?"

"The job! A job!"

"On a Sunday?"

She laughed. "This town operates on strange rules. Mostly that there aren't any. I was down in one of the bars on the Strip, having a sandwich with Ellanya David, you remember her?"

She was another model, formerly based in New York. Peter was becoming more amused by the moment. "You hated her! Why were you having a sandwich with her?"

"Oh, well, that was then." MJ giggled. "But now she's down here, and she's stuck in this real awful relationship, and I really feel sorry for her. Anyway, we're having this sandwich, and a guy came over and joined her. His name is Fletch, and he's from one of the big agencies, one that turned me down. We started talking, and Fletch found out that I knew Ellanya in New York, and he had just fired her—"

"This is getting very complex," Peter said.

"It gets worse. Or better. So Ellanya had to leave, and another guy, a friend from a different agency came along, and Fletch introduced us to this other guy, his name is Joel. *He* works for an agency called Up N Over. And Fletch talked Joel into hiring me because I knew Ellanya."

Peter blinked. This was hardly the first time he had felt he needed a program or scorecard when trying to keep track of MJ's professional connections. "Uh, I'm seriously confused now."

"You're not alone. But Joel hired me; he said I had great planes." MJ giggled again. Peter shook his head in mute amazement. "And he gave me a retainer, right then out of the cash machine. He handed me five hundred bucks, *cash!*"

"If you produce results like this in a weekend," Peter said, "I'm going to be interested to see what you can do on a weekday."

"Well, we'll find out."

"So what do you have to do for him?"

"It's standard couture. They've got a campaign coming up for one of the magazines, all high-tech scenarios, and they're going to be shooting up by IBM in Boca, and along the Space Coast. And get this: at Kennedy, too!"

"The Rocket Garden?"

"Is that what it's called, where all the rockets stand around? Probably. But Boca's first, and we leave tomorrow!"

"So you won't be commuting, then." He hadn't had time to see much of her the last couple of days; now it looked like there wouldn't be time this week, either.

"No, Tiger, you know how it is. Until they get the rhythm of the shoot established, it's going to be eighteen-hour days. The commute would be crippling. We'll be in Boca the first couple of nights . . . then Kennedy after that."

"You're going to be up there for the launch, then?"

"I think so, if I understand the timing right. But Joel wasn't sure. He said he still had to settle the timing with the director, and get all the people together for this—he was looking for three other models as well."

"MJ, this is dynamite! How long is this going to last?"

"I'm not sure. But money's money."

"And the deal's good enough to please you?"

"Not quite what I would be making in New York at the best of times, but—" She giggled once more. "This isn't the best of times . . . and this is better than nothing. So I'm coming right over. Where's the albatross?"

"The albatross?"

"Vreni."

Peter laughed. "She's got plans of her own this evening."

"Well, that's just fine. I'll be right over. And we'll have some dinner out."

"That much anyway," Peter said. "I had kind of a late night . . ."

"You've got your second wind—I know you. Until you have dinner: then you'll fall over." She chuckled. "I'll be there to catch you . . . and then—"

"Then?"

"Then we'll see where our negotiations lead us." He could hear her smiling.

So it all came to pass. They had a splendid dinner down in the hotel's fancier restaurant, which specialized in Caribbean-style food. Then they negotiated. And four or five hours later, in the hotel room, MJ turned and snuggled up against Peter and said, "So tell me about your day."

He told her. When he finished, she looked at him with some concern. "Sounds like you're starting to get close to what's going on."

"I hope so," Peter said. "I'd like to get to the heart of whatever's about to happen *before* it gets serious."

There was a little silence. Then MJ said, "I could almost wish this job hadn't come up right now."

"Why on Earth not?"

"Well, what if you need me or something?"

He chuckled. "Good point. I may need you to hold the Lizard down while I web him up."

"Peeeeter!" MJ grimaced. "It's just . . . I don't like it, that's all. When I got married, I promised to stay with you when you were in trouble—that's the 'worse' part of the for-better-for-worse. What if I'm not there for when you need me? When you need my help? Suppose the Lizard beats you up a little? Who's going to strap your ribs up and tell you you did okay anyway?"

There was more coming, but Peter put a finger on her lips and said, "I know. I know you're worried. I'll be okay. And you having a job, and making money to keep us both afloat—that's important. It's also important for me to know that you're doing things you like to do. That you're happy and busy. Those things are important to me."

"I don't know," MJ said. "I just . . . Never mind."

"It's going to be all right," Peter said. "It's been all right until now."

"Mmm," MJ said, not sounding entirely convinced. But then she smiled, and snuggled closer to him. "Never mind."

Peter reached over to pick up the phone and arrange for an alarm call, and saw that the red message light was flashing. He dialed for the front desk.

"Hi, this is Peter Parker, room twelve thirty—any messages for me?"

The operator tapped at a keyboard for a moment. "Uh—yes. 'Breakfast club is off.' Does that make sense?"

"Yes, it does."

"Right. 'Breakfast club is off, lunch instead—'" The operator paused. "This may not have been spelled right. 'V-r-e-n-i.'"

"That's right."

"What an interesting name," said the operator.

Peter chuckled and agreed, and took another moment to set up his wake-up call, then hung up and turned to MJ . . . and found her already asleep. *Typical,* he thought. *The one morning when we could sleep in, and we can't—she has to leave early.*

Oh well.

He turned out the light.

FOUR

He woke up suddenly to light streaming into the room, and looked over in panic at the alarm clock. It read *8:30.*

I thought I took care of the alarm call! Peter thought. *What the—*

Then he saw that there was a note on the pillow. "Ran out to do an errand," it said in MJ's small, neat handwriting. "Back about 9, see you at breakfast."

Peter chuckled. Sometimes she was an early riser, and there was just no stopping her. This was plainly one of the times. He got up, showered, dressed, and went down.

She was there waiting for him, already halfway through a plate of scrambled eggs, with an angelic look on her face— that settled and cheerful look that she wore when she had a job, any kind of job, these days. Peter's heart clenched a little at the sight of it, and not for the first time, he wished he had a job that paid enough that MJ could work when and as she wanted to, rather than because she had to. This look of sheer pleasure was priceless for its own sake.

"You should try the pancakes," she said. "They're great." And no sooner had Peter sat down than MJ said, "And I have a present for you!"

"What?"

"Here." She handed him a box wrapped up in gift paper.

Peter tore the paper off as tidily as he could and stared at the outside of the box. It was a cellular phone. He opened the box and got the little creature out of its Styrofoam nest. "MJ! How much—"

"Not that much," she said. "They're on sale. With the connection fee and everything. It's one of those new netwide ones—it'll still work in New York."

"MJ," Peter said, still in shock.

"Now, I want you to take this with you everywhere," she said, "because they've given me one of my own. I have it right here." She got another one, twin to Peter's, out of her purse, and dangled it in front of Peter, and giggled. "Isn't this trendy?

Here, write down the number." She showed it to him, on the little sticker on the back of the phone.

Dutifully, Peter got out his little address book and wrote the number down. "I want you to call me every five minutes," MJ said, "until I get back. You understand?"

She was enjoying this, Peter saw, but there was also a slight twitch to the corner of her eyes, a narrowing that said she wasn't kidding. "If anything happens," she said, and lowered her voice, "anything at all, I want to know."

"You'll be the first."

"Somebody else is usually the first," MJ said, raising her eyebrows. "Someone whose name starts with S. But never mind. Right after him—I want to know. Promise?"

Peter desperately hailed a passing waitress.

"Promise?"

Peter looked at MJ and smiled and gave in to the inevitable. "Promise."

MJ smiled and started playing little tunes on her phone's key-pad, while she finished her scrambled eggs. Peter rolled his eyes, then smiled at the waitress and ordered breakfast, wondering at how complicated life could become without warning . . .

South of Miami proper, the Florida coastline trends gently southward and westward and becomes slightly less developed. Parkland appears, dotted here and there: places like Biscayne National Park, and Homestead Bayfront Park near the air base. Farther north, though, about fifteen miles south of Miami proper, Matheson Hammock Park rests against the water, a beautiful, flat landscape of wetland and cypress leading down to a wilderness of salt grass, and finally to the dunes and the white sand beach of the coast. The coastline itself is a long, wide welter of tidal washes, little bays, and tidepools, alive with sea life and the land-based animal life that comes down to catch it. The busy surburban and city life of south Florida seems very far away.

Such places at night can be very quiet and very lonely. Some people count on that.

The little boat came nosing in to shore without a sound, nor a light. Northward and inland, Miami lit up the sky with a faint golden glow; southward, the lights of Homestead and Coral Gables glittered, distant sparkles flat on the edge of the flat world, unsteady through the warm night air. There was no sound but the rush of the waves.

One of the two men in the little boat peered through binoculars at the coast, saying nothing. He was a big husky man, dressed in shorts and a windbreaker. When his companion got close enough to see him, in that uncertain light, the other's face was as closed as a shut door.

Dealing with that face's owner made Satch nervous. But he was stuck with him for the time being, and so just sat, used the oars to keep the boat steady, and said nothing.

Half a mile away, on the beach, there was the merest flicker of light. "Right," said the other. "Start rowing."

Satch rowed, not arguing the point; when this man told you to do something, you just did it. Or else you got as far away as you could, as fast as you could, before he found out you hadn't done what you were told.

The other kept his gaze fixed on the coast through the binoculars, and Satch rowed steadily on. The two of them had done this run before, several times now, though in different spots, so that there was now a kind of routine. They would motorboat down from Dinner Key, say, or up from Coral Castle, and loiter when they got to the right spot—just a couple of fishermen out for the afternoon. But they wouldn't come back in. Darkness would fall, and they would wave at anyone who stopped, and say "Night fishing . . ." This was common enough. Lots of people around here night-fished for pompano and blues. Occasionally, by night or day, a police boat would hurry by on business. Satch's gut would always clench when this happened, but the other man would just wave and shade his face with the bill of his cap. There wasn't a lot of Coast

Guard activity around at the moment. Satch had been very relieved at that. He hadn't known quite what to make of it when
the other told him that the Coast Guard were "being taken care
of." If money had changed hands, well, that was common
enough. But how much money did it take to buy off a whole
Coast Guard cutter? Satch often thought about that, and shook
his head.

"Come on," the other said, "get a move on!"

"I am, I am," Satch said, muttering. "If you're in such a
rush—" He was about to say, "Why don't you row?" At the
look the other gave him, though, Satch shut up and concentrated on rowing faster.

Another ten minutes' rowing and they were into the
combers. The bottom didn't shelve evenly here: there were
dips, and there was an undertow, and Satch had to work twice
as hard as he had earlier. The other man cursed at him. "Can't
you go any faster, goddammit?"

Satch didn't bother answering, just grunted and rowed.

Sand hissed softly under the keel as the boat came to shore.
He could see them waiting, just above the high water. They
were pretending to be fishermen, too; a couple of lawn chairs
were set up on the sand, and fishing poles were stuck in the
sand next to them.

Nearby, as Satch and his companion stepped out of the boat
into the backward-rushing water, Satch could see evidence of
recent digging, being hurriedly covered by another man. There
also were the things they had come to fetch—the three small
drums.

Satch's companion gave him no help with the boat. He simply strode up through the water to the beach, and up to the others. As he went, he pulled something out of his belt. Satch
looked at it with some concern. He hadn't known Lugers came
that big. He didn't want to *see* any that came that big. He didn't
want to *see* this one now, or in this man's hands, where it
might wind up pointed at him.

"How long have you been here?" he heard his companion say to one of the other men.

"About an hour. What kept you?"

Satch's companion gestured back at him with his head. "He's not exactly an Evinrude," he said. There was some snickering about that. Satch chose to ignore it. There were a lot of things you had to ignore about this business if you wanted to keep doing it, keep making the money. And Satch had a family to support. Hard enough to find honest work these days, and any other kind, even that was hard to hold on to . . .

"Okay," Satch's companion said. "Here." He reached into one pocket, came up with an envelope which he handed to one of the two waiting men.

"You want to open one up and have a look?" said that man.

More chuckling at the suggestion. Satch's companion laughed. "You want to count that?"

Less chuckling. But the man now holding the fat envelope did it nonetheless. "Price is going up, seemingly," he said, conversationally enough.

Satch's companion shrugged. "Supply and demand. When's the next pickup?"

The counting man shook his head, tucked the parcel away. "You'll be notified in the usual way."

Satch's companion showed no change of expression. He turned to Satch. "Come on," he said, "get these in the boat."

Satch sighed and did as he was told. He went to the first of the barrels, beginning to roll it slowly, edge-on, across the soft sand. Satch grunted with the strain; he never got used to how heavy these things were for their size. And when you got them down into the wet sand, it was even worse. Satch huffed and puffed and set himself low, as best he could, and grunted as he got the first barrel heaved up into the boat.

The others were speaking in low voices now as Satch made his way back for the second barrel. He could never shake the feeling, on these outings, that they were talking about him.

That some dreadful joke was being made at his expense. He wondered if it had been smart for him to take this job at all . . . wondered whether he was actually playing the part of one of the poor schmoes in a pirate movie, who digs the hole and does the work to bury the treasure, and then gets shot or buried alive to keep the secret. Certainly, if he saw any indication of that coming, he would run like hell. But in the meantime, the money was good enough. *Besides,* he thought, *it's not like anybody's getting killed . . .*

He got hold of the second barrel and started rolling it back to the boat. *At least the hours are okay*, Satch thought. It wouldn't take much longer tonight. They would row a little farther down the coast until they met the boat that would make pickup on this stuff. Then they would collect their own payment and be gone. His companion would set him ashore down at the docks, and he would catch a late bus back and see Marie and the kids.

Satch heaved the barrel into the boat, turned, and started slogging his way back to the shore. His back was killing him. His companion had turned a little away from the others and was looking toward him. "Hurry up!" he hissed. "You want to be here all night?"

"Yeah, yeah," Satch muttered. He grabbed the third barrel, said "Oof—"

Someone else went "Oof" too. Surprised, Satch looked up. One of the three men they had met, the one who had been covering up the dug hole, was standing strangely, with a shocked look on his face, and he looked taller than usual, somehow. Or there was something dark behind him, a shadow. Satch thought it was a trick of the light, at first, but there seemed to be something sticking out of the man's chest—

But there was. The breath went out of Satch with a whoosh as the scene suddenly made sense. The something was black, and it glistened in the moonlight, and then vanished as swiftly as a snake's withdrawn tongue. The man fell. The other two, and Satch's companion, took several quick steps back from him as a fifth form rose over the crumpling body.

It was a guy in a black suit, a big guy, with some kind of design or logo painted on the front of him. Satch swallowed as the thing grinned, white in a black face, and grinned, and grinned—a mouthful of great knifelike fangs that seemed to go right around to the back of his head, until the top of it looked likely to fall off because of that dreadful grinning.

Satch's companion pointed that huge shiny gun at the man. He never got a chance to fire. Satch didn't even see what happened. One minute the gun was in his companion's hand. The next minute there was a dreadful choked-off scream, as hand and gun were flensed off by some kind of knife that leapt away from the guy in black. Satch's companion bent down. Another breath, a half a scream, and that knife—it wasn't a knife at all, it was an arm or tentacle of some kind, and another one followed it, how could anyone have so many arms?—whipped out from the man's body, seemingly from a place where there hadn't been anything a moment before. It whipped itself around Satch's companion's head.

The other three men turned to run. Satch was frozen where he stood. Running did the others no good. More of those weird flexible arms shot out like glistening black rope, knotted around the men, pulled them back leisurely. The man who screamed the loudest stopped screaming first. Satch had to watch it, had to watch it all. He didn't move. He couldn't move. He just watched.

The thing in black dropped the second man and went for the third. It spent more time over him, like someone savoring a lunch break. Eventually he let the rest of the pieces fall, and turned to Satch.

Satch stood and watched. He couldn't move. The thing in black came to him, grabbed him by the lapels of his poor polo shirt. It shredded in the grip of the claws that held him. Odd, though, how delicately they did it, as if intent on doing him no more harm than was absolutely necessary.

"Now, then," said a horrible fangy voice. "We want you to take a message for us. Take it to your boss, to the person who pays you. Tell him we said, 'Cut it out.' Tell him Venom says so. You do recognize us?"

"Fuh, fuh, muh, muh," was all that Satch could say.

Those claws came up, and patted Satch's cheek, almost an amused gesture. "The dangers of celebrity," Venom said. "And you—you cut it out, too. So you have something to tell your grandchildren about. We won't tell you twice."

Venom let him fall. Satch collapsed to his hands and knees in the wet sand, panting, and didn't dare move, because if he did, he would see what had happened to the others . . . and then he would throw up. He hated throwing up. But mostly he felt as if he should just be very still and small, do nothing, make no sound. He held still.

That dark shape stood above him, and the voice said, very deep, very amused: "Now. About *these* . . ."

It was dawn before Satch got up off his hands and knees, mostly because he had to; the tide was coming in. An early jogger was approaching him along the beach, and Satch thought it would be good to get away. As he stood up, as the jogger got closer, and saw what was on the beach, and ran toward him with a horrified look on his face, Satch looked around and saw that the drums were gone. The boat was gone. Everything was gone.

Downtown Miami can be a very chic, very stylish-looking place on a Monday morning. Well-dressed people come and go, hot cars and expensive ones pass by, and everything is beautiful.

Richard C. Harkness was one of those who found it all beautiful, as a matter of course—as something he deserved. He had worked hard on his way up the corporate ladder, had sucked up to the right bosses, signed the right reports and found ways not to sign the others, and had kept his nose clean in the best corporate tradition. He was good at what he did, which was making money without getting his hands dirty.

He drove his Porsche into the parking garage at 104 West Seventh, one of those sleek glass-and-steel constructions that had risen above the smaller, less grandiose buildings of Miami these last few years. He stowed the car in the space with his name painted on it, pulled the thin briefcase out of the back, shut the car, set the alarm, and walked away. Only six steps or so took him to the executive elevator. He stepped into the shiny little lobby, put his key in and signaled. The elevator arrived quickly. This, too, was something he deserved and which he now accepted as a matter of course: the right not to have to waste time waiting, not to have to be crammed in an elevator with people in the company's lower echelons on his way to his office.

The elevator whisked him up to the thirtieth floor. Harkness stepped out, crossed the hall to the glass and gilt entrance to the front lobby. The door opened for him. The receptionist, sitting behind her big glass-brick and Italian plate-glass desk, nodded deferentially to him as he passed. "Good morning, Mr. Harkness."

"Morning, Cecile." He didn't ask her about any messages; she wouldn't be trusted with such. Down the cool gray hall, along the thick maroon carpet toward the executive offices, he made his way. There was the thick mahogany double door that had his name on it. It opened in front of him, Cecile having alerted Mary Ellen that he was coming.

"Good morning, Mr. Harkness."

"Good morning, Mary Ellen. Twenty minutes, and then you can come in and give me a report."

"Yes, sir."

He walked past her desk, past the door of the little anteroom in which her own secretary worked. The door to his private office was shut. No one touched it without his permission. He opened the door, tossed the briefcase onto the leather sofa next to it, shut the door behind him, and turned to examine, with the usual great pleasure, the view out onto the morning city, the sea, the world of business into which he had fought his way and which he handled so well.

Between him and the window stood a tall black shape. Harkness's mouth fell open in outrage and astonishment. On his five-thousand-dollar Persian carpet stood three big dirty wet barrels, shedding sand and muck onto the Kilim weave.

That dark shape looked at him, took a step closer, and said, "We believe these are yours."

Peter met Vreni that afternoon for lunch, but it was less of a lunch than he had been expecting. He stood around at the entrance of the restaurant, waiting for her, and finally at about twenty after twelve, went in and sat down, got himself a Coke, and waited. At nearly twenty of one, she appeared, hurrying across to his table. She didn't sit down.

"I have some things to take care of this afternoon," she said. "It's not stuff that I'll need pictures of . . . not yet anyway. Do you mind taking the day off?"

"Mind?" Peter laughed. "No problem. When should we meet again?"

Vreni thought, then made a helpless gesture. "I couldn't say. I'll leave you a message, okay?"

"Fine."

And she was off again, half running. As Peter watched, it occurred to him that he didn't remember seeing her ever go anywhere at anything less than a fast walk. She drove herself the way she drove her car. Possibly the secret of her success. *Or possibly*, he thought, as the waitress stopped at his table, *it has more to do with being shot at* . . . That was something Peter could sympathize with.

All the same, it left Peter with an extra day to call his own. Among other things, he could spend a little more time poring over the Connorses' bank statements. And there was also the matter of his piece of smoke. Which to attack first?

The smoke, he decided—if only because it was more mysterious. Peter had a sandwich and a salad, then headed up to his room to make some calls, and have another shower—this was one of those sticky mornings; even in the hotel's air-conditioning, the humidity got at you. While undressing, he flicked the TV on to one of the news channels to see what the world was up to.

"—reports of Spider-Man being seen in the east Everglades have been confirmed by Ochopee police this morning. The enigmatic superhero, or villain, depending on your sources of information, made a brief appearance near Deep Lake—"

Peter chuckled and headed into the bathroom. But he had no sooner gotten into the shower than a voice said from the next room, "Dade County police are this morning investigating an incident scene near Matheson Hammock Park. Early reports are that a jogger stumbled on the aftermath of a massive assault. Police are questioning one man, Arnold Warren Campden of Miramar, who, initial reports say, was found near the scene of the incident. Police sources say that at present they have no confirmed suspects, and no indication of a motive, though there is speculation that the crime may have been drug-related—"

This by itself would have sounded fairly dry, had Peter not climbed far enough out of the shower to look around the door into the room and see, on the TV, the news channel film crew's shots of the beach area. A patch of beach some forty feet by forty was yellow-taped off. The sand there was much churned up, as if by a struggle, and great brown splashes of blood were everywhere. Off to one side was a hole which seemed not to have been completely filled in, and there were marks in the sand leading to or from the beach, as if something heavy, several somethings, had been dragged a short distance.

Peter got back in the shower, frowning. The thought of all that blood was on his mind. He knew people who left such scenes behind them. *If* people *is the word I'm looking for,* he thought.

Never mind that now. He got out, toweled off and dressed,

sat down at the room's table again, and tipped out the contents of the "thermos" once more. As MJ had, he poked it, found that slight springiness, but it gave only so much. There was an odd strength to it, for all its ephemeral appearance.

Peter reached for the room phone with one hand and his address book with the other. *What I need,* he thought, *is a specialist in materials science. And I don't know any materials scientists.*

He paged through the book for a moment. *At least it's Monday, there'll be someone up there.* He picked up the receiver, dialed nine, and then a longer number.

After some ringing, there was an answer. "Empire State University."

"Hi. Physics department, please?"

"Thank you." A pause, then another ring. "Physics."

"Rita? It's Peter Parker, from Biochem."

"Peter! How you doing? You were in last month, but you didn't stop by."

"It was a little crazy, Reets," he said.

"Tell me! With Hobgoblin and Spider-Man and Venom ripping the place up? That's one word for it. Who're you looking for?"

"I was wondering if Roger Hochberg was on campus right now."

"I think so. I certainly saw him yesterday. Any idea what department, though?"

"Not sure . . . he was talking about changing majors."

Rita laughed her deep dark laugh. "He does that about once a week. Wait a minute! Renee? Renee, by any chance do you know where Roger Hochberg might be?"

"Uh—" said another voice.

"Tall skinny guy, glasses. The one with the weird haircut."

"Oh, him! He's up in the main research library. I saw him go in about an hour ago, anyway."

"Pete? Did you hear that?"

"Yup," Peter said. "Can you put me through?"

"Sure thing. You come see us, now! It's not like you're that far away."

Peter laughed. "I'm in Florida at the moment."

"Oooh, how'd you swing that? Never mind, don't want to know. Putting you through. Bye!"

"Bye, Reets."

Peter waited, while yet another number rang and a seagull planed past outside his window, burning white in the sun. "Library."

"Roger Hochberg, please? I think he's up there in the stacks."

"Just a moment, I'll page." He heard the library's soft paging system say Roger's name, and then the librarian said, "Oh, there you are. Call for you." The phone changed hands.

"Hochberg."

"Rog, it's Peter Parker."

"Hey, how ya doing?" said Peter's former lab partner, his ever-present smile almost audible through the phone. "Haven't seen you for weeks."

"It's been busy. Listen, I have a question for you. What looks like smoke, but it's solid?"

"Huh? What do I win if I get this right?"

"A cookie at least. I saw this stuff the other day—on TV," he added, to avoid complicated explanations, "and I've never seen anything like it before. It's been driving me crazy. I've got to find out what it is."

"Okay. Sounds mineral, rather than animal or vegetable."

"I'd say. But past that I wouldn't venture a guess."

Peter described the stuff to Roger in more detail, and finally—on hearing about the stuff's odd unsolid look, and its minuscule weight—Roger said, "Wait a minute. You saw this on TV? I see! They must have gone public."

"Who? With what?"

"I'll tell you. There've been papers about something that's supposed to look this way. It's called 'hydrogel.' "

"What's it for?"

"I don't think anyone's sure yet. They cooked this stuff up

out at Livermore Labs, out west—I think as part of their superconductor research program. The stuff is apparently no good as a conductor, but they think it may have other uses. I don't know much more about it, it's not in my line. I only read the article abstract."

"Okay. Rog, who would I talk to about this stuff—to get some detail? I'm working on a story right now, and it may actually be of some use."

"Well, let me think." A pause. "Trouble is, he's not exactly local."

"Well, define local. I'm not at home, either. I'm in Florida."

"In this weather? Jeez. You poor guy. Never mind; Florida's not bad. There's a guy I know, an alumnus, who could probably talk you through what you need to find out—he was always such a journal hound, he'll *have* to know about it."

"Where is he?" Peter said, hoping the man wasn't up in the panhandle somewhere.

"South of Miami, I think. Wait a sec—" There was a moment of scrambling. "I've got the laptop here with me. I think I have his address."

"What's this guy doing now?"

"Food science."

"Good Lord," Peter said. He got an image of someone who designed the sugar for doughnuts.

"No, he's good, don't worry." Faint keyboard clickings ensued, and then Roger said, "Here we go. Doctor Liam Kavanagh." He read off an address in Coral Gables, followed by two phone numbers. "Liam was always such a research junkie," Roger said, "that I can't believe he doesn't know about your hydrogel—lots more than I do. Will that help?"

"I think so. Rog, you've saved my life."

"Just our usual service. When are you going to get back here and go out with some of us for dinner? There are people here who want to heckle you about not finishing your doctoral project."

Peter moaned softly. "Let's not get into it. I might be back in a couple of weeks . . ."

"Call me, then, and we'll get together. Say hi to Mary Jane for me."

"Right. Thanks again, Rog."

Before Peter could hang up, the phone rang. After a moment, he realized it was the cellphone MJ had given him. He picked it up, fumbled with it a moment, not quite sure how to turn it on. At last, he found a button that said Receive, and hit it. "Hello?"

"Peter!" MJ said. She sounded a little breathless. "How's your new toy?"

"I haven't had a chance to play with it yet—been too busy this morning."

"With what?"

"The 'smoke.' I've got at least a hint about what it is, thanks to Rog Hochberg. He says hi, by the way. Anyhow, I have to go see somebody down in Coral Gables, if he can make time for me. Listen, MJ, I've got to try and talk to this guy right now if I can."

"Okay."

"Where are you?"

"On the way to Boca." Peter heard, quite clearly, the sound of MJ rolling her eyes. "I'm going up with one of the staff vans—we stopped for a rest break. The director for the shoot," she said more softly, "is, uh . . . a character."

"Oh? Good or bad?"

"I would say he had the brains of a duck, but that would be an insult to ducks everywhere. Can't seem to make up his mind about what he wants, generally. This whole thing may turn into a disaster."

"Hope not."

"We'll see. Where are you?"

"The hotel."

"Where's your friend?"

"Vreni? She had something to do this afternoon. So I'm going to Coral Gables alone."

"Right. Oh, gosh, here they come. We're leaving. Bye bye, Tiger! I'll call you later."

"Bye," Peter said, and turned the phone off, pocketing it. He got the feeling that whatever he did, MJ was going to call him every five minutes for the next while. *New toys, indeed*, Peter thought, and grinned. He picked up the thermos and the other bags and headed down for the car.

Coral Gables was south and west of the city. Kavanagh's building was near a road called Killian Parkway, which Peter found without too much trouble. The drive down was studded with odd road signs suggesting that Peter go to places with names like Parrot Jungle, Monkey Jungle, Orchid Jungle, and the peculiar name he remembered hearing that morning, Matheson Hammock Park. The image of a forest festooned with tropical hammocks stayed with him for a while.

Kavanagh himself, when Peter had managed to reach him on the phone, had been succinct almost to the point of eccentricity. Peter explained to the scratchy voice on the other end that he had been recommended by a friend at Empire State, and the response was, "Oh, God, not that dump!"

"Dr. Kavanagh," Peter had said, "I have a research problem—"

"Don't we all, my son, don't we all. Well, bring it along." Kavanagh had issued him directions which sounded more like a football play than anything else—I-1 to 41, 41 to 826, 826 to 874, then east to 174th . . .

"So far so good," Peter murmured as he got onto Route 874. Then something in his pocket shrilled, and he jumped almost out of his skin. It was the phone.

Peter pulled over and answered it, knowing perfectly well who it was. "Joe's Deli," he said, "Joe ain't here."

"Peter!" MJ said. "Can I kill somebody?"

"Hmm. Don't think Florida state law permits that at the moment. Why?"

"The director. Maurice."

"Maurice."

"The ducks would be right to be insulted, honey." She was whispering now. "The man does not know what he wants. My hair is right, but the light is wrong. The light is right, but the wind is wrong. Nothing is ever all right at once. He's infuriating."

Peter sighed. *This new toy is going to be a mixed blessing,* he thought. "And also," said MJ. "Is my hair 'carroty'?"

That one brought him up short. MJ's hair was one of his favorite things about her. When they first met at his aunt's house all those years ago, it was the first thing he noticed. The blaze of it in the sunlight was a conflagration in the evening, like embers. "Well, I call you 'carrot-top' every now and then, and you don't seem to mind."

"You don't make it sound like the vegetable associations of the word should also be applied to the hair's owner," MJ hissed. "Which Maurice does."

"Ignore him," Peter said. "He's a loony."

"Murder would be quicker. He suggested I go blonde."

"Definitely a head case," Peter said. "Plainly having difficulty with reality."

MJ sighed. "It's good to hear you say that. Oh gosh . . . here he comes. I'd better get on with it. Thanks, honey."

"*De nada.* Have fun."

She snorted at him, and hung up.

Peter put the phone away again, resisting the urge to turn it off. *This is the first day she's got hers,* he thought. *If I turn it off, she'll kill me. I can cope with one day of this.*

As long as that's all it is . . .

He finally reached Kavanagh's address, turning into the parking lot of a small professional building, the kind where doctors and dentists have their dwelling. Its lobby even had a corrugated noticeboard. Even as he had thought, there were indeed three doctors, two dentists, a chiropractor, an orthopedist, and a company called Dextro Sugar International. Underneath, in smaller letters, the sign said "DR. LIAM KAVANAGH." Peter raised his eyebrows, wondering how all the dentists felt about the company name, and went upstairs.

Peter walked up the single flight of stairs to the next level of the building, and walked around past the dentists and so forth to the door of Dextro Sugar. He knocked.

The door was pulled open by one of the single tallest people Peter had ever seen. Liam Kavanagh was seven feet tall and a bit. He stooped—Peter suspected this was likely to be a habit—and looked down at Peter the way Gulliver would have looked down at Lilliputians. "You Parker?" he said.

"That's me."

He took Peter's arm and pulled him in, then slammed the door behind him as if there were enemy agents outside. Peter managed not to react to this as if he was in a fight situation—mostly because Kavanagh was just too unusual to take seriously. He looked like a beanstalk wearing a polo shirt and jeans and a white lab coat, and big horn-rimmed glasses—the biggest and thickest ones Peter thought he had ever seen. *No one,* Peter thought, *could possibly be that nearsighted without needing to wear a radar box around their neck.*

"You want some coffee?" said Dr. Kavanagh. His accent was purest New York Bronx.

"Uh, thanks, I just had lunch."

"It's good coffee."

"Do you make the sugar for it?"

Kavanagh smiled. It was a wry smile, one that spoke of a very wicked sense of humor. "Caught the 'Dextro,' did you? No, I drink mine black."

"Milk," Peter said, "and two sugars. Thanks."

Kavanagh produced a couple of mugs and poured coffee from a filter-coffee set on one side. "It's a general tag," he said, "that's all. Our kind of life runs on dextro-rotatory molecules, ones that bend light to the right when crystallized out.

Levo-rotatory ones don't do us much good. The 'sugar'—" He shrugged. "It's a private joke. What is it exactly that I can do for you, Parker?"

"May I show you a specimen of some material I found?"

Kavanagh sat down in a chair by a desk with a computer and many books on it, and leaned over to clear off a spot on a small side table. "Right there, if it can sit on a table unprotected."

Peter produced the thermos. Kavanagh looked at it and said, "Nice! European."

"Is it really?" Peter said.

Kavanagh nodded. "Better than our local brands, by and large. Whatcha got in there?"

Peter opened the container, and on the clean, white composite tabletop, dumped out the piece of smoke. Kavanagh leaned over it like a vulture examining a potential piece of prey, his eyebrows going higher and higher as he gazed. Then he glanced up at Peter. The expression was not entirely interest or surprise; there was some envy mixed in it. "West Coast connections?" he said.

"I have a few," Peter said, though he doubted they were the kind that Kavanagh meant.

"You are a genteel and nonviolent-looking young man," Kavanagh said, leaning back in his chair again. "Normally not one who I would assume was involved in industrial espionage, or any other kind. Otherwise I would have to ask you serious questions about how you got this out of Livermore. They were the last ones to be working seriously on hydrogel that I know about for sure."

"Can you tell me something about this?"

"Sorry?" Kavanagh said, looking at Peter for a moment as if he had just arrived from Mars. "You've stolen this, but you don't know what it is?"

"I didn't steal it," Peter said.

"Let's put it this way, then," Kavanagh said, leaning farther back and folding his arms. "You have—come by? come into?—

a piece of a substance which is presently sufficiently rare that stable examples of it exist in only three places on the planet. Not that the technique of its making is a secret. It's simply involved, and requires a lot of specialized equipment and expertise. But you don't know what it is . . . and you've come to me to ask me to tell you about it."

"That's about right," Peter said, getting slightly annoyed. "Can you help me? Or should I try the orthodontist next door?"

Kavanagh gave him a long look, and then began to laugh. He took a drink of his own coffee, and then toasted Peter with it. "All right," he said. "This is a peculiar situation, but not illegal—that's my gut feeling. But when we're finished, I wish you'd tell me where you got this. For real."

The doctor sat down by the table again, and prodded the hydrogel. "It's an accident, you know," he said.

"It is?"

"Was, originally. They were looking for a spin-off from clathrate technology. You know what a clathrate is?"

Peter nodded. That was fairly elementary biochemistry, and he was much more than an elementary biochemist. "It's a sort of latticework or cage of atoms of one element, sometimes more than one. The cage holds another atom, a guest atom, trapped inside. The substance produced by that structure often has properties that don't have any relation to what a normal compound of those elements would behave like."

Kavanagh nodded. "Right. They were looking at ways to extend clathrate structure, make it more complex—possibly increase the number of atoms which could be held in one of these cages, thereby producing materials with new and unpredictable behaviors. So they tried something unusual. They mixed oil and water."

"Can't have gotten them very far," Peter said.

"Well, at normal heats and pressures, it wouldn't. Specifically, they were using silica oils, which are not structurally similar to normal oils or lipids. Then they added water, and fractional amounts of other compounds, and they mixed them together under high temperature and considerable pressure." Kavanagh grinned. "And when they did that, something happened." He nudged the little piece of smoke. "This."

Peter looked from it to Kavanagh. "What's it do?"

"Do? It doesn't *do* anything. It just sits there." Kavanagh took another swig of coffee.

"No, I mean . . . what's it for?"

"Ah!" Kavanagh said. "They're still working on that. But what I can tell you is that this is one of the most stable compounds ever to be produced. I don't mean nonreactive, as such, nor do I mean inert. I mean *stable*. It resists being changed. The whole molecular structure of the thing simply resists being shifted out of its present state into any other, and that makes it very valuable."

"Why?"

"Here. Have you held it?"

"Not for long . . ."

Kavanagh picked it up, felt it for a moment, and then slapped the piece of hydrogel into Peter's hand. Once again he felt its great lightness. It hardly felt there at all. There was also a strange, friendly warmth to it.

"Interesting, isn't it?" Kavanagh said. "The *Scientific American* articles mentioned that odd feel in the hand. They called it 're-ambient heat.' Like something else is there, isn't it?"

Peter nodded, almost reluctantly. "I'd think it was alive, if I didn't know better."

"No chance of that. However, you don't need to be alive to be useful."

He turned away from Peter and went over to several very crowded cabinets, deeper in the office. "Ah," he said, reaching up to one, and came down with a big square-headed hammer. Peter looked at it, and Kavanagh said, "May I? Thank you."

He took the hydrogel, put it up onto a workbench. "Here," Kavanagh said. He took the sledgehammer two-handed, and swung it at the hydrogel with all his might.

The hammer bounced. The hydrogel compressed no more when struck than it had when Peter poked it with his finger. "Care to try?" Kavanagh said.

"Uh, thank you, yes—" Peter took the sledgehammer, took aim, and hit the hydrogel, hard—no doubt much harder than Kavanagh suspected he hit it. The hammer bounced. There was a spatter of sparks from where the hammer hit the bench top, but nothing else. The feeling of hitting the hydrogel was like hitting a mattress, but one with more bounce.

"Not strictly an inelastic collision," Kavanagh said. "Not elastic, either. Like something yielding under the pressure, and then throwing the hammer back. Interesting, isn't it?"

Peter nodded.

"Watch this," Kavanagh said. He took the bit of hydrogel off the countertop now, came over, and handed it to Peter. Then he turned away, and when he turned back again, he was holding an orange canister with a crooked nozzle. He thumbed a ring valve by the nozzle, struck a match on his countertop, and lit the nozzle. Hissing, a blue flame leapt out.

"Now wait a—!" Peter started to say, but it was already too late. Kavanagh had already brought the flame down on the piece of hydrogel in his hand. He flinched—then realized that flinching didn't matter. The flame splattered and spread an inch and a half above his hand, and he felt almost no heat at all. No heat whatsoever was transmitted to Peter through the hydrogel itself.

"Go on," Kavanagh said. "Put it down there." Peter put the hydrogel down on some papers on Kavanagh's desk. Kavanagh lowered the torch to the hydrogel again, held it there.

Nothing whatsoever happened, to the hydrogel or the papers; nothing scorched or even curled. "Pick it up," Kavanagh said to Peter.

Peter did, waving a hand over it first to sense any residual heat. Nothing. He touched it with a finger. It was cool. The hydrogel sat there in its smoky uncertainty, completely unchanged.

He picked it up and looked at Kavanagh. "It doesn't hold heat."

"It's a peerless insulator, certainly," Kavanagh said. "So the *SciAm* article said. It's mechanically stable, chemically and physically stable, and as you see, stable in terms of molecular vibration—heat and, I would also suspect, radiation."

Peter put it down between them and sat down again, looking at it. "What you could do with this stuff . . ."

"Yes, but it's not easy to make. A lot of heat and pressure is required, and the process as described in the journals is very labor intensive. But once made, the substance resists everything you can do to it. It can't be broken, bent, marred, eaten, or even touched by most forces known to us. To cut it like that—" He shook his head. "How they did that I don't know: it might be a little more manipulable when it's new. Later, I suspect the molecular structure would have so robustly asserted its new integrity that it wouldn't allow any further manipulation."

He paused for a moment. "Applications—I know, because they mentioned it in the article, that they were thinking of using it for the tiles in the Space Shuttle."

"Really!" Peter said, straightening.

"Sure. You felt how light it is. An average Shuttle tile is much heavier. Shape that into a tile of the same size and thickness—" Kavanagh shrugged. "You could decrease the Shuttle's weight by, oh, eighty percent. Think of how much more payload the beasts could carry then. They *might* actually become cost-effective." He smiled. "But think of all the other industrial uses, for example. This—" He gestured at the little piece of smoke. "This stuff could change our world. It's simply one of the most extraordinary compounds ever invented."

Peter nodded.

"So, the only question I have for you at this point," Kavanagh said, leaning confidentially toward Peter, "is—where exactly did you find it?"

Peter opened his mouth, and shut it, and then opened it again and said, "In a swamp."

Kavanagh snorted, and then smiled. "You would do me a great favor," he said, "if, in return for this information, the next time you're passing through that swamp, you would pick me up a bit. This isn't exactly Livermore—" He looked around the rather shambolic combination of office and lab space in which they sat. "But I wouldn't mind taking a run at this stuff myself. Trying to work out how to make it on the cheap. An indestructible substance, light as a feather, tougher than steel, impervious to anything you can throw at it—" He shook his head, and looked slightly wistful. "The world ought to have this stuff."

Peter looked at him. "We could try leaving you a sample," he said.

They did try, for about half an hour. But no scalpel, tome, or other implement in Kavanagh's lab, not even his Swiss Army knife, could get so much as a chip or a sliver off the hydrogel. "It's too bad," Kavanagh said sadly, at last. "Take it away before I'm tempted too far. And whatever you do—" he looked at Peter seriously "—don't let the world at large know you have this stuff. I would imagine there are people who would do quite a bit to get their hands on it . . . and wouldn't deal kindly with you if they knew it's with you."

Peter nodded, knowing this was almost certainly true. *Curt,* he thought, *why did you have this stuff? What's going on out there?. . . .*

Peter thanked Kavanagh for his help, got back into his car, and drove back north.

There's got to be a pile of money behind this, he thought, as he pulled back onto the freeway. *There's no way that this kind of materials engineering happens on the cheap. Either a lot of money was spent to steal this from Livermore, or a lot was spent to produce it somewhere else.*

Kavanagh had given Peter a copy of the Scientific American article, which gave full enough instructions for a careful chemist to synthesize it on his own, given the proper equipment. *And Curt had had it. Stolen from someone else . . . or synthesized by Curt, for his own purposes?*

But the Lizard was carrying it. It was hard enough to communicate with the Lizard at all, let alone make it act like some kind of courier—

The phone rang. Peter picked it up. "Hi, MJ—"

"Peter! Oh, gosh!"

"What's the matter? Where are you?"

"Up on the shoot. Oh, honey!"

"MJ, what's wrong?"

"Venom!" she said.

"What?!"

"He was on the news just now. He was up in some skyscraper—intimidated some executive, it looks like, and just walked out afterwards. By the time the police got there, he was long gone."

"Oh, that's just *wonderful*," Peter said.

"I thought—"

"MJ," Peter said hastily, "not on the cellular. People can eavesdrop on these things. Are you busy tonight?"

"No . . . they're putting us up at a hotel here. Do you want to come up?"

"I might do that. Which hotel?"

"The Splendide, on North Collins." She chuckled. "It's about as splendid as a landfill, but never mind. Around eight-ish?"

"I'll be there."

He hung up, and thought bad words, many of them.

Venom!

They had tangled last month, several times; in the middle of it, Hobgoblin had been added to the equation. Finally the alien creature had been put out of harm's way, and with Hobgoblin carted off as well, Venom had announced that, since he had other business to handle in San Francisco, he would leave Spider-Man to his own devices for the moment. *He must have handled it by now,* Peter thought. *And now that the media are announcing I've turned up here, he must feel he has leisure to come back this way and settle my hash. Not on his own turf, of course—but this isn't exactly mine, either.*

Damn! Why can't he leave me alone?

It didn't seem likely, though. The symbiote to which Venom was bound was one that Peter had rejected when he realized just how alive his new "costume" was. It had gone hunting a new host, and had found one—and the symbiote did not forget the pain of its rejection. It held a grudge, and Eddie Brock was only too glad to help the symbiote deal with its own anger. Venom had nearly killed Spider-Man several times now, and so far luck or skill in fighting had saved him. But he couldn't count on it forever.

And now they're here.

And what about the Lizard? Peter thought. *If Venom runs across him, who knows what he'll do? He thinks he's just a crazy monster, likely to harm the innocent.*

It occurred to Peter, ever so briefly, that it would be an interesting fight to watch. While he wasn't exactly invulnerable, neither was anybody going to tear the Lizard up like wet paper, not even Venom. But he very much doubted he'd have the leisure to watch any such fight, since if Spider-Man were anywhere in the neighborhood, Venom would happily put the Lizard on hold until old business had been dealt with.

Peter sighed. *I really needed this,* he thought. *Well, if he crosses my path, I'm gonna do my best to trash him. I've almost managed it, a couple of times before. Then the police can have him.*

It probably wasn't very compassionate to want so badly to pound someone into a pulp. But Venom had been making Spider-Man's life difficult for some time now—and Peter Parker's, too. Venom had not scrupled to try to get at Spidey by frightening MJ. That, if nothing else, earned him a good thrashing in Peter's opinion.

Just this once, he thought. Seeing Venom locked up in the Vault would do him no end of good.

But then there would still be the Lizard.

Curt, Peter thought, as he swung south onto the freeway toward Miami, *what's going on?*

Not surprisingly, the few structures standing in the Everglades have a temporary look. Heavy building materials are not easy to get in and out, and the weather makes any building situation unpredictable. The swamp and marsh are endlessly malleable by the elements. Canals that were passable last week may be drowned and lost today; ground that was dry yesterday may today be under two feet of water. And, even if you *do* manage to get your materials in and get something built, there's no predicting when or if a hurricane will come screaming through and rip up everything you've done.

As a rule, it isn't easy to see buildings in the Everglades. The lush growth makes even a cleared site look like primeval forest within a matter of years. And if you go out of your way to hide a structure, then only the spy satellites will know where you are—and even they have to be told where to look. There are places in the wetlands called hammocks where trees seed themselves prolifically, and they and their rootling trees grow so closely together that there's no seeing what lies inside the little self-contained island they create. The temperatures in such places, sealed off above by a thick canopy of leaves and surrounded by a wall of many trunks, soar far higher than elsewhere in the landscape. Rare flora—air plants, bromeliads and orchids—grow wild inside such hammocks, a kinder environment than any greenhouse.

Entering a hammock is like walking into a close, dark, humid room. The occasional song of a bird, the shriek of a shrike, are the only sounds to be heard in the acoustically close little place, and the only illumination are the few turning spots of light shifting and flowing along the interior as the sun moves. Hammocks can be as small as twenty or thirty feet in diameter, or quite large.

There was a large one, covering maybe half an acre, some miles north of Big Cypress and about ten miles from a town called Felda. No one in Felda knew much about it. In that wilderness of canals, that "river of grass," as the poet called it, filled with wetland, dry land, poisonous plants, and snakes, it was difficult enough to really know the landscape around your home, let alone that ten miles away.

But someone had found this biggest of the local hammocks, and someone had used it.

Inside the palisade of cypress, bald cypress and dwarf cypress, mangrove, and tangled banyan, a little, long, low building had been erected. It was a temporary structure of the kind built by people who supply pre-fab trailers and so forth to construction sites. It had two levels, the second accessed by a stairway up the outside. It looked as if someone made a half-hearted attempt to keep it clean, but the fiberglass of the outside was rapidly becoming festooned with Spanish moss and bromeliads, which considered the exterior of the building to be just another kind of tree trunk. The building had no windows. It was not built for pleasure or convenience, but for a specific purpose.

Upstairs in the small building, in a blank-walled office that looked just like so many others he had worked from in his time, a man in a lab coat worked busily at a personal computer. The screen was displaying an automated computer-assisted design program. He placed his left hand on the specially designed mouse—a necessity, since he had no right arm, and the typical mouse was designed for right-handed use. He clicked, and on the screen a diagram of sticks and balls, a complex molecular structure, rotated itself. The man picked up another stick and ball from a pile of them on one side of the screen, mouse-dragged them into the diagram, and hooked them onto one side of it. The new stick and ball bounced away, there was a soft chime, and the computer—using a sound-file lifted from a well-known television series—announced, in a chaste, cool female voice, "This procedure is not recommended."

The man sighed deeply. Using the mouse, he picked up a different color of ball, another stick, plugged the stick in, then thought for a moment, squashed another ball into the first one, and applied them both to the stick. There was another soft chime, but this time no protest from the autoCAD program.

The man sat back in his chair and let out a long sigh. He was good-looking, with dark hair and fine features, eyes with the slight, smile-created downturn at the corners that suggested a kindhearted, thoughtful person. Under the lab coat, his clothes had an inexpensive look to them. They had not been tailored to accommodate his uneven proportions; the right sleeve simply hung limply. Considering what frequently happened to his clothes, Curt Conners didn't see any reason to spend a great deal of money on them when they might be torn to shreds at any moment by an annoyed Lizard—the thing at the bottom of his soul.

The lab door opened, and he glanced up to see Fischer walk in, if Fischer could ever be said to merely "walk" anywhere. To say that he hulked in might have been a more accurate description. Curt thought he had never seen shoulders so broad. On some superheroes possibly, but not on an ordinary human being. Fischer always looked as if he belonged in an action-adventure movie.

He tended to prefer wearing camouflage clothing. His hair was cropped in a Marine-style crew cut, his eyes were an astonishing, photogenic frozen blue in a broad face with high cheekbones, a big, square jaw, and a thin-lipped mouth that could wear a deceptively wide smile. He was a most improbable-looking man, and most improbably handsome, but he was real enough. He had certainly become one of the realities of Curt Connors's life in the past six or seven months. And he had to be dealt with, whether Curt liked it or not.

"How's it coming?" Fischer said.

Curt nodded. "The substrate's in place," he said, "but the beta-N ring structure is giving me some trouble—"

"I don't need the jargon," said Fischer. "How close are you to being *done*?"

Curt sighed. The man's obtuseness about science was deliberate, rather than an inability to handle it. Fischer just didn't see science as anything a reasoning being would get interested in, any more than he would get interested in, say, a screwdriver or a telephone. It was a tool, not a source of pleasure in itself.

"Very close," Curt said. "It might be a week, it might be less. Depends on how quickly I can finish putting this together. Some of it—" he shrugged, a regretful gesture "—is just a matter of trying all the pieces in different configurations until they work. And some of it, I'm afraid, genuinely does require a certain level of inspiration."

Fischer stared at him with those cold blue eyes. "Well," he said, "you'd better get inspired. Once we manage to arrange another delivery of the administration medium—"

Curt met the stare without flinching. "I don't know what went wrong with the last one," he said, "and there's really no use dwelling on it, is there? Even before the installation, the Lizard was unpredictable enough. But now that," he raised his eyebrows, "your favorite gadget's been installed, it's hardly his fault if something goes wrong. You want to have a word with the programmer. Or whoever else wrote the code. Or your pet surgeon, who put the thing in. If one of the neural implants—"

"Shut up, Connors," said Fischer. He said it jovially enough, but the tone of voice would have been more reassuring if Curt didn't know, from previous experience, that if he didn't shut up violence would follow. To Fischer, the use of force was just one more form of conversation, and Curt had seen what happened to other people who didn't shut up when Fischer told them to.

His guts began to roil a little inside him. He despised this necessary pretense of cowardice; he would have liked to wait until the inevitable happened—and then calmly take this man apart with the Lizard's bare claws. That much he would enjoy. But it would destroy the whole point of this exercise, and so he restrained himself from even thinking about what was hopeless and couldn't happen.

"Programming isn't at issue," Fischer said, leaning back against one wall with his arms folded. "What is, is that the Lizard picked up our consignment. And then he lost it again. Not very good. It's going to take us another few days to get any more. It's going to be tougher than last time, and even then we attracted enough notice."

"But you will manage it?"

"Oh yeah, we'll manage it."

"And then?"

"Then the surgery will go ahead as scheduled," said Fischer, again jovially, "assuming you have the kinks worked out of that by the time we get it."

"It's not so much working them out as working them in," Curt said ruefully, looking again at the molecular diagram on the screen. He had been hanging D-benzene rings all over the long-molecule structure like blown-glass ornaments on a Christmas tree—but no Christmas tree had ever been such a delicate construction, or so easily misbalanced. Too many balls on one side and the structure of the molecule came apart, or twisted itself into some odd configuration he hadn't planned.

Already this week he had constructed some enzymes that might prove extremely useful in the genetic engineering of vegetables, and at least one proteolytic structure that might possibly someday be part of a cure for cancer. But that wasn't the cure he was looking for, and so he put it aside—having first carefully noted the structure, and resolved to write a paper about it someday, when he was back doing normal work again. He had to hold that hope in front of himself. If he ever lost it, ever let go of it. . . .

If that ever happens, I'll cease to be human, he thought. *Since I'm only sporadically human these days anyway, I'd better hang on to the little that I have.*

"Anyway," Fischer said, "Certain People will be very glad that you're making such good progress. Certain People wouldn't like to be kept waiting very much longer. They have their own agenda, and your price is rather small."

"I understand that."

"Good."

There were other things on Curt's mind, though. He was beginning to feel rumblings of something he knew all too well now, an array of sensations superficially like an epileptic's aura, a certain change in the way things looked, a shift in the perception of colors, a metallic taste that heralded changes in the sensorium.

"It's going to happen again shortly," he said.

Fischer's eyes widened just slightly. That was as much of a surprise reaction as you could get out of him. "How long?"

"Soon. It's never very consistent."

"All right, then. You'll want to get yourself out of here. You wouldn't want to wreck the joint after seven months of work, would you now?"

"No," said Curt. "I just want to back this up, before—"

"Fine," said Fischer. "I'll leave you to it. Just be careful not to lose anything."

"Believe me," Curt said. "That's the last thing on my mind."

Fischer turned and bulked out of the room again. Curt waited until he heard the footsteps receding down the metal stairs outside the building—probably going off to warn the rest of his people, he thought. Only when the man was safely away, for just a moment he lowered his face into his hands and breathed out a long, soft sound. A moan.

Martha . . . he thought.

It would be easier for him, so much easier, if he was the kind of person who could just forget about people, let them go or even shut them forcibly out of mind and memory. Keep them at arm's length. But that wasn't the way he had been raised. His parents had been loving, his relationship with his family had been good. They cared about each other.

His parents were both dead now, and his family separated; but all of them kept in touch by phone, and he knew, on the rare occasions when he called them, that they were always glad to hear him. But there was always a note in their voices that said, "Why have you become so distant? Why have you drawn away? Is it something we did? Tell us, and let us make it up."

It was, of course, nothing he could ever explain. There had seemed no point in spreading the pain Martha already suffered around the rest of the family. So he became the somewhat-lost brother, the distant uncle, the cousin who was a bit of a black sheep, who didn't keep in touch, who no one really knew much about anymore. He knew that when his relatives spoke of Martha and William, they shook their heads, and sighed, and felt sorry for them.

Not half as sorry as he did.

For maybe the ten thousandth time, Curt thought back on the day the experiment went wrong, and he wished as hard as ever that time was reversible, that you could point at a given moment, a causal linkage, and just explode it. To delete it, to hear the cosmic voice saying "That procedure is not recommended," and watch the elements of the dumb move, the Big Mistake, separate and float back to the side of the screen, waiting for you to do it again, and this time, do it right—that would be worth almost anything.

But reality had not been so kind.

Curt opened his eyes and gulped. The taste at the back of his mouth was wrong, and the colors in the room were shifting. Hurriedly he began to take his clothes off—there was no point in ruining any more of them than he absolutely had to—and silently, looking as erect and proud as he could look when he knew that inside of ten minutes he would no longer be a man, Curt Connors went outside to await the inevitable.

Fischer watched, from his position leaning against a thick-trunked mangrove, as Connors edged sideways out of the hammock into the relatively open air, paused, then stepped down into the smooth brown water and swam slowly away. He moved with a fair amount of splashing. That gave the water moccasins and the cottonmouths a chance to get out of the way before he changed into a form less hospitable to the native wildlife.

Without looking away, Fischer beckoned over his shoulder. One of his men, a slighter version of himself, materialized at his elbow. "Get Dugan and Geraldo. Tell them to get a boat and keep an eye on him. I want to make sure that what went wrong last time doesn't happen again."

"Who's on the remote?"

"You take it."

"You want us to do anything while he's—out?"

Fischer considered, then shook his head. "No. He's been a little visible this week already. Let things quiet down. Then next week, if he's still here—" he smiled slightly "—we'll knock off one of the convenience stores in Ochopee. Go on."

The man went, and Fischer leaned there on his tree, pulled out a cigarette, tapped it against the trunk, then put it in his face and lit up, waiting for the roar.

SIX

T he next afternoon, Peter returned to Miami from Boca Raton, where he had spent the evening with MJ, and spent a long time reassuring her about what he had been up to. Or trying to, anyway; where Venom came in, she was difficult to reassure.

"I don't really like the idea of you and Venom even being in the same state," she had said as they prepared for bed.

"If I find him," Peter said as he got in beside her, "he won't be in the same state for long. I intend to pound him flat and dump him on the police and get him out of my way. I've got other things to think about just now."

MJ laughed, even though it had an uneasy sound. "Nice trick if you can do it," she said. "It's just . . . You know me. I worry."

"You do. And usually over nothing."

"Not over nothing," MJ said. "Venom is a legitimate problem."

"I guess so. But tell me how the shoot is going," Peter said.

MJ laughed at him. "Don't be changing the subject or anything, Tiger." Her smile went wry. "But I have to admit, this isn't going the way I'd hoped. The director . . . He's not exactly psychotic, but I'm going to be very glad when this job is over."

Oh dear, Peter thought. *That bad.*

"He really just doesn't know what to do. I think that's part of the problem. He seems to have a lot of trouble making up his mind. The minute he hears any suggestion from somebody else, he takes it. Even if his first idea was better. It's making a complete shambles of the shoot."

"Well," Peter said, "stick it out as best you can. But if you really can't work with this guy, you should leave."

"No," MJ said. "I went out to bring home this bacon, I went out for it on purpose, and I'm not coming back without the whole pig."

"You have the soul of a poet," Peter said.

"I'm modest, too. And gorgeous."

"Gorgeous I could have told you about. But you should try to keep from killing the director."

"Someone else may beat me to it. He's got more than one way to drive everybody crazy."

"More annoying than chronic indecision?"

"Uh-huh. He's a health nut." Peter looked at her, confused. "Look, Tiger, I don't mind people eating healthy. I mean, it's smart. And smoking is obviously a protracted act of suicide. But this guy—you can't so much as put a hamburger in your face without him screaming about saturated fat! You can't eat anything much more complex than whole brown rice without incurring a lecture."

"Sounds like a bore," Peter said. He knew that MJ had something of a taste for junk food on shoots. It was hardly her fault, either. Sometimes there wasn't much of anything else to eat, especially if the shoots had a poor caterer, and he knew how fond she was of the occasional burger.

She chuckled at him. "At one point this morning, I had this image of calling Venom—"

"Excuse me?"

"Well, if I knew his phone number. I wanted to say—" and she made a "phone" with pinky and thumb—" 'Forget about my husband. Do you want some nice health food? No artificial additives, no preservatives. No brains.' "

"Oh, MJ, really! This is not a nice thing to wish on a fellow human being!"

"I have my doubts about the human part," MJ muttered. "But I just keep telling myself, 'The money's good. Stick with it.' But it's not easy. Maurice is so—I don't know—unpredictable. The sudden changes of mind and tack and God knows what else are getting on my nerves—and everybody else's."

Peter thought for a moment. "It wouldn't—" He stopped, then said, "He's not *on* anything, is he?"

MJ laughed hollowly. "Not likely. The boy doesn't even like aspirin. He saw one of the models using an inhaler this morning, and climbed all over her frame for putting unhealthy artificial substances into her body. Never mind that they were substances her doctor had prescribed—she's asthmatic, and the air quality wasn't great up there today. I thought he was going to carry on for about an hour. Also—" She shook her head. "Odd, but I get a feeling he doesn't want to go shoot up by Kennedy, particularly."

Peter looked at her oddly. "Why?"

"He said something about the Shuttle making him nervous. You told me, didn't you, that there was something atomic going up on it?"

"It seems so. NASA's denying it, but they're protesting a bit too much."

"Well, he was complaining about that to Rhoda, that's the AD, this morning. If he thinks antihistamines are unnatural substances, you can imagine what he thinks about nuclear fission. To hear Maurice talk about it, you'd think all of Kennedy was one big bomb about to go off."

Peter wondered about that for a moment—then put the thought aside. *Just my own paranoia,* he thought. *Lots of people are worried about any kind of nuclear at all.*

"Well. You don't really want Venom to come and eat Maurice, do you?" Peter said.

"No," MJ said, though she sounded somewhat halfhearted. "No, I can put up with him for a *little* while longer."

"All right," Peter said. "Enough about him. What about us?"

"Yes," MJ said, and smiled slowly at him.

Peter woke up early the next morning, not entirely because he wanted to. His body still felt dog-tired, but the back of his brain was worried enough to wake him up with its own musings after only about six hours of sleep.

He lay staring at the ceiling for a few moments with a feeling of dislocation. It took a few seconds to remember where he was, why he was there, and what he had been doing.

He would have to get back to Miami. Vreni might need him today. He rolled over, saw that MJ was still sound asleep. This was unusual—usually as soon as he woke up, she did too, unless she was completely worn out.

He looked at her for a moment. There were shadows under her eyes. She looked as tired as he felt. *She really hates this work, and that wears her out. I wish she didn't have to do it.*

Peter dragged himself out of bed, showered, then switched the television on softly as he passed. The weather report was blathering about a continued spell of calm weather. That was good enough news for him. Once he had done whatever work Vreni required of him, the good weather would make his continued search for Curt a little easier.

The question, of course, was where to look? That had been niggling at him since before he went to sleep. He was pretty sure that the Lizard would not turn up again too close to where he had been a couple of nights ago. There was still too much police attention there. Judging by the news briefs, the area was apparently being searched again this morning. But if not there, where?

His dreams had been troubled by the recurring thought of the bank statements. He was sure they held the key. His first run at them hadn't been too conclusive. Curt seemed more than anything else to hit the machines down in Ochopee, but he could hardly just go and lie in wait near a bank machine.

Once Vreni had made her police connection, Peter was tempted to share a little of his information with her to see if the police could get more details on Curt's access to the machines. Most of the First Florida Bank's cash machines were now fitted with cameras, and he was hoping that somewhere within the range of the camera's lens they might be able to turn up a recurring car license plate, or maybe an actual warm body who was accompanying Curt to the machine.

Because Peter couldn't get rid of the idea that Curt Connors was, once again, being used. That strange description of Mrs. Bridger's, of him stopping and starting, kept coming back.

Like someone was using him, or as if someone was attempting to control him in some strange way. It was all a mystery, but Peter hoped to get to the bottom of it.

When he was scrubbed, and shaved, and generally feeling much better, he sat down on the bed and shook MJ gently. "Honey? MJ?"

"Nnnngh," she said, opened her eyes and looked at him blearily. "What time is it?"

"About eight. Sweetie, I have to get back down to Miami."

"Okay, Tiger," she said, and reached up for a hug.

After a few seconds, Peter said, "Now, about this phone."

"Yes, dear," she said, in the voice that said she knew a lecture was coming, and that the amount of attention she would pay to it was negotiable.

"I think it would be smarter if when I'm wearing my other hat, so to speak, I shut the phone off. So if you don't get an answer sometimes, don't be surprised. Tonight in particular. I'm going out looking again."

"Okay," MJ said, though she stuck her lower lip out and pouted slightly, for effect. "But as soon as you're out of costume again, you call me. Understand?"

"I will. You can leave messages on the mobile system, anyway, even if I've got the phone shut off. I'll turn it on and pick them up when I can. But I don't want the thing going off in the middle of a swamp again."

"All right, all right." She blinked. "Eight o'clock, huh? I'd better get up and start putting myself together."

She got out of bed and stretched. "Oh, my back!"

"Is the bed too firm?"

"Not this bed," she said, "and firmer than you think. I spent the better part of yesterday tastefully draped over a large scenic rock. If Maurice asks me to do that again, I'm going to tell him to take his rock and—"

"MJ!"

"Yes," she said, "I know." She went to Peter and hugged him again.

He kissed her hard. "You're going up to Cocoa today?"

"That's right. I'll call you and let you know about the changes in plans," she said with a grim smile, "because I know there'll be some."

An hour and a half later, Peter was back in the hotel room in Miami. Vreni, when he got there, was already gone, and had left him a message saying she wouldn't be back until late. *Still chasing her police connections, I wonder?* Peter thought. *She seems awfully hung up on that.*

But he was pleased enough to have the spare time. Peter sat down at the table with the map he had picked up, and with the list of bank statements. He located Ochopee and Sunniland and several other branches of First Florida where Curt had stopped. All the bank branches sat in towns that were, in essence, along two sides of a triangle. The third side was empty of banks, empty even of towns—it ran through the heart of the Everglades.

He looked at that third side. *Martha is probably right,* he thought. *There are more usages of these two machines than any others. Curt must be closest to them, and doesn't see any point in trying to go out of his way.*

Peter was sure now that Curt wasn't staying in a town, but had found some quiet hideaway. He couldn't prove the hunch conclusively, but short of going to every tiny town in this area and asking questions, he had to let the assumption stand.

Peter gazed thoughtfully at the third side of the triangle and picked a spot about halfway along it. Whoever was working with the Lizard—if indeed there was someone at all—seemed to be keeping him fairly active. Normally, if the Lizard had a choice, he preferred to hide during his transformations, rather than be seen by people. But this time he was being seen, all right.

I have to start somewhere, Peter thought. *It's a chance: there's a lot of territory to cover there. Still . . .* He chuckled to himself. *A day out on the webs, working out these aches*

148

*and pains, will do me good. And anyway, I don't know what
else to do.*

A couple of hours later, Peter was in the Everglades, web-
slinging to his heart's content—and looking. You could cover
a lot of ground in this part of the world if you just kept moving
fast and kept your eyes open. Once you got a sense of what fit
in, he figured, you would quickly start seeing what didn't.

And so he spent the best part of the day swinging around
and trying to get the same feel for the 'Glades as he had for
the city streets of New York. There were kinds of movement
you soon came to know as normal and natural. Simple traffic
patterns: the way pedestrians walked when they were untrou-
bled, the way cars moved when the streets were clear of acci-
dents or gridlocks, even the general sound of the place.

Here there were no pedestrians, but there was plenty of life.
Peter quickly learned to recognize the different flight patterns
of quite a few birds, the panicky movement of those flushed
from cover by his approach, and the more leisurely evasions of
others already in flight. He soon knew that a quick swirl of
ripples in still water meant the same thing as a ponderous,
low-slung shifting of the undergrowth, and kept well clear of
the alligators both movements concealed. He even saw a couple of Florida panthers—the first was no more than a lithe,
half-seen movement in the trees, but the next one was swimming. That surprised him a little, thinking the big cat had
somehow fallen in or even been grabbed by a 'gator, until he
saw the same thing again later in the day, and this time the
panther seemed to be actively enjoying its dip.

He started near Ochopee, not too far from the Melendezes'
farm, worked swiftly northward until he got as far as the Everglades Parkway about ten miles east of Deep Lake, crossed it
at a quiet moment—having had to wait a while for that—and
made his way over into the other side of Big Cypress, toward
Sunniland. After that he moved on until he hit what he esti-
mated were the boundaries of Corkscrew Swamp Sanctuary.

There being no signs, he turned back and started working downward again a little farther east.

It was hot, and very sticky. The sun slid leisurely across the sky, and birds flapped heavily or hastily out of his path, occasionally squawking their disapproval at the intrusion. It was surprising, though, given the way this place teemed with life of all kinds, how very quiet it was.

And so it went for most of the day, as the sun dropped toward the western horizon and things finally began to cool a little. Spidey was glad enough of that. His uniform was definitely going to need a rinsing, and working in such humidity for long periods drained even his enhanced strength, as well as sweat. The sky was clearing now: earlier he had been forced to stop his swinging and head for some sort of cover, when the lowering heavens opened and the rain came pouring down in a near-solid wall of water, and lightning slashed out of the leaden sky to strike the water or, occasionally, a tree.

But the storm had passed quickly enough, and he went on again while the afternoon slipped into early evening and the sun was swallowed up by a great cloudbank to the west. Anywhere else, things would have gotten quieter with the approaching nightfall, but not here. The song of the frogs and the bugs began, peeping and shrilling and calling. The day shift of hunters and food-seekers in the animal world checked out, and the night shift took over: creatures that moved more quietly, less obviously. In the hour or two of lingering dusk before day gave way to darkness, Spidey began to get used to them, too.

He crossed the highway once again, swinging south toward the middle of the Everglades. *I could get to like this,* Spider-Man thought. *No cars, no trucks—or at least, not all over the place, like New York. Just frogs and bugs.*

He paused in the topmost branches of the cypress and looked around. It was too early for the moon, and there was only the faintest shimmer left of the sunset. A little south of him something big and silent floated by. An owl, he thought. Hawks didn't fly this late. He watched it go, perfect in its silence. *Low-tech stealth technology*, he thought, and grinned inside his mask.

From the south came a long, low roar, and with it a mild buzz of his spider-sense. The unseen grin vanished. Spidey stared into the gloom. He couldn't see anything, but he heard the roar repeated, just once. He knew that roar; it was neither 'gator nor panther.

He started swinging as fast as he could in the direction of the roar for about fifteen or twenty minutes. Then he heard another roar, much closer, and made a course correction. At a guess the source was no more than half a mile away, and he poured on some speed. He was coming into an area of fewer cypresses—more open water, with islands both solid and semisolid floating in it like dumplings in soup.

Where I can't swing, I can spring, Spidey thought, and went bouncing along, more excited now that the day's frustrating search seemed to be paying off. Only a couple of hundred yards away from him, hidden by stands of reeds, he could hear thrashing, splashing—and not just one roar anymore, but two. The first was the sound he had been tracking, the second a deep, hissing grunt. *Now what the . . .*

He leapt from one island to another, burst through the screening reeds, and found himself face-to-face with an alligator-wrestling match. It was not precisely wrestling: one 'gator lay on a nearby reed island, upside down with its stubby, taloned legs waving impotently and its jaws snapping at the air. But only its front legs. There was no movement from its back legs or its tail, and Spidey suspected its back had been broken.

In the water, waist-deep, the Lizard was advancing slowly, snarling, toward a second shape that was circling him. This second 'gator was bigger than the first. Its snout, eyes, and ridged, scaly back were all visible above the surface like the hull of a submarine, but its tail was lost in the swirling froth of churned-up water.

Then Spidey saw it suddenly change course, surging toward

the Lizard. With two beats of that massive tail it was on top of him, jaws gaping wide, but the Lizard sidestepped the clumsy rush and grabbed the 'gator as it plunged by—then roared, strained briefly, and lifted the whole beast clear of the water and up over his head. The shocked 'gator produced that bizarre hissing grunt again, and its tail lashed from side to side, but its target was inside the arc of its swing and safely out of reach.

Spider-Man crouched down and stayed very still for a moment, sure that this was no time to distract the Lizard—no matter how much he wanted to have a chat. Then the Lizard dropped the 'gator. At first Spidey thought this was an accident, but in a flash the Lizard had grabbed the bigger saurian between his left arm and his side, holding its jaws tight shut. *He knows!* Spider-Man thought with a touch of grim pleasure. The muscles that closed a 'gator's jaws were ferociously strong, but those that opened them were much weaker.

The Lizard brought his right arm around, grabbed his left arm with it in a sort of awkward hammerlock, and began to increase the pressure. The 'gator thrashed, unable to even hiss now. Then there was a sudden, grisly snap, and the 'gator's thrashing became reflex flopping, then shuddering, until finally the huge reptile hung limp. The Lizard flung its carcass aside and roared in triumph.

Warily Spider-Man stood up, tensed and ready to dodge. "Nice going, scale-puss," he said. The Lizard whirled at the sound of his voice and threw himself at Spidey. Spider-Man leapt out of the way, tsking in disapproval. "This is no way to greet an old friend!"

The Lizard wasn't concerned. As Spidey leapt, he leapt after him. For a few seconds that part of the swamp would have looked, to an outside observer, like a particularly lively pogo-stick competition, Spidey leaping from islet to islet and the Lizard bounding after him with snake-strike speed. "Curt, listen to me!" Spidey called from a safe distance. "Listen! Stop! I just want to talk. I don't want to—"

—*fight with you!* he finished internally, springing sideways again as the Lizard pounced straight at him, claws out. His roar had scaled up and up until now it was almost a scream, a sound like sheet steel being torn in two. *It's as if it does hurt him,* Spidey thought, reluctant to be reminded, *but I won't—I can't—treat him as if he's going to be the Lizard forever. I don't want to acknowledge that identity. I've got to get through to the man inside.*

Once more the Lizard jumped him, so fast and from so close that there was no time to web him. Spidey had to club him aside, as hard as he could. The Lizard came down with a splash, half in and half out of the water, his upper body sprawled across one of the little reed islets. As he lay there dazed, Spider-Man bent down beside him. "Aw, damn," he muttered. "Curt?"

The Lizard rolled over, hissing in pain, and stared blankly at the darkening sky, slit-pupiled eyes dilating and lipless reptile mouth stretching into a snarl. Spider-Man glanced up—then threw himself sideways just as fast as he could. Even then, he was missed only barely by the pseudopod, sharp as a knife, that thudded into the reedy dirt where he had been crouching a second's fraction before. He came down on his back in the water and struggled to his feet. Even if he hadn't recognized the tendril for the alien creature that it was, he'd have identified his attacker based on the total lack of warning from his spider-sense.

"Don't you know it's dangerous to be out in a swamp after dark?" said Venom softly, and tendrils from the symbiote came boiling at Spider-Man. He jumped again, slightly hindered by the water and the clinging mud beneath, and made it to one of the islets, looking around him desperately for something to shoot a web at. There was a cypress about fifty feet away; he targeted that, and pulled himself out of the way just in time as Venom came after.

"We might have known we'd find you here," Venom said. "Well, you just keep your distance for the moment, while we deal with this." He turned back toward the Lizard. "It's ruined enough lives in its time. Now that happy chance throws it in our way, we shall put an end to it."

"*No!*" Spider-Man shouted. He charged back at Venom, leaped off one small island that was barely more than a dry patch in the midst of the water, and shot web from both hands as he passed, tangling the pseudopodia that reached out toward the Lizard to slash and kill.

The Lizard moaned, rolled over, and struggled to push himself up on his arms as Spider-Man locked off the web and used it to jerk Venom toward him. "It's not his fault!" he snapped, shooting more web—faster, he hoped, than Venom could claw it away. "None of this is his fault!"

Venom tore himself free of the webbing. "Who are we supposed to blame, then? Society?" He started toward the Lizard again.

Spidey launched himself at Venom, feet-first this time, and hit him chest-high. They went down in a heap, grappled one another, and rolled splashing in a tangle of webs and pseudopodia. "You're supposed to be such a tough guy. How come you have to try hitting people when they're down? Not very chivalrous. Not very kind to the innocent."

"Innocent?" Venom hissed, as claws and pseudopodia grabbed Spider-Man by the head and began to pull him closer to that dreadful fanged, slavering face. Spidey pushed himself back as hard as he could, but the grip was crushing. "He's no more innocent than you were when you ruined our life. If he had an accident, well, isn't that just too bad . . ."

Spider-Man pushed and pushed, desperate to break that lock. There was a noise on the edge of his hearing, a sound like the buzzing of bees. He couldn't make out what that would be at this time of night. "Believe it or not," he said, "I no more meant you harm than he means it to anyone. He can't help himself when he's like this. But you . . . You're like this on purpose. He'll turn back to Curt Connors, sooner or later. You're the way you are because you like it!"

Venom roared and went for him, clutching him tighter. Spider-Man was having a hard time keeping his distance from that awful grin. The tongue streaked out, looped around his neck, and began to tighten. Spidey braced himself against the pull of the tendrils and the strangling grip of the tongue, intent now on not blacking out; but his ears began to sing, and that buzzing got louder and louder, and his vision began to go dark around the edges.

Then there was a splashing noise nearby, and suddenly the inexorable pressures on head and throat were released as Spidey was pushed backwards into the water. He scrambled up and out of it, tangled in reeds, and looked around him. A hundred yards or so distant, he could see a low, hunched figure, indistinct in the twilight's last gleaming but with a faint sheen of water and scales about it.

It was the Lizard, heading for the horizon just as fast as he could. Venom was after him, leaping as Spidey had from tussock to tussock, but as Spider-Man watched, the Lizard dove into and under the water, cutting it as cleanly as a thrown stone. The surface closed over him, and he was gone. *Go, Curt, go!* thought Spidey as Venom continued into the darkness on the same line as the Lizard's final dive, thrusting pseudopodia into the water as he went, feeling for his quarry.

Spider-Man was distracted by that buzzing noise, now definitely not a sound from inside his battered head, but rising to a throaty mechanical drone. He turned; behind him a boat was approaching, a low, flat-bottomed boat with one of those big, wire-caged fans mounted at the stern, skimming along the open, reed-thickened water of a nearby canal. A searchlight was flickering from it, and as the beam swept from side to side it caught him square.

Fight or flight, he thought, then shook his head and stood his ground. *No. These guys are on my side, whether they know I'm on their side or not. I'm not gonna run.*

The heavy drone of the big propeller-fan died to a sound more like a domestic lawn mower as its engine was throttled back, and the boat settled down onto the surface of the canal and coasted to a stop near him. They were only vague outlines beyond the glare of the searchlight, but Spidey guessed there were about six police officers on board; he could hear the sound of rounds being racked into shotgun chambers. Then one of the figures leaned forward and said, "You again?"

He recognized the man's voice. It was the officer he had spoken to the other night, when he'd run into the Lizard earlier. "I was just passing through," Spider-Man said somewhat lamely.

"Spare me," said the officer. "We could have heard you a mile away tonight, even without all this listening-gear. Who's your buddy?"

"What? You mean the Lizard?"

"No. I mean the other one, the big one in the black suit."

"Hardly a buddy," said Spider-Man, "in my system or anybody else's. I'm afraid that was Venom."

There was a moment's silence, and a suggestion of half-seen movement as the men on the boat looked at each other. "You're keeping bad company, Spider-Man," said the cop. "And I thought we asked you to stay out of this area."

"I was looking for a friend."

"This time you *do* mean the Lizard. Company's getting worse and worse."

"Believe me," Spider-Man said, "if you had a choice between the Lizard and Venom, I'd advise you to take the Lizard any day. At least he'll run, if he has the chance. But Venom . . ." He shook his head. "He'll run too—but he'll go through you for a shortcut first."

If Spidey had hoped his flip remark might lighten the tense atmosphere, the attempt failed miserably. There was an awkward, distinctly unamused silence, and then the cop cleared his throat. "I'll choose not to regard that as a threatening statement," he said grimly. "Normally we don't give warnings. This is your second. I'll make it simple for you. Get out of this area. Stay out of this area. You're not wanted here. You're complicating a crime scene, and it's not making our jobs any easier. Do I make myself understood?"

"I understand you just fine, Officer."

There was another silence, and during this one Spider-Man could practically hear the cop thinking that though Spidey understood, he hadn't yet agreed. "Then you'd better be on your way."

For a moment the thought crossed Spidey's mind that, if he moved fast enough with his webbing, he might be able to tie them all up, leave them here safe enough, and continue his pursuit. *But no,* he thought. "Good night, officers," he said, and took off.

Their engine powered up again, and a few seconds later the flat-boat zoomed off in the direction taken by the Lizard and Venom. Spider-Man went after them, and despite the racket from the boat's engine and propeller-fan, he remembered what the cop had said about listening-gear, and moved as quietly as he could, trusting as always in his spider-sense to guide him. It was hard to avoid splashing near the water or crashing in the trees, but he took a Great Circle route, arcing out away from the cops and then back around to where it should intersect with Venom's and the Lizard's.

But it was too late. The Lizard had vanished into the swamp, without leaving any trace that Spidey—and hopefully Venom—could see. And as for Venom, there would be no tracking him down either, since his spider-sense never gave any hint of where Venom might be. He had often puzzled about that; probably it had something to do with the symbiote having been tailored originally for him and his special abilities. Right now the question was academic at best. They were both gone. A night's work wasted, the police even more seriously alienated than they had been before, and he was no closer to finding out what Curt was up to.

He stayed in the swamp for at least another hour, playing cat-and-mouse with the police-boat as he worked his way back toward Curt and Venom's trail—and then without warning, something shrill-voiced shrieked right beside him. For a moment, after the day's quiet, he thought it was an exotic nightbird, or a tree-frog of some kind. Then it shrilled again, in exactly the same key, and he realized it was the cellphone.

"I do not believe this," he said under his breath, and hastily pulled it out before it could ring a third time. *I cannot believe that, after all that, I forgot to turn it off!*

In the middle distance—too middle, not enough distance— he could hear the changing engine-note of the police flatboat, and then its searchlight came flickering toward him. "Hello?" he whispered.

"Peter!"

"I can't talk right now. You know," he said quietly, not saying her name, "I really wish you wouldn't call me at work!"

"Why? I thought you were going to turn the phone off when—"

"I forgot," he said, "and you can laugh at me later."

"Where are you?"

"Near some people who are getting very interested in me. What's up? Make it quick!"

"Well, we're done with . . . work where I am," she said. He heard the sound of MJ being cautious. "We're staying here tonight, and then we're going . . . farther north, tomorrow."

"Good," he said.

"That, er, garden you mentioned."

"Gotcha. Look, call me back in a couple of hours, all right?" That searchlight was getting closer, and he had a nasty feeling that its flickerings weren't as random as they had been.

"Right. 'Bye . . ." And she was gone.

By the time the police flatboat got close enough to get a positive fix on him, Spidey was gone, too. He made away at his best speed, and soon enough the light swung away and the boat's drone faded, as the cops turned back onto their original trail. This time Spidey didn't follow them. He was fairly sure that, listening-gear or not, they weren't going to find anything, either.

He sighed, and slowly made his way back to where he had cached the car, at a Seminole-run rest stop on the road—a small and amiable tourist trap kind of place that sold fry bread and souvenirs to the passersby. Anyone passing that lonely spot would have been surprised to see the figure in the red and blue costume standing there by the beat-up little phone booth. But no one passed, and no one was left at the rest stop to see or hear as he dialed.

"Hello?" It was Martha.

"Martha," he said, "it's Spider-Man."

"How're you doing?"

"Well, good and bad. I, uh, I saw Curt this evening."

"You saw *Curt*?"

"Well, the Lizard. We had a brief set-to."

"You didn't hurt him, did you?"

"No."

"And he didn't hurt you . . . ?"

"Not so it counts. Unfortunately, Venom ran into us before we could get into any serious conversations, if you know what I mean."

"Oh, no!"

"No, Martha, it's all right. He got away. I very much wanted to be able to follow him, because sooner or later, he would have led me back to wherever Curt is keeping himself. I just wanted to let you know what happened, though, because some of this may turn up on the news later. I had a run-in with the police."

"Are you all right?"

"I'm okay. It's just that—well, we're no further forward."

She sighed. "Thanks for letting us know, anyway. It's better to have real news than these hints and rumors."

"Whatever he's up to, Martha, it's definitely something down in this area—if only because there's a limit to the distance he can travel in a few hours as Curt, and he can't stay the Lizard all that long. At least I don't think so." He did not say that there were some things about Curt's behavior that seemed to have changed considerably since Spider-Man had seen him last. There was no point in getting her worried about something he didn't himself fully understand yet.

"You'll keep looking for him?"

"I will." He couldn't say anything more promising than that, though he wished he could.

"You know we really appreciate your help. Both of us do. William likes to make a great virtue of self-sufficiency."

"No question that it's a virtue," Spider-Man said softly. "But tell him to leave *me* something to do."

Martha chuckled softly. There was the strength of the woman: despite all the terrible things that had happened to her family, she never quite lost the humor. "I will. You take care."

"Bye, Martha."

She hung up. Spider-Man sighed, then took himself out of sight again, into the brush behind the rest stop, and changed gratefully out of a costume that was now not just itchy but muddy and smelling of an unsavory mixture of sweat and swamp-water. *Glad I brought a spare,* he thought, as he got wearily into the car and started the long drive home. *At the rate things are going, I don't think there's going to be time to stop and do the laundry.*

SEVEN

He woke up the next morning with a massive ache in his neck and shoulders, left over from Venom's friendly embrace. Peter took a couple of aspirins, then went and stood under the shower and took mental inventory.

On the surface, it seemed to have been a wasted day. He had no new information about Curt, or about what was the matter with the Lizard. But, on the other hand, he was now a lot more comfortable with at least part of the 'Glades. Peter had a feeling that this was going to be useful, and sooner rather than later. But at the moment, he was a little weary of life in the swamp.

And then a plan materialized with a snap. *I'm going web-swinging this morning,* he thought. *Among nice neat shiny skyscrapers, for a change. Since I'm here, they might as well see me. If the cops want to do anything about it, let them chase me up the side of a building.* At the very worst, he would have a nice therapeutic swing around town, and see some of the sights. It would be very relaxing. Skyscrapers were much simpler and more reliable to swing from than cypress trees. Nor were there alligators waiting beneath them, waiting eagerly to catch you as you fell.

Peter felt instantly happier. The next problem, of course, was where to go to change, in a strange city. This hotel was one of those with windows that didn't open: otherwise he would simply have gone straight out.

He left the hotel and drove north a little bit, on Biscayne Boulevard, to the big Omni shopping center. Peter had seen pictures of it in the tourist magazine in his own hotel, and had thought MJ might like to go there.

The place was very busy—they were having sales. *Yet another reason to bring MJ here, I guess—before she finds out about it, and accuses me of having known about it and not telling her.* He drove into the deepest level of the underground parking lot, and tucked the car into a shadowy corner. There he changed.

He exited then, calmly enough, in broad daylight—spidering his way along the ceiling, upside down, totally unnoticed by people as they walked out or drove in. The Questar and his other valuables he had left hidden in the trunk of the car.

Spider-Man scuttled along the ceiling to the parking lot's entrance, and then went straight up and straight out, right up the side of the main building—twenty or thirty stories of hotel and offices. He concentrated on going up only in front of closed windows; no use in ruining some jet-lagged tourist's morning by the sight of a superhero going about his business. There was a brisk wind coming in off the water; a seagull squawked, startled, as it passed Spidey while skimming past the plate-glass skin of the building.

He shot a line of web up to the top of the Omni after a while, hauled himself up, crouched briefly at the very top, and launched another webline at the nearest skyscraper, across Biscayne. It anchored and he began to swing.

It was amazing how relaxing it could be to fall back into the old routine. Building-corner to building-corner, swinging along, noting with amusement that Miami people looked up no more than New Yorkers did. There were fewer skyscrapers here, and they tended to cluster close. Most buildings here were low, as if people were reluctant to shut away the sun even though they already had so much of it. But he could still exploit the center of the city well enough to get a good look at the place—wide boulevards, traffic a little more easygoing, to his eye, than the standard New York brawl and rush of cabs and trucks. On a bright sunny morning, with the humidity not yet out of hand and the temperature still only in the 80s, it was very pleasant. Spidey smiled under the mask.

On a day like this, he thought, *it's nice to be Spider-Man—*
That was when he heard the sound.

It was familiar, and his grin got even broader under the mask. It was amazing how little real gunfire sounded like any of the sound effects in the movies, so much so that he wondered, sometimes, where they got those sounds in the first place. Bullets didn't whine: they went "pff" past you, unless they hit something and ricocheted—and even then the sound was no Lone Ranger "wheeeeenng!" but a sharp brief scratchy sound. Rifles made a sound more like someone smacking a ruler on a wooden desk, and automatic weapons generally sounded more like someone backspacing repeatedly on an old Olivetti than like the "buddabuddabudda" beloved of comics letterers.

Now Spidey heard rulers being smacked on desks, several of them, repeatedly, and fairly nearby, to judge by the way the echoes were racketing off the surrounding skyscrapers. He briefly consulted the memory of the city map in his hotel room. The sound was coming from over by North West Seventh and Flagler.

Spider-Man swung over in that direction in a hurry, fastening his web for the second-to-last swing to the top of a building with an unusual sheared-off, diagonal face. He swung low past the front of it, catching the occasional astonished look from people gazing out through the glass, and dropped down thirty or forty stories to see what was going on.

The situation was fairly serious. North West Seventh was blocked off by police cars to the east and west, about a building over in each direction. The sidewalk in front of the building to which he clung, and in front of the building directly across from it, was conspicuously empty. Across the street was a car, and from his high vantage point he could see a group of men huddled down behind it. Parked to the car's right, slewed sideways and up onto the sidewalk, was an armored car, its back doors open and smoke wafting out of them.

This was a scenario Spider-Man had seen often enough. Smoke bomb into the car's air intake, force the crew out. The details would differ, but there would always be armed men waiting nearby, wearing gas masks and ready to jump into the car and drive it off. *Not while I'm here*, Spidey thought.

He looked down and considered briefly how best to proceed. A hail of bullets was flying in several directions down there, the four men behind their car ruler-whacking and backspacing at great speed. Behind the police cars across the street and to either side, police officers crouched and returned fire, but with little effect.

Spider-Man shot a line of web over to the top of the other building, swung over, and took care to keep himself high and out of anybody's notice. Then he came up against the far building—a bank, as it happened—clung a moment, looked straight down. Only four men: he had wanted to be sure. He scurried down the face of the building until he was about ten stories above the men behind the car.

There he paused. Two of the men were firing mostly forward; the other two were firing each to his own side. None of them was paying any attention to the space behind them, which they apparently thought they had secured.

This was a mistake. Spider-Man considered his choreography for a moment—then dropped right down behind them, silently. The problem with being a stressed-out gunman, blazing away at everything you see, is that it's very hard for you to hear someone coming up softly behind you and shooting a big gob of sticky web over your head—which was what Spider-Man did to the first man, the one on the left-hand side as he faced them. He pulled the man sharply over backwards. As he fell, another jet of web hit the gun. Spidey yanked it out of his hand, released the web, and let the gun and the webline fly off to one side, well out of reach.

The man immediately to that robber's right reacted to the sudden cessation of gunfire, turned openmouthed to see that his companion was gone, spun around staring behind him, saw Spider-Man, and sighted on him. The next jet of web caught this man full-face. He staggered forward, firing, and plate glass shattered, but it was no use—Spider-Man was already somewhere else, about twenty feet to the left. He pulled on the rope of webbing.

The man went down hard, face forward, and Spidey shot

another webline at the gun and fastened it down immovably to the concrete.

The other two had noticed him now. One of them, a man in a T-shirt saying "Nuke the Whales," whirled, firing an Uzi at him. Spider-Man bounced and rolled, changing course twice on the way toward him. He then shot web in two directions, one at the Uzi-carrier, to snatch the machine gun out of his hands and toss it over Spidey's shoulder, the other at the fourth man, to web him and his gun solidly to the car. The one man still standing, the one who'd had the Uzi, jumped at Spidey.

"Waste of time," Spider-Man said softly, and simply decked the man in midair. Vectors add, after all; by his rush, the man added his own energy to the punch that would have hit him to begin with. He crashed to the ground, and Spidey looked down to see if he would move again. He didn't.

"It's a dumb T-shirt, too," Spider-Man said with some satisfaction. He stood still then, for uniformed cops were hammering toward him from all directions, now that the guns were silent. Casually enough, Spidey lifted his hands in a nothing-to-do-with-*me* gesture as they closed in on him.

"Gentlemen," he said, noticing that there were still a fair number of their weapons trained on him, "tell me if I'm wrong, but this looked more like a withdrawal than a deposit."

Some of the cops chuckled, but no one moved much until another man, one in a suit this time, came striding up to Spider-Man. He looked over the site, and then broke into a large grin. He was a big man, dark-haired, broad across the shoulders, with a big mustache over the grin, and a broad, intelligent face. When he spoke, another New Yorkish accent came out, or at least a northeastern one, so that Spidey began to wonder whether this state was entirely populated by refugees from colder climes.

"Spider-Man," he said. "Heard you were in the neighborhood. Didn't think we'd have the pleasure."

"The pleasure was all mine," Spidey said. "Detective—"

"Anderson," the detective said. "Murray Anderson."

They shook hands. "Well, on behalf of the city of Miami and the department, let me thank you," Anderson said. "Because I would have seriously disliked seeing any of my people get shot by one of these guys." He looked around at the four men, whom his officers were detaching from various globs of web, handcuffing, and taking away.

Another uniformed cop came up to them and said, "The guards in the van are coming around, sir."

"Good. Do me a favor. Run them downtown and take their statements—and have somebody from Medical come down and look them over. They might have some smoke inhalation."

"Right." The cop went off.

Anderson turned back to him. "Should I be thanking the City Tourist Bureau as well?" he said. "Are you here on vacation? Come to think of it, do superheroes get vacations?"

"Not as such," Spidey said, and laughed. "This morning I was on busman's holiday, if anything. The trip is mostly business."

"Oh really? Anything we could help you with?"

Spider-Man smiled inside the mask. "Well, since you asked . . ."

"We don't have to discuss it here," Anderson said. "Always wanted a chance to talk to one of you guys. Come on, I know somewhere quiet."

Anderson's unmarked car was nearby. He drove them down Biscayne Boulevard to Brickell, and from there to Bayfront Park. Murray pulled up in the parking lot there, picking a spot where they could look across at the low flat green line of Key Biscayne, and, beyond it, to the Atlantic.

"Pretty spot, detective," Spider-Man said.

"Call me Murray. Yeah," he said, leaning back in his seat and grinning, "I've sat on stakeout a lot down here. Now. What can I help you with? You strike me as a man who may

have some kind of problem, seeing you're out in uniform—"
he smiled "—so far from home."

Spider-Man thought for a moment, and then said, "Among
other things, I'm investigating certain . . . anomalies in security up at Canaveral, at Kennedy Space Center."

To his surprise, Murray nodded. "Word does get around
fast, doesn't it?"

"How do you mean?"

"Oh, they've had some problems recently. Something went
missing, some days back—something they were taking delivery on, that *should* have gone on the shuttle. It vanished."

"The Cape," Spider-Man said carefully, "has been saying it
hasn't had any security problems."

"They'd hardly broadcast it if they did. I know that's the of-
ficial line. But we have our own sources up there. Some of the
people in security, meaning only the best, make sure we find
out things that we need to know about. Even if their bosses
don't necessarily like the idea. We're all on the same side, for
cryin' out loud."

"What happened, exactly?"

"Something jumped up on one of those big delivery barges
they've got there. Decked a bunch of people, hurt some of
them pretty badly—busted some arms and legs, poked a big
damn hole in the barge—then took this object, jumped back in
the water with it—was gone. They did everything up to and
including drag the Banana River, but there was no sign of
what was lost."

"Any reports of what this person looked like?"

Murray laughed, just a breath. " 'Person'—that's not what
the APB says. Six foot two or higher. Massive build. Green.
Claws. Fangs. Tail," Murray said, with emphasis. "Not
many perps down here answer to that description. And no
'persons.' "

Spider-Man nodded. "It's the Lizard," he said.

"No kidding." Murray looked delighted but also concerned.
"But he's crazy, though, isn't he? I thought."

"If you mean he doesn't have any control over himself," Spidey said, "yes, that's right." *As far as I know.*

"Hey, a super-villain on my turf!"

"He's not much of a villain, really," Spider-Man said. "Not in the classic sense."

Murray nodded, said nothing for a moment. "It wasn't accidental, then," Spidey said, "that I ran into some of your colleagues looking specifically for him, the other night?"

"Nope. The APB's been out for days. Now that there've been a couple of sightings, *everybody's* looking. Those who want to catch him, anyway." Murray's look was sly, and suggested that not everybody would particularly want to find the Lizard without ample backup on hand.

"What exactly was it that he took?" Spidey said.

Murray shook his head. "Our sources haven't been willing to say."

It was all very confusing. Theft—the Lizard shouldn't be capable of it. Unless Curt has managed to achieve some measure of control over him again. But that seemed very unlikely, given that he'd shown no sign of being conscious of his inner humanity, or even capable of being reasoned with, the last two times they'd met. Just that mindless rage.

"I have to say," Murray said, "that a little of the, shall we say, edge of immediacy has gone off the issue of the Lizard at the moment. We seem to have a bigger problem."

Spider-Man looked at him. "Venom."

"Venom," Murray said. "Now, that is *serious* trouble— somebody in full control of his faculties, and crazy as a jaybird. Or worse, crazy like a fox—and very unpredictable, especially to members of my fraternity. We've heard enough reports of what happens if you get between him and somebody he's chasing."

"At the moment," Spider-Man said, "I think that's probably me."

"Well," said Murray, "I was going to mention . . . You might want to be careful about the height of your profile for the next little while. You want to limit the collateral damage, you might say. To innocent bystanders—if Venom catches up to you."

"Oh, believe me," Spidey said, "the bystanders are high on both our lists. Possibly the only good thing I can say about Venom."

"And you're sure it's you he's after."

"I *think* so," Spider-Man said.

"But you don't sound certain."

"No," Spider-Man said, "I'm not. Venom doesn't do things without a reason. They might not be what you or I would consider sane reasons, but he has them. These two little escapades—that guy in the skyscraper, and the people on the beach—"

Murray frowned. "We haven't yet released any information about Venom having done it."

"I know what scenes look like after Venom's been there," Spider-Man said. "A crime scene that looks like that one did, paired with a definite sighting of Venom a day later—the coincidence is too big."

"You sound like you have inside info."

"No, I just know Venom," Spider-Man said, and shuddered just a little. "Too well."

"Either way," Murray said, "the modus for these crimes isn't clear. Our one witness has been hard to get anything out of. The doctors say he's in traumatic incurse, whatever that is. Mostly it seems to mean that he can't do anything but stammer. And as for the bank executive—" Murray shrugged. "There seem to be some smuggling connections; they're being followed up. But the guy's very white-collar, and whatever tracks he might have left are well covered. So . . ." He shrugged, and looked out across the bay.

Spider-Man gazed out too, for a moment, and watched the boats go by. "Did you hear about his last appearance in New York?"

"A little."

Spider-Man told Murray something about the CCRC connection on which he and Venom had stumbled when they last ran into one another—the smuggled radioactives and so forth. "It's a name we know," Murray said, "but not for hot stuff. Or not from that kind of hot stuff, anyway."

"Oh?"

"DEA has been investigating them," Murray said. "We've had a few liaison meetings with them, and the Coast Guard. Again, the trail is very well covered, and they haven't been able to pin anything really conclusive on them. A lot of talk, a lot of rumors, but no smoking gun, as yet, nothing concrete. Then this vice president in charge of buffed nails at this German bank gets attacked by Venom, and even the DEA has to start asking itself, why him? Why out of the blue? So the investigation will heat up again now. There's a little annoyance," Murray added, "in the Department at the moment. My department, you understand. Venom brought some barrels along to the scene, the second one. DEA came in and confiscated them."

"Barrels," Spider-Man murmured. There had been a lot of barrels of toxic waste stowed around various CCRC buildings and caches in New York. "Something radioactive?"

"I truly don't know," Murray said. "They just came in there and took the stuff before there was anyone on the scene really senior enough to stop it. Jurisdiction problem. Messy," he said, and chewed his mustache reflectively for a moment. "You think they were nuke stuff?"

"Could have been," Spider-Man said, "but it's a wild guess at the moment. I'd have to see them."

"Tough to do," Murray said, "unless you want to break into DEA HQ and try."

"No, thanks."

"And another thing," Murray said, shifting in his seat. "They've sold that bank."

"Who?"

"CCRC, if I understand the scuttlebutt correctly. The ownership is incredibly convoluted, of course, there are about eight shell companies involved. But the German bank's parent company divested itself of them two days ago. And the 'parent' is a 'child' of CCRC. Apparently the rumors about shipping illegal stuff didn't bother them—I'd bet every big bank in this town has such, sooner or later. But this was apparently too much for someone several corporate levels up. Sold." Murray made a "skrit" noise and a throat-cutting gesture. "To some Arabs, I think. Just like that."

Spider-Man digested that. "What were these rumors?"

"Mostly about illegal shipments coming into the Miami area. Other materials going out again. But no one knew what."

"Where was the cargo supposed to be going after Miami?"

"That," Murray said, "was the peculiar thing. They weren't going anywhere, at least nowhere that could be traced. We do get, from the DEA, estimates of what's coming into the U.S. from the so-called 'southern gateway.' That's the whole stretch of land and water between here and the Leewards, every month. They're rough estimates, of course, but these shipments, whatever they were, would come in, and there would be no sudden jump in the local market, the way there almost always is." Murray chewed his mustache again. "If someone was caching contraband for later use," Murray said, "that would fit the picture. But they almost never do that. Too much chance of the stuff being found, by the competition or by us, and then their investment's shot. In any case, DEA, and police all over the state, are watching for any large sudden movements of merchandise. It's all we can do."

Spider-Man shook his head. "I would bet that those barrels, and those other shipments you're discussing, have something to do with radioactives. Probably toxic."

"There's a nasty logic to it," Murray said. "After all, the channels for smuggling the stuff are already in place. The handoff points, the clandestine transport, everything's ready. But then—" It was Murray's turn to shudder. "The thought of toxic waste getting loose in the Aquifer . . ." he muttered.

"The whole state would be glowing in the dark in a matter of days. And it would take centuries to get rid of it."

"We'll just have to make sure it doesn't happen," Spider-Man said, somber-voiced. The thought haunting him at the moment was not of CCRC specifically, but of Hobgoblin. He'd thought Hobby had been the major mover behind much of the business that CCRC had gotten itself involved with. But Hobby was in jail now, and those illegal operations had been shut down—he thought.

Someone else is managing this, Spidey thought. *Not Hobgoblin. Who?*

"Murray," Spider-Man said, "would you be willing to help out a guy in need of some information?"

Murray laughed. "I thought I had been."

"You have . . . and I'm grateful. But I may need some more. Is there somewhere I can reach you privately? There may be some info I'll need badly in the next few days. It may make a difference either to the Kennedy problem or to the Lizard situation. Or the one with Venom."

Murray fished out a business card from his jacket pocket. "That's my home machine. You leave a message on that, tell me where to call you, and I'll call you back as fast as I can. My pager number's on there, too."

Spidey pocketed the card. Murray said, "Anytime, you let me know. I'll do what I can for you." And he grinned like a little kid. "I don't often get to deal with superheroes, after all."

"Aw, shucks," said Spidey.

Murray smiled and started the car. "They used to tell me, you stay in Miami long enough, you'll see every kind of person there is. Now I believe it."

Spider-Man webbed his way back to the Omni, back to his car, and had changed back to Peter Parker with no hassles. Peter drove back down to his own hotel, checked in, and found messages from Vreni and MJ waiting for him.

"Call me," MJ's said simply. Peter, bemused, took out the

phone—which he had been carrying with him that morning—and turned it on again, half expecting it to ring instantly, then glanced at the other message. It said, "Interesting high-finance connection. Meet me Howitzer's, Miracle Mile . . ." and an address.

Peter looked at it and tried to see the map in his head again. That was over toward Coral Gables, he thought. More interestingly, that was where Regners Wilhelm, that German investment bank, had its main offices. The message had come in about twelve-thirty; it was one now. Peter got moving.

Howitzer's was a little coffee bar in the Mile, in the shadow of yet another tall, handsome, concrete-and-steel confection: though it was not as huge and obvious as some of the buildings downtown. Vreni was waiting for Peter with a cup of coffee in front of her, and was scribbling furiously on a notepad.

"How are you holding up?" she said.

"Pretty well. I'm about to go find a developer for most of my film. If you have any requests, I'll take care of them today before I drop the stuff off."

"That's exactly what I was calling for. I need you to get me some of that building over there." She pointed at it with her chin.

"Got a hot tip?"

"As hot as any so far. I *finally* made some police connections down here. Why are you smiling?"

"Nothing, just a passing thought. Sorry. What did you find?"

"Well." Vreni sat back. "That bank over there—very respectable for a lot of years—has more rumors going around about it than any other bank in this town, I think. Mostly regarding money laundering."

"Oh, really?"

She nodded. "So far, only one genuine conviction—a very very junior accounts executive, fired about a year and a half ago. But there are persistent reports of illicit funds transfers, stolen and counterfeit cashier's checks, money going missing. And then something very strange happened in their computer department, just a little while ago. An employee was fired. A virus invaded their accounting computers, trashed *everything*. The usual thing: a grudge, the employee left a Trojan, as they call it, in the system where it would go off if he didn't deactivate it periodically. Sort of a computer version of a nasty dead-man's switch."

"Bad," Peter said. "But you can always restore from the backups."

"Not if the building containing the backups is torched the same night," said Vreni. And she got that feral grin.

"Tell me," Peter said. "This was just before some kind of investigation happened?"

"Federal," Vreni said. "RICO."

Racketeering as well, he thought. It was all getting very tangled.

"The destruction of the backups was complete," Vreni said. "The destruction in the computer itself was a little more selective. What the virus ate seems mostly to have been material pertaining to a company called CCRC."

Peter's eyes widened. "What are they up to?"

Vreni shook her head. "I hope to find out. This story is a lot bigger than even Kate thinks—that I'm sure of. I have a suspicion that the whole Cape Canaveral story is going to come in second to this." She finished her coffee, closed her notebook. "Come on, let's go get your pictures."

Peter went out with her and snapped the exterior of the building, then got some long-lens exposé-type shots of the building's reception area and of a guard glowering at them through the half-mirrored glass of the entrance. "This is all we're going to get from these guys," Vreni said. "Once they realized what I was interested in, they very politely threw me out. I've got stills of their executives from the one of the corporate yellow pages sources, though. They'll do all right."

Peter shot the end of his last roll and got it out of the camera. "What's next, then?"

"I'm going to go interview that junior executive who got

fired," Vreni said. "He's out on bail, somewhere in the area. Meanwhile, the Shuttle launch is getting closer." She looked suddenly tired. "And my sources don't seem able to tell me anything about what's going on at Kennedy."

Peter stood still and quiet for a moment, considering. Finally he said, "I had a favor that I was able to call in." He told her, without attributing the information, what Murray had told him about the Kennedy situation. Vreni produced her pocket recorder and listened to what he had to say, then looked at him sharply when he finished. "Is this source reliable?"

I only met him this morning, Peter thought. *It's a fair question.* But aloud he said, "In my opinion, yes. I *could* be wrong—"

Vreni looked at him. "I think your judgment is trustworthy. I wish I knew what to make of it all. I thought the Lizard was just—" she shrugged "—sort of a crazy thing running around, not something that you could order to do things. But if he's actually committing thefts . . . How is he doing it?"

Peter shook his head. Vreni smiled again. "This story is not only resisting being investigated," she said, "it's damn well taking the Fifth. I *love* it."

Peter was glad she was enjoying herself so. His problems were unfortunately not quite so abstract.

"All right," Vreni said, as they walked away from the Regners Wilhelm building together. "I've got some more interviews today, then starting this evening, I'll be in the hotel. We're getting close to our first deadline. I suspect I'll spend the afternoon hunting down this Jürgen Gottschalk, our fired exec."

"Right," Peter said.

The Intercoastal Waterway runs up between Miami Beach and Miami proper, starting at the Port of Miami and flowing up past the opulent houses and hotels of Miami Shores and Bal Harbour. Between Biscayne Boulevard on the "mainland" side, and Collins Avenue on both sides of the Waterway, many a beautiful house leans down to a private pier or a dock.

The palms around them sway and glitter when the sun hits their polished leaves, the landscaping looks pincushion-perfect, and an odor of exclusivity clings to white houses and pink bungalows and mansions done in peach stucco and glass brick. Here and there such houses rise above a strip of private beach.

One such house, shaded by palm and bougainvillea, perched by the bay shore, lights gleaming from inside as the dusk settled in. By a blue pool surrounded by pink paving, raised above the line of the waters of the bay, a man sat at a white cast-iron table, drinking an iced tea and staring out at the water.

He was quite young, blond, with a thin, fine-featured face, and very blue eyes. He had been sitting by this pool, staring at that bay, for almost three weeks now.

House arrest was a polite name for it, but that was what it was. There were police outside his front door, police outside his side doors, police staked out in boats down by the water. Some of them were not police officers per se, but federal agents of one kind or another. If he put a foot outside his property, they all went with him—and they let him know that they didn't like him to go outside, not for very long. So mostly he didn't bother going out. If the phone rang, he didn't answer it because he knew it was bugged—a friend on the force had tipped him off before the court order went through, and he had had just time enough to slip out and make a few vital calls from a pay phone before the house arrest started as well.

He sat still and did nothing, because others had told him to. It would all be straightened out in a while, they'd said. Be patient. The heat will come off. The feds will get off your case. He had not inquired how, or why—he was sure that money was changing hands somewhere. Money *always* changed hands. Not even the feds were invulnerable to that.

Evening was fading into night. He looked at the glitter of lights across the Bay Causeway and thought how very much he just wanted to get onto the Causeway, drive until he got

down to the airport, catch a Lufthansa flight home to Munich . . .
But there was no point in it. Even if he could get away from
the house without his watchdogs—highly unlikely—even if he
managed to successfully exit the country with one of several
spare passports the others had given him, the German government would only extradite him right back here again. They
were entirely too willing to show cooperation to the U.S. in
these matters.

No, better to sit still. He got up, strolled over to the edge of
the terrace, and leaned on it. Twenty feet straight down was
the water, and not too far away was the police boat. He gave
its occupants an insouciant wave and strolled back to the table,
sat down again. He lifted his iced tea.

Under the nearby bougainvillea there was a rustling. *Palm
rats,* he thought, exasperated, and turned to look.

The breath caught in his throat. His mouth dried. From the
darkness under the big spreading tree came something darker:
a man's shape, tall, broad in the shoulders, wearing some kind
of dreadful-eyed mask, horribly fanged. A white design was
plastered across the front of him. A spider—

The mask smiled, and a long, slime-dropping tongue flicked
out. Jürgen Gottschalk gulped, and choked, dry. He watched
the news. He knew who this was. More, he knew what had
happened to his colleague in the Miami satellite office of Regners Wilhelm just the other day.

Slowly, Venom advanced on him. He stood up.

"No point in running, Mr. Gottschalk," said that soft, deep
voice, a voice with teeth in it.

Jürgen's mouth worked, but no words came out. The blank
eyes, the awful grin, transfixed him as if he were a spotlit deer,
with someone sighting down a rifle along the beam. "Some
people we know," Venom said softly, "suggested we go talk to
your friend Mr. Harkness the other day. He told us some
things we needed to know, but not as much as we had in mind.
We had to check some of his files before we left his office,
just to reconfirm some of the things he didn't tell us. And your

name figured very prominently. We think we should have a talk."

"Aba . . . ba . . . bout what?"

Venom sat down very casually in the other white iron chair at the table, picked up the iced-tea glass, and sniffed it. "No alcohol," he said. "That's good. We like people who have their wits about them when we talk to them." Those blank eyes fastened on Jürgen's. "Those files," Venom said conversationally, "indicated times and dates for some very interesting meetings out in the water which have been taking place of late. We attended one of those meetings the other night. It was fascinating."

Jürgen swallowed. He had seen the news report. *Fascinating* was not the word he would have chosen.

"Now," Venom said, leaning in, and a pseudopod rippled out of his upper arm and patted Jürgen on the cheek, while Venom leaned his chin on his hand, "we're afraid we weren't able to get those people to deliver the message we gave them. We suppose it's better to do such things oneselves, after all. We were going to tell their boss to cut it out." He smiled more widely yet. "It was rather distressing, though, that we couldn't get them to tell us anything about the source of the barrels they were handling that evening. And the people who had come to pick them up couldn't help us very much—well, we gave them a chance, but it's the usual problem: keep the lower echelons in the dark and they can't spill too much information. They may spill something else, of course . . ."

That grin spread wider, until it seemed to have more teeth in it than a museum of dentistry. "We weren't able to investigate those barrels too closely," Venom said, "but we want you to tell us everything about what was in them, and where it comes from, and where it goes. . . ."

Jürgen shook all over. "Now, we know what you're thinking," Venom said. "You're thinking that if you tell us, the people who you're involved with in this business will kill you. And so they probably will, eventually. At least they'll try.

What you need to know, though, is that if you don't tell us, right now, we will kill you." The pseudopod, wavering in front of Jürgen's eyes, sharpened itself into a thin stiletto, and delicately, delicately traced a line across the front of his throat, just enough to let him feel the nick of the razor's edge.

"We can make it take quite a while," Venom said. "You won't be able to yell for help, because your larynx is one of the first things we'll cut out. After that—" Venom shook his head and shrugged. "We could be here all evening, couldn't we? The people in the boat down there won't come up here unless they see or hear some reason to. Your guards out in the street won't bother coming in—they know there's no way out except by the front or side doors, and they checked those long ago. No, we'll just have a lovely evening together. The longest one of your life."

"It's ruh . . . ruh . . . ruh—" Jürgen's mouth was just too dry to get anything out.

"First word?" Venom said helpfully. "Sounds like? Here." He pushed the iced tea toward Jürgen.

Jürgen clutched the glass and drank. When he set it down a moment later, gasping, it hadn't helped all that much, but he was able to croak. "Radioactives."

"What kind?"

"Transuranics."

Venom waved that knife-pseudopod casually in front of Jürgen's face. His eyes fixed on it as if it were a snake about to strike. "Do be a little more forthcoming, or we'll start getting the idea that you're being purposely obstructive."

"Oh, no, no!" Jürgen said, "*nein! Ich weiss nicht—*"

"English, please," Venom said gently. "We never did finish that last Berlitz course. Life got too busy."

"I don't know!"

"You'd better. What kind of radioactives?"

"It's waste of some kind. Radioactive waste."

"You're telling us," Venom said gently, and a bit of deadly edge was beginning to show in his voice, "that someone in

Florida is shipping toxic radioactive waste out of the United States in those little barrels? Not a very cost-effective way to do it. Where is it going?"

"No, it comes in—"

"Where is it coming from?"

"Eastern Europe. I don't know where, exactly. Russia, maybe."

Venom's blank eyes narrowed a little. "And they're shipping it to Florida?"

"Brazil first."

"From Brazil to Florida. And then what's happening?"

"Then it gets shipped back."

"Not as toxic waste, surely."

"No. Treated—reclaimed—refined somehow."

Venom nodded. "We only know of one plant that does that kind of work," he said. "It's in Europe, in England, at Sellafield. The THORP facility. Nasty filthy thing," he said softly. "Think of all the fish in the Irish Sea that one can't grill without counting their heads first, because of the waste from that place. But never mind that for the moment. You're telling us that there is a nuclear waste reprocessing plant. A secret one, for no government would be so stupid as to try to site such a thing here openly—"

"I didn't tell you that."

"Oh, but you implied it. Clever, to let me draw the conclusion, so that you can truly tell your masters, when they catch up with you, that you didn't tell the main part of the secret." Venom leaned closer. That pseudopod rippled out again, forked, grabbed a pinch of Jürgen's cheek in it, and wiggled it back and forth playfully. "Very clever indeed. You may survive this. So. Toxic waste is shipped from Eastern Europe, heaven only knows how many miles overland, and then to some seaport, and then is shipped thousands of miles to Brazil in those drums—labeled as what? Industrial oil? Fertilizer? And then shipped again, from Brazil up through the Caribbean past the Leewards and the Windwards, some of the most deli-

cately balanced ecosystems in the world, and up to Florida—
and then stored here. In what have to be fairly significant
quantities, to produce—what? Plutonium, surely, is what
would be extracted if there was enough waste of the right
kind. And no one would bother for anything less. It's much
too much trouble."

Jürgen nodded.

"And then," Venom said, "that refined plutonium is shipped
back the same way, all that distance, mislabeled as who-
knows-what, through some of the world's most crowded
sealanes, and across the Atlantic, where the currents would
carry this material, if it leaked, halfway around the world before anyone knew. Killing everything in the water where the
concentration exceeded a part per billion in the seawater. But
then, back to Europe—and someone in Europe is getting significant amounts of plutonium, 'unmarked' as it were, leaving
no records with the various atomic energy commissions of the
countries which deal in such things. And there it vanishes."

Venom grinned, leaned even closer. "Into the hands of . . .
Well, there are too many people who would pay good money
for untraceable weapons-grade plutonium, here and there.
Very slick indeed. And then your bank launders the payments
for these services. Isn't that how it works?"

Mute, Jürgen nodded, took another drink of iced tea.

Venom stood up. Jürgen cowered down against the table,
covering his head. If he was going to die now, he didn't want
to see it coming. From above him, the dark, deep, smiling
voice said, "You've been fairly helpful. We won't kill you just
now. That might suggest to your bosses that someone's getting
too close to them, and they would attempt to elude us. We
don't want that. Anyone so careless with the lives of billions
of innocent people deserves to be caught totally by surprise—
by me. So, no warnings. You will speak of this meeting of
ours to no one. Anything that makes us think that you have
spoken, and we'll be back." Venom chuckled. "No one will be
able to stop us. No one will be able to get to you in time to

stop what will happen, or even to cut it short. All you need to do is be quiet."

A long silence ensued. It was nearly twenty minutes before Jürgen dared look up. That dark presence was gone. The city, unconcerned, glittered across the bay.

Jürgen staggered to his feet, then fled back toward the house, ran into the bathroom, and threw up.

EIGHT

"**T**wo more days down in Cocoa," MJ's voice said.

Peter sighed. It was the next morning, and he was just out of the shower again, getting ready to go meet Vreni before she retreated into her room to write for the day.

"So you're not going to be up to Kennedy for the launch tomorrow?"

"No," MJ said, "I don't think so. Maurice isn't a big fan of early mornings anyway, and the Shuttle goes up at—I think it must be seven-thirty."

"That's right," Peter said. "So you're not going to do the Rocket Garden after all."

"Maybe the day after. He *does* keep changing his mind. The other production staff, the AD and the wardrobe people, they're going crazy. No sooner are they ready for one shot, everything set up and the lighting right, than he changes his mind and wants to do something else."

Peter shook his head and reached over to the table for the top contact sheet of many on the pile he was looking through. "Sounds like you're beginning to think it would have been smarter not to take this job at all."

"Pleeease," MJ said, and she sighed too. "I thought we were going to see each other every night."

"Oh, I know. But look, I appreciate what you're doing."

"I know you do, Tiger. At least the clothes are nice. And the swimsuits are really lovely." Peter could hear the wicked smile in her voice even though he couldn't see it. "You'd like the swimsuits."

Peter secured the phone between shoulder and head while he riffled through the contact sheets again. "*Sports Illustrated* swimsuit issue, huh?"

"Not quite that high quality, maybe, but pretty neat anyway. The only problem is, we can't swim in them."

"Why not? Will they shrink?"

"No, that's not the problem. They've been having shark alerts all up and down the coast."

Peter came up with one sheet, the pictures of his first fight with the Lizard, and put it aside. "Don't let me hear that you've been trying to lure Maurice near the water," he said. There was a pause, and then MJ chuckled.

"Don't tempt me. Still, if I got a nice big bucket of low-calorie tofu and threw it in."

"That's the spirit," he said. "Always assuming the AD is expert enough to take over."

"Oh, she is. It's amazing she hasn't already tried to electro-cute him. I'll tell you, though, I'll be glad to be done with this."

"What? You're shooting on the beach! That should be wonderful!"

"Oh, please. Between coating ourselves with sunscreen and getting sand in every orifice, we all look like a bunch of jelly doughnuts by the end of the day." Peter burst out laughing. "It's easy for you to laugh, buster! Miss one spot, and it burns! Being out in the sun all day is no joke. And we don't even have a tent or a marquee to shelter under. Maurice decided we wouldn't need it. It's the only permanent decision he's made all this week."

"Well, you make sure you cover up as well as you can. I don't like jelly doughnuts when they're overdone."

"Trust me, it's on my list. How're you doing?"

Peter laid one hand on the pile of contacts as if to hide them from himself. "Officially I've got another quiet day," he said. "Vreni's writing."

"That's 'officially.' But . . ." MJ trailed off.

"Oh, of course," said Peter. "I have other business to attend to." He had grown cautious about saying anything out loud or in the clear, since it had occurred to him the other night that it was possible the hotel operators could occasionally listen in on their clients' conversations. "I have to go looking for our miss-ing friend this evening."

"He's still missing, is he?"

"Uh-huh. But I think I may have a slightly better idea of where to look for him."

"Oh, really?"

"Well, while I was swinging through town the other day—" MJ giggled a little "—I met a gent who's been able to help me cut through some red tape. I'll tell you all about him when we get around to seeing each other. But he's really been extremely useful, and he's given me some equipment that's going to be very handy for what I'm doing."

"What, better than that big goggle-eyed thing you've got?"

"Please!" Peter rolled his eyes. "I've done some nice wildlife photography with it, but nothing much else. Not so far, anyway. Tomorrow morning I think I may do better."

"Going to take it up to the launch, then? I wish I could be there."

"You'll be close enough; you'll be able to see it go up. It'll take off right over your head."

"Assuming the woodpeckers don't get it," MJ said.

Peter laughed. A lot of people at Kennedy still hadn't gotten over the embarrassment of the aborted STS-68 launch, when it was discovered, just a week before launch date, that the insulation cladding of the main fuel tank had nearly a hundred holes drilled in it by woodpeckers—one of the local varieties of flicker, actually—and *Discovery* had had to be moved back inside the VAB so that the damaged fuel tank could be swapped for a new, unpecked one. The Wildlife Management people had put up decoy owls and broadcast flicker distress calls in an attempt to drive the birds away. It seemed to have been successful so far, but the Kennedy Center falconers had been standing eighteen-hour watches for the past three days, with instructions to get rid of any flicker that showed its beak around 39-A—with extreme prejudice, if necessary, but at least to run them well downrange. Local radio stations had been getting a good deal of mileage out of the story over the past few days; for Peter's part, he doubted he would have been quite so lenient with the woodpeckers.

"Look, honey, I've gotta go—or I'm gonna be pecked to death by angry reporters. She wants a look at the contacts to pick the best one for her story, then I'm going to have to run and find a processor who'll do me some reasonable prints for less than an arm and a leg. The people who did these contacts were really terrible."

"That's funny. I would have thought with all the modeling shoots around Miami, you could have found people who'd do decent prints."

"Don't bet on it," Peter said regretfully. He had tried to travel light on this trip, and now he was wishing desperately that he had brought his entire darkroom setup with him. "They seem a little slipshod down here, at least by New York standards, but never mind. Look, I'll probably be in and out for most of the day. You can safely try to reach me until, oh, mid-afternoon, but after that . . ."

"I won't call you," she said, more or less in the voice of an annoyed child forbidden to play with a new and favorite toy. "But if you don't call me, I'm going to get worried."

"You're just going to have to be worried, then. MJ, I'm doing all right."

"No you're not," she said. "Venom is in the neighborhood. 'All right' is at best an inadequate description. I don't like the thought that he might get anywhere near you."

"Don't worry. If he does, I'll kick sand in his face. Or something."

"Promises, promises," MJ muttered. "You call me tonight."

"I will."

Peter spent all that morning and the better part of the early afternoon going over the contacts with Vreni. She was in a bad mood, and she didn't like any of them. The angles were wrong, the lighting was poor, they were underexposed or overexposed, they included more material than she wanted or excluded things that she claimed would have made a better shot, they were badly composed, they had too many verticals or too few . . .

Peter sat and listened to her carping criticisms and wondered if this was the kind of thing that MJ was putting up with from Maurice. *Maybe I should offer to introduce them.* About twenty minutes into the critique session, Peter looked thoughtfully at Vreni and said, "How's the article coming?"

She fixed him with an unfriendly stare. "Better than these pictures."

"Now, Vreni." Peter smiled at her and he meant it. She sagged back in the chair on the other side of the table in her hotel room, and sighed.

"All right," she admitted, "I'm not happy with it. Not at all. There's material about this whole mess that I'm missing. I've found a lot of guns, but none of them are smoking. Lots more interlocking company registries, and shell companies, linking CCRC and the German merchant bank. Public records seem to indicate that they've been selling these shell companies back and forth as a way to launder money. But no one seems any too sure where the money's coming from."

"Don't tell me," Peter said. "The information got lost when their computer had its little fit."

Vreni nodded. "That seems to be the story. And the information on where that money is coming from is really the heart of the whole business. As for the security situation at Kennedy, I haven't been able to find out any more than we already know. Whatever happened, whatever was taken, *everyone* is stonewalling."

Peter sat quiet for the moment. He found himself wondering if his meeting with Murray was an example of the Old Boys' Network in action—with the emphasis on the "boys." It would be annoying if it were. Then again, his connection with Murray seemed to stem from Murray's excitement at working with a real-live superhero, gender notwithstanding. Still, he could see how frustrating this must be for her. "Vreni," he said, "I don't know what to tell you. You're the reporter, and I'm sure you'll find out what you need somehow in time for Kate."

Vreni looked at him blearily. "From your mouth to God's ear," she said.

"Meantime," Peter said, spreading the contact sheets across the desk again, "you're going to have to make some kind of choice from these. I've got to go to the processor and try to beat some kind of decent results out of them. Look here . . ."

They spent the next half hour or so with their heads bent over the contacts, until finally Vreni came up with five or six shots that she liked for the feature, and four or five second-string photos as standbys. Peter jotted down the exposure numbers, but looked up at one point to find Vreni gazing thoughtfully at one of the shots of the Lizard.

"Anything more on why he's here?" Peter said.

Vreni shook her head. "Some of my sources think that there's some connection with Venom." She was ticking off the exposures one by one, and her pen paused by one exposure number, the picture of Spider-Man and Venom which had been taken by his little camera. "That Questar," she said, impressed, "does get some brilliant results. I could swear you were right on top of them."

"It's a good piece of equipment," Peter said, which was undeniably true.

"OK," Vreni said. "Take that last one, that should hold Kate. Could you have this stuff ready by—" she looked at her watch "—six o'clock? That's the latest the courier company can pick up."

"I'll have them for you then."

At something like ten of six, Peter came tearing back into the hotel again with an envelope under his arm. He was suffering from a case of extreme annoyance. It had taken him most of the afternoon to find a processor who would even admit to being able to produce professional-quality color stills before the end of the business day. It had taken the rest of the afternoon to bludgeon them into doing the prints correctly, sending one picture back four times because the developer kept pushing it too hard. *It's a pity,* he had thought at the time, *that I can't just get these done at Kmart. But it's too late now. Even Kmart needs a couple of hours.*

He took the elevator up to Vreni's floor and jog-trotted down the corridor to her room. When he knocked on the door, she snatched it open at the first tap. There was a Federal Express envelope already in her hand. "Are those them?" she said ungrammatically. "Here. Hold this." She shoved the FedEx wrapper at him, grabbed the prints, sat down at her desk, and started to leaf through them. "Yes," she said "yes, yes, yes, yes—no!"

"What d'you mean, 'no'? It's just the way you wanted it."

She groaned and put her head in her hands. "It's so underexposed!"

"You should have seen it before I made them redo the print. Four times." Peter glanced around. The room looked very much as if a small localized hurricane had passed through it, littering the floor with pages torn from notebooks and crumpled bits of paper, and her laptop computer was standing open on the table, beeping a plaintive complaint about low batteries.

"All right," Vreni said finally. "It'll have to do." She squared the photos' edges and slid them back into their manila envelope, grabbed the FedEx pack from Peter and jammed the manila into it, and sealed the whole thing up. "There," she said. "Let's get it down to the front desk and meet the courier. And then I am going out."

"For a night off?" Peter suggested.

She looked at him sardonically. "Not a chance," she said. "I have a date with a cop, whom I intend to question thoroughly. What are your plans for the evening?"

"I'm going to call MJ and let her harangue me about her work conditions," Peter said, "and then I've got an old friend to look up out of town."

Vreni locked her room and they made their way down to the

.

front desk together, where Vreni broke into a run and did a good imitation of someone trying to qualify for the hundred-yard dash. She caught up with the FedEx courier just as he was walking out the front door of the hotel. Airbills were exchanged, the package was taken away, and Vreni came back sighing with relief. "That's something, anyway," she said. "The story's already up in the *Bugle's* computer, so Kate will have the hard copy and the comp boys will have the electronic. And here comes my date!" Peter turned, and was very hard put not to react. It was Murray Anderson.

"Peter, this is Murray Anderson. Murray, this is Peter Parker, the photographer who's riding shotgun with me on this jaunt."

"Pleased," Peter said, and shook Murray's hand. He glanced from him to Vreni. "Where'd you two meet? Have you known each other a while?"

"Since yesterday afternoon," she said. "We ran into each other downtown."

Murray smiled slightly. "Rear-end collision," he said. "Fortunately, not too serious."

"It seems to have turned into a beautiful friendship," said Vreni, "even if he did give me a ticket. The swine." She managed to both smile and glower at him; it was an amusing effect. Vreni took Murray by the elbow and steered him away from Peter, then paused and looked back at him. "If you want to join us . . ."

"Thanks, but no. Other plans, remember? And that friend of mine is expecting me. But have a good time."

About two hours later, darkness had fallen almost completely in Big Cypress, and a silent figure in red and blue was webswinging through the trees, intent on picking up a trail that had gone cold. But now, at least, he was better equipped for cold trails—or for hot ones. When he had spoken to Murray the second time, the policeman had sounded thoughtful.

"Can't be easy," he had said, "chasing people around in the 'Glades with just your naked eyes."

"Well," Spider-Man had said to him, "what are you recommending I use?"

"Can you meet me down at Bayfront Park in, say, about an hour?"

"No problem."

Spider-Man had met Murray there, the cop having taken the precaution of slipping into a private little space created by a stand of sword-leaf palm. Spidey, webbing in, had joined him there and found Murray holding something that looked like a cross between a pair of binoculars and a VR eyeset.

"Here," Murray said, holding it up for him to see.

"Infrared night glasses?" Spider-Man said curiously. "Or a starlight 'scope?"

Murray shook his head. "Better than both. This is a thermal imager."

Inside the mask, Spider-Man raised his eyebrows. The gadget was military—or in this case, more probably SWAT—technology, something that made it possible to see people and vehicles by their own heat emissions without using an active infrared source to illuminate them. It would work in fog or smoke as well as darkness, and, unlike standard low-light optics, needed no light at all.

"If you're going to be out in the 'Glades again," said Murray, "and especially at night, this should do you some good. Most animals run hotter than people, and most of our local reptiles run cooler. At night they'll be cooler still. A little practice and you'll be able to tell one from the other easily enough. This—" he tapped a small knurled wheel at the side of the big lens-cover "—is an adjustable thermograph. Right now it's set between 95 and 100 degrees; that should catch most people."

"As low as 95? I thought everyone was 98.6?"

Murray laughed. "That reading's based on an average taken from a hundred people nearly a hundred years ago. Not what

I'd call a very representative sample. So the default setting is 95 to 100. Once you've found out the temperature of the person you're trying to find, you can fine-tune the viewer to find that signal in your field of vision, tag the target with a color or an ID letter, even—" he turned the viewer over and pointed to a row of tiny buttons "—keep track of up to six different traces at any one time."

"Murray," Spider-Man said, "where did you steal this from?"

"Steal?" Murray said, drawing himself up and looking offended. "Hardly. The word you're looking for is requisition."

"With extreme prejudice?"

Murray laughed. "Not that extreme. The DEA guys use these for surveillance, and they've left us a couple. But I signed this out in my name, so for God's sake don't lose it, and whatever you do, don't break it!"

"Is that worse than losing it?"

"Probably. Losing it I could explain as someone else requisitioning it from me. With extreme prejudice. Breaking it, though, and I'd have to explain how it got broken."

"That settles it," Spider-Man said. "If worse comes to worst, I'll lose it."

"Please don't!"

"Only kidding. I'll bring it back to you safe and sound. With, I hope, some answers."

Now, he was swinging along through the cypresses, doing his best to retrace his way to the spot where he and Venom had clashed. Once he found that, he could also find the bearing on which the Lizard had taken off, and follow that. And then . . . That was always the question. And then what?

What will you do when you catch him? Spidey asked himself as he swung. *Hit him over the head, tie him up, and take him home to Martha and William? It's not likely to be that simple. You'd better hope the police are nowhere near when you find him, because they'll just hit him over the head, tie him up—and then toss him in jail.*

There are worse possibilities, he mused. *What if he's actually getting close to finding a cure? What if, wherever he's hiding out here, he's close to the solution? Whatever else has been going on with him*—and again Peter thought of the old lady's strange description of the Lizard stopping and starting, like a machine, like something being run by remote control—*he has a right to go about his own business. But what if it's not his business? What if he is being used as a tool to commit crimes? That's gotta be stopped. And not just for other people's sakes; for his too.*

It was all so tangled, and the thought of the hydrogel was on his mind, too. Was the hydrogel somehow wrapped up in the issue of Curt's cure? That wasn't an idea Peter particularly liked. It suggested that Curt had acquired at least enough control over the Lizard that he was stealing for a purpose.

"No," he said aloud. "I don't believe it." Then he slowed down and looked about him in the darkness. This was the place. He dropped down onto one of the small islets where he, the Lizard, and Venom had fought, recognizing the torn and trampled reeds and the place where one of the alligators had fallen. There was no sign of that 'gator now. Whatever else you could say about the scavengers in the Everglades, they were both efficient and thorough.

He pulled out Murray's present, which had been webbed to his back, carefully put it on and lowered the visor. At first it was a little difficult to get used to focusing both through the eyepieces of his costume and the lenses of the viewer, but he managed at last, and drew in a sharp breath.

These weren't like the stark, pallid infrared pictures of a TV wildlife show, or even the ghostly green visuals transmitted through starlight scopes during Desert Storm. Instead they were color images that showed up as clearly as on a cloudy day, or maybe even a bit brighter. Trees and undergrowth all had their colors; not exactly those of nature, but the mini-computer built into the headset recognized each separate heat wavelength in its programmed temperature band and assigned each source its own specific color. Cool was dark, warm was light, but only the water and the sky were dead black.

Slowly Spidey turned his head, getting his bearings—and also getting used to the slightly skewed perspective of a landscape illuminated by heat instead of light. It would not be comfortable to use this visor for long, especially on the move, but if he was lucky he wouldn't need to use it for very long.

He took off along the line where he had last seen the Lizard swimming, heading more or less due east. A moment later, as he swung slowly along, webbing his way from tree to tree with more care and less speed than usual, he saw that under the image a faint line of data was giving an inertial tracking readout that even included latitude and longitude. The visor had its own satellite tracker built in, and displayed the exact location of whatever object was centered in its field of view.

Very handy, Spidey thought, becoming more determined than ever not to drop or break this thing. If he had thought the Questar was expensive, the thermal viewer was an order of magnitude more so. He paused under one cypress to fiddle with the temperature setting on the right temple of the headset, and as he clicked it up and down, various parts of the landscape—a tree here, a reed-bed there—flared brighter or dimmed down.

That was all very well, but to make best use of the visor, the one piece of information that he needed was the one he didn't have. What was the Lizard's body temperature? The question probably came in two parts. Was Curt's metabolic rate as the Lizard closer to the human or to the reptilian end of the scale? And was that the modern, cold-blooded reptilian metabolism, with its reliance on ambient temperature, or was it that of a small, warm-blooded dinosaur?

Spidey shook his head and adjusted the readout to "see red" at 95 degrees. Without any hard information, splitting the difference might just work. He went off on the Lizard's trail again, holding to that due-east course and watching the water, studded with reedy islets, as he went.

Of course, there was no hope at this late stage that he would find any trace of the Lizard's passage actually left in the water. The day's heat, the night's cold, the currents stirred up by passing alligators, and the slow percolation of water through the aquifer would all have long obliterated his trail so far as temperature was concerned. But if he just kept his eyes open, there was a chance of spotting the less high-tech traces of broken branches or trampled undergrowth.

He headed steadily eastward, and after about twenty minutes of swinging, he paused and looked around him. Nothing but a soft, hazy glow near the horizon, like sunrise. It was a little late in the night for that—or a little early—but he kept going east, and as the minutes passed, that glow on the horizon grew. Through the visor it was an astonishing light, rapidly becoming blinding. Spider-Man swung on toward it, sweeping the visor from side to side. He went on that way for a long time, seeing no sign of anything in the temperature range he had set.

The visible-light end of the spectrum showed him an alligator sluggishly pulling itself up and out of the water before flopping its scaly bulk down onto a reedbed. Here and there an owl or a night-hunting kite went by in a brief, brilliant blob of light that left a trailing afterimage across his vision. And the glow in the east got brighter and brighter, until it was like looking at the dawn.

Shortly Spider-Man stopped. He was running out of trees, at least for the moment. Farther east he could see several small clumps of them gathered together. These, he had found out from one of the tourist books, were the "hammocks" that Hammock Park had been named for: knots of trees growing so closely together that they formed a living palisade, with a little isolated biosphere inside each one. He sprang toward the area where the hammocks began, passed the first one, and kept going. The first limb of the moon came up over the flat edge of the world, looking molten-white through the visor.

Spider-Man paused on one island of trees to turn the gain down, readjusting for temperature as he did so. As he jiggled the click-stopped wheel it went too high for a moment, right up over the hundred mark. The rest of the cool, nighttime world went briefly black, but far off to his right a heat source glowed, then faded as he adjusted the control again.

What the . . . ?

Spidey held still for a moment, staring toward the visual memory of that spark of light, and delicately racked the visor's setting back up again. The spark grew again, then stabilized, radiating at 106 degrees. *At this time of night?* he thought, for it was well past midnight.

He made for the pinpoint of light, and as he closed to within five hundred yards, he could see it for what it was: a hammock, but a huge one. Spidey noted the latitude and longitude on the tracker display, and memorized it. *This,* he thought, *is distinctly fishy—or reptile-y. Whatever.*

About a hundred yards away, he paused, lifted the visor—blinking under the mask as he did so—then removed the entire headset and re-webbed it to his back. While other hammocks that he could see had a somewhat higher ambient heat than their surroundings, even at this time of night, none of them had been this hot. There was something in there worth looking at.

Let's just take a little peek, he thought, and moved in. As he got closer, the islets gave way to larger patches of firm ground, at least on this side. Little rivulets made their way through, but one strip of water was a canal, cut through a stand of reeds, fairly deep from the looks of it, and leading toward the hammock. *Very interesting,* he thought, and leapt across it.

Something hit him chest-high, and knocked him backwards into the water with a splash. Something else hit him again, adhered, grabbed him, and pulled him with brutal speed and strength out of the water and onto firmer ground. He struggled against what held him, but his arms wouldn't work. Spidey strained again, and this time felt strands part.

It was webbing. Very familiar organic webbing which,

along with the lack of a spider-sense warning, clued him in as to his attacker's identity in short order.

Alien tentacles whipped around him but didn't manage this time to pinion his arms. *Two can play at that game,* he thought, grabbed a bunch of the pseudopodia, and pulled hard. What might have started as a leap ended as a crash as Venom came cannoning into him and they went down together, half in and half out of the water and the reeds.

"Same old places, same old faces," said Spider-Man as he struggled to his feet, threw off the rest of the web, and bounded twenty or thirty feet to one side. "Here I thought I was on vacation by myself, and it turns out I'm on a package tour with you! Don't you have any initiative? Is following me around the only thing you can do?"

"Don't flatter yourself, Spider-Man!" Venom hissed. His awful prehensile tongue came out and stroked along the fangs in his open, grinning jaws. "We're ready enough to stop for lunch, if you insist." Tendrils shot out at Spider-Man, but he wasn't there anymore. From something like ten feet in the air over Venom's head he shot webbing, two-handed, straight down, fast and hard. It tangled about Venom's head and shoulders, and plastered the first wave of pseudopodia to his body before they could extend far enough to be a threat to Spidey.

Down he came on the other side, rolled and bounced as Venom struggled in the webbing. It was only a matter of seconds, Spider-Man knew, before he would break free. As regarded webbing, they were fairly evenly matched.

"I don't have time for this, Venom," he said, bouncing again as the first strands of web shredded and more pseudopodia came streaming out at him. "It's not you I'm after!"

"Oh, no doubt. Just where is your confederate the Lizard?" Venom burst free of the last length of web and went for Spidey in a rush. "We'll have that information at least, before we rip your useless head off!"

"Haven't got a clue, fang-face," Spider-Man said, avoiding Venom's rush. "Right now I'm a lot more interested in what's cooking in the kitchen over there." He pointed at the hammock. Venom came down in a crouch about a dozen feet distant, and simply stared at him for a moment, breathing hard.

"Indeed?" said Venom, and his voice filled with menace. "Then why—"

Crack! The first shot went between them. Spider-Man, warned by his spider-sense, had gone down flat before the gun went off, and Venom followed suit immediately thereafter. It was a good thing they did, for a second later the unseen gunman switched his weapon to full automatic and the air above their heads was filled with the whine and crackle of high-velocity rounds.

To Spider-Man, it sounded rather like the bank robbery the other morning—except that instead of being safely above it, he was slap in the middle, in the dark, in an unfamiliar place, with Venom not ten feet away. There was more firing, a lot of it and from more than one gun, then the roar of engines starting up. Spidey could hear the droning propeller-fans of flat-boats like the one he had encountered the night before, and another, deeper bellow like a big outboard motor. The engines revved up, then came blaring toward them.

"While they're moving!" Spidey said. "We may not get another chance! That reed island over there. You lead a bunch of them away from it, that way. I'll go the other. We'll meet up there—" The rest of what he might have said was drowned by the hammer of more gunfire, short, controlled bursts from several automatic weapons, so that the neighborhood began to sound like a busy night in Sarajevo.

"Even you," Venom growled, "have a good idea occasionally." He took off northward. Spider-Man headed south, jumping, rolling, and occasionally crawling through reedbeds and stands of brush, slowly working his way back around to the island he had indicated to Venom. Two of his pursuers were fan-boats, and one of them was a kind of amphibious craft.

He jumped to the other side of the canal, ran farther southward, then doubled back on his tracks while out of sight and ducked deep into a thick raft of cattails. The two fan-boats droned past, closely followed by the amphibian. Each of the fan-boats was carrying about six men; from a quick glance through the cattails, Spidey could see that they were dressed in dark camouflage coveralls with their faces blackened. Every one of them was carrying an assault rifle, and it was obvious from the way they were spraying out fire that they weren't paying for their own ammunition.

When they were safely past and the ripples were splashing up against the cattail raft where he was hiding, Spidey hurriedly made his way—very low, very cautious—back to the reedbed he had shown Venom. He slipped into it and lay flat for a moment, just getting his breath back, then put his head up. A pseudopod snaked silently out of the darkness and pushed it back down again, as another of the boats came back.

The roar of its engine died down to a throaty rumble and then fell silent as it lay rocking in the water no more than twenty feet away. "Where'd they go?" somebody said.

There was a short crackle of static from a walkie-talkie, followed by another voice grumbling, "One went north an' the other went south like cats with scalded tails."

"Question is," said the first voice, "who were they?"

"Doesn't matter. Pretty sure they're gone now."

There was another burst of static, and then a third voice spoke from another walkie-talkie. "We gotta timetable here. We can't linger."

More static, and a fourth voice. "I don't like it; they can't have gotten away that fast. We should take a look around. Anything this close needs killing."

Very close to him, Spider-Man could hear a rustling as if someone was gathering himself to rise. As softly as he could, he said, "Don't do it!"

Venom growled as softly. "If we do not kill some of these people, they will not show us proper respect."

"Not after they're dead, that's for sure," Spider-Man hissed back. "And after they're dead, we can't follow them anywhere either. You just lie still for a minute."

The boat had gone quiet. "You hear something?" someone said. There was another pause, the silence dragging out so long that Spidey was tempted to say "Ribbit!" just to relieve the tension. But he had no idea of the quality of his frog imitations, and with half a dozen military-level automatics no more than a long spit away, he didn't dare risk producing a bad one. He concentrated very hard on nothing bad happening.

Spidey heard another squirt of static. "Come on, you guys. We've got a lot of ground to cover, and things to blow. North unit, echelon left; south unit, echelon right. Warm up, let's move out!"

"That's a roger," said the man with the nearest walkie-talkie, and returned it to a cradle on his belt.

"He just loves to sound so damn military," said another voice, a scornful one, from the boat.

"Yeah, sure. And if you don't want to give him the chance to use that military on you, get this thing started." There was a cough as the engine turned over; then it caught and roared into life again. The flatboat spun neatly on its axis and headed off due east, so close to their reedbed that the reeds whipped and gusted in the prop-wash of the thing's eight-foot fan. Had any of the men been looking behind them, they might have seen two prone figures lying in the reeds pushed flat by the wind. Then the reeds stood up again, and the boat was gone.

Spidey elbow-walked in the direction from which the pseudopod had come, and pulled some of the reeds aside. He found himself looking directly into Venom's fanged face; not the most charming view.

"Now," Venom said. "Where were we?"

"You can't be serious!" Spider-Man said. "Didn't you hear those people? They're going to blow something up. Don't you think it might be nice to find out what, just in case there are some people on site who'd rather not be blown up with it?"

Venom looked at him coldly. "If we thought you were half as concerned for the innocent as you pretend to be . . ."

"We don't have time for this conversation right now. And, I might ask, what brings you here?"

"It was close to here that we lost the Lizard last night," Venom said, sounding annoyed. "About two miles south, to be precise. But we have other reasons to be here."

"Something to do with that little hot-box in there, huh?" said Spidey, nodding toward the hammock.

"Is it there indeed?" said Venom.

"Is what there?"

"The base from which your precious Lizard has been working. We thank you for the information."

Oh Lord, Spider-Man thought. *What have I told him?* But aloud he said, "Glad to be of help. But don't you think we have something a little more important to think about just now? What are those guys going to blow?" Then the thought came to him, and his mouth fell open under the mask as he made a little strangled noise that made Venom shoot him a suspicious look. "Oh my God," he whispered. "It's tomorrow morning. Only a few hours from now."

"What?"

"The Shuttle launch! They've got plenty of time to get there."

"What is this about the Shuttle?" Venom said.

Spider-Man told him, quickly, about the security breaches at Kennedy. "Something funny is going on," he said finally. "There's something very hush-hush about this particular launch, despite the fact that they're trying to make it look like there's not. Now, these guys are going off saying they've got 'something to blow'—it *can't* be a coincidence."

"That may be," Venom said, getting up. "But we've let them gain enough distance. And we have other concerns. Craft very like that amphibian are being used to smuggle certain substances in and out of this country, under circumstances that will endanger many more people than a Shuttle launch gone awry." And he leapt off eastward after the people in the boats.

Spidey went after him. "I wouldn't bet on it!" he said, as, going low and carefully, they chased the boats east.

The argument went on for a good while. Those boats were moving fast, but they couldn't do better than thirty or forty miles an hour in the clear, and this was not the clear. They had to pick their way, zigzagging from canal to stream to canal again. The amphibious vehicle did better, going up and over firm ground sometimes, but mostly for speed's sake, it stayed in the water as well. Spider-Man and Venom were able to keep up with them at a safe distance.

Nearly an hour went by, and part of another. Then a much broader stripe of water lay in the near distance before them. "It's the Miami Canal," Spider-Man said. The boats were racing down a smaller waterway ahead of them, heading for where it met the canal.

"This goes north and south, does it now?" Venom said.

"That's right. Northward it empties into Lake Okeechobee, and connects to the river and canal network northward. Southward it heads for Miami and the Intercoastal Waterway."

The boats roared into the canal—one group heading north, the other south. "Come on, Venom!" Spider-Man said. "The Shuttle!"

They were leaping along the southern bank of the smaller canal which joined the Miami. "No," Venom said, "we think not. Our business takes us south. Besides, if you and we both go north, who will follow those? And as you say—who knows what they may be about to blow?"

Spidey stopped for a moment then, and looked at Venom. "Good hunting, then," he said.

Venom chuckled. "Oh, we always have good hunting. And after we deal with them—let's see how *you* like being the hunted."

He leapt off southward and swiftly vanished into the moonlit landscape. Meanwhile, the other flatboats were buzzing off northward. Spider-Man said a word under his breath, one that superheroes should not be heard saying. Nearby, a frog said reproachfully, "Ribbit."

Spidey breathed out, just a breath of a laugh, and took off after the boats.

Another two hours passed. The boats went on through the night, and Spider-Man followed. He was getting very, very tired. Only his spider-strength was keeping him going now, and even a spider's patient, mindless endurance would be tried by keeping a pace like this. At about the two-hour point, the boats stopped, and he stopped too, watching. The pause was only a brief one—they were refueling from gas drums cached on a reedy island. Spider-Man crouched under a cypress, about a quarter-mile behind, and watched, panting.

Heaven only knew how many miles he had covered since parting with Venom. Not that that had made Spidey very happy, either; the thought of what Venom might be getting up to down south somewhere, for what purposes, made him twitch. But what made him twitch more was the image of something bad happening to the *Endeavour*, something much worse than woodpeckers.

The boats started up again, headed northward. He followed.

The canal network of mid-Florida is a tangled thing, full of unexpected connections. Once it was much used for freight; now pleasure boats plied it constantly, and local county authorities were constantly digging new connections, with their eye on the tourist industry. It was possible to go from the Everglades to Lake Kissimmee completely by the inland route. But the people whom Spider-Man was pursuing didn't opt for that. Instead, once clear of the Miami cityplex, they "hung a right" out of Lake Okeechobee into the Saint Lucia Canal, which comes out in Saint Lucia Inlet. From there they headed up the eastern coast, on the inside of the Intercoastal Waterway, in the shadow of the long thin island which runs just down the eastern coast sheltering the Florida mainland from the sea. Spider-Man followed them.

Many times Spidey wished he were driving; other times he wished he could just stop and catch a bus. Still, he plowed onward through marshland and grassland, swinging from high-tension towers and radio masts and buildings when they were handy, and bounding through wetland and dry land when they weren't—upsetting the wildlife and the occasional late driver who saw him. *But a lot besides wildlife will be upset if I don't get to Kennedy when these people do . . .*

Spider-Man was sure that was where they were going. He became even more certain when, at Cocoa Beach, they veered even farther inland on the west side of Banana Island, and ran up the coast near Titusville and Mims, making for the northernmost, unrestricted part of the Cape. *That clinches it,* Spidey thought, and concentrated on narrowing the gap.

He was slowing down, though, and he knew it. What frightened him more than anything else was when he heard the engines stop. He had been tracking by sound; he would have to rely on sight again.

He caught a flicker of motion off in the flat wetland, toward Kennedy. Tonight, the lights were on down there. Pad 39-A had all the big Xenon spots trained on the Shuttle. There it stood, looking small at this distance, but blazing jewel-like in white and black and the orange of the main fuel tank. Between it and him, Spidey could see running forms, crouching, going fast.

He went after them. After a very short time, Spider-Man found himself looking at a barbed-wire fence, with a sign nearby that said U.S. GOVERNMENT PROPERTY. TRESPASSING PROHIBITED. In the fence, someone had cut a hole big enough to let two people go through at once. Spider-Man stopped. He could hear no alarms, no sounds of trouble of any kind—and that was the worst news of all. They were in, and somehow nobody knew about it. *Isn't there some kind of perimeter security out here?* Spidey wondered, as he leapt the fence and went after the mercenaries. *Or have the damn budget cuts affected that, too?*

Softly, ahead of him, something went BOOM.

Leaping was the only form of locomotion left to him at this point; in this vast flatness, there was nothing tall enough for him to swing from. Away Spidey went, at top speed. As he went, he hurriedly got out Murray's widget again, and slipped it over his head. He had to stop just for a moment, to readjust.

The moon was no longer a problem: it was high enough in the sky to be out of his view. *Endeavour* itself, sitting there proud and shining, was not much of a heat source at this point. But the intense hot spotlights shining on 39-A were as unbearable to look at as the sun. Spider-Man turned the gain down, and then cautiously adjusted the scope's heat levels.

There. Four or five shapes, running, white, silhouetted against the indigo and super-dark green of the grass. They were running away from a blocky shape that radiated some residual heat—not at body temperature, but lower. A building. From it a glowing fog billowed upward.

Spidey bounced toward it as fast as he could. As he approached it, he could see more shapes, brighter, hotter ones— jeeps, glowing brightest from under the hoods and at the exhausts. They came roaring toward him down a service road from the direction of 39-A. Yellow hazard lights flashed on them. He could hear sirens. Searchlamps scanned ahead of them.

Spider-Man came around the corner of the building and stopped, shocked to see the amount of heat it was radiating. A bomb of some kind had exploded against the side of it, and had made a huge crater in it. Whether the building housed someting vital, he couldn't tell. He turned.

Over his head, Spider-Man heard the whistle of a single bullet, and then a fraction of a second later, the *crack!* of its firing. Spidey stood very still and put his hands in the air as the spotlights of the approaching jeeps came to rest on him.

Three jeeps pulled up, and shortly Spider-Man found himself surrounded by more pointing guns than he ever wanted to see. Some of the people in the jeeps were in Air Force uniform, and others were wearing NASA windbreakers, and they all looked very grim indeed.

Four people got out of the jeeps and came over to him slowly: three men and a woman. "Who are you," said the man in the lead, a NASA security man, "and what are you doing here?"

"Before we get into that," Spider-Man said, "it's not me you want, it's those eight people who just scattered in all directions after doing this." He glanced at the building. "They're probably re-forming up behind you even as we speak. This wasn't anything important, was it?"

"We're not going to discuss that with you," said the man. "But all the same—" He looked at the people in one of the other jeeps and jerked his head back toward the way they had come. That jeep took off, and someone in it started talking rapidly into a walkie-talkie as they went. "Now," the man said. "About you—"

"I'm Spider-Man," he said, "and I'm here about your hydrogel."

The people with the guns looked blank. But the man who had spoken, and the woman, in Air Force uniform, exchanged a shocked glance. "Yes," Spidey said. "The stuff the Lizard stole from your boat the other night. The stuff that's supposed to go up on the Shuttle this morning."

Silence. The man and woman looked at him. "The Lizard," Spidey said impatiently. "Big green guy? About six feet? Scales? Tail?"

The woman stepped forward. "A friend of yours?"

"People keep asking me this," Spider-Man said. "Let's just say he's an acquaintance. I know where the hydrogel is, and how it can be gotten back to you. But rather more to the point, what are you going to do about those people? They do not mean well, I'm here to tell you—if you need more evidence than this." He jerked a thumb at the cratered building. "And if you don't go after them, something very bad may happen. They just made a very concerted effort to kill me and someone else I know earlier this evening, because we were in a position to overhear what they had in mind. They said they were going to blow something."

The man turned quickly to the woman. "Let's put him under guard and get out of here. We've got a situation."

She looked at Spider-Man—a cool look out of a still, pretty face. "No," she said. "He's coming with us."

"But he just broke in here!"

"I don't believe so. Put a guard on him if you like, but put him in our jeep. He's coming with us. You," she said to Spider-Man, "if you please—you have some explaining to do. Tell us who those people are, and make it quick."

NINE

T he moon was gaining height when the mercenaries split, one group going north and the other south. Venom went after the southbound ones, in a very mixed mood.

He had been ready to kill Spider-Man again, and once again he had been distracted from that. It was a perfectly straightforward intention, and he couldn't understand what kept going wrong with it. If he had been of a less materialistic turn of mind, or more superstitious, Venom would have suspected there was some bad planetary aspect in his horoscope these past couple of months. Or maybe it was sunspots. All around him he could feel the symbiote twitching with frustration. It had been so close to a satisfying, messy, violent end for its worst enemy, and the sweet satisfaction of dining on part, or more likely, all of Spider-Man, before the night was out. Now once again it would have to wait.

Be patient, Venom said within himself. *It'll be worth it. When this is all over, he will still be there.*

The wave of annoyance that came back to him from the symbiote suggested that it found the reassurance less than satisfying.

Venom settled into a steady pace along the canal bank, following the mercenaries. He found himself wondering whether the symbiote had started showing any signs of its taste for blood while still with Spider-Man. Was this something these creatures normally developed? Or was this simply a byproduct of its thwarted desire to bond with Peter Parker? He supposed it made sense that the symbiote's desertion by the being for whom it had tailored itself could very well have deranged it. It was Spider-Man's blood it really wanted, and if it couldn't have it by way of partnership, it wanted it for lunch. If it couldn't have Spider-Man's, it would have other people's. This was not a substitution that made it really happy, but a stopgap measure, until the day it achieved its heart's desire. And someday it would . . .

Not tonight, though, Venom said silently to his partner. *For the moment, we have other business.* His group of mercenaries—two of the fan-driven flatboats—sped down the Miami Canal for the better part of an hour, southeastward. He followed them as steadily as he could, alternately bounding and webswinging along the canal's western bank, occasionally veering inward to avoid a house or a farm. He wished not to be seen by anyone, neither the group he was chasing nor the people in the towns and villages they passed. The innocent could, after all, be easily frightened by them, even though he meant them no harm. As for the guilty, they would see him soon enough. And if Venom had his way, he would leave none of them alive except one, some single messenger, to take his warning back to his masters as before—making it plain what happened to people involved in such ugly business. *And I only am returned to tell thee.* . . . Watching the boats skim ahead of him in the moonlight, Venom smiled and continued his pursuit.

He had been very busy working with various sources in the past few days. Miami's underworld was full of people who knew more than was good for them, people who tried their best to get their fingers into the pie. It was a town where dirty money was rife, and where at any hour of the day or night you could be sure to find something illicit going on, if you knew whom to ask. Venom knew whom. Or more to the point, he knew how. And he had some help from an unlikely source: the media.

Word had gone out quite quickly that he was here. As a result, there was almost no illicit bar, numbers parlor, gambling den, or other nest of crime where he would not get instant and terrified cooperation should he put in an appearance. For anyone who had not seen the TV pictures of the spot he had visited on the beach a couple of nights ago would have heard about it by now. Rumor, decorated with tongues—in this case, one large, slime-drooling, prehensile one—had already gone streaking through the city streets, making its way into the darkest recesses, telling what had been found on that beach, and what shape it was in. Because of this, whenever Venom turned up at some shady address or some dingy alley, or (in other cases) in polished boardrooms or exclusive offices, the inhabitants had been only too glad to talk to him. Some of his informants babbled information so fast that Venom would have been tempted to think they were making it up, except he knew they wouldn't have dared.

His investigation of the CCRC connection had proved particularly fruitful. He still found it hard to believe the massive recklessness of the local environment that was embodied in CCRC's importation of toxic waste here. The people running the corporation must certainly know that when the government caught them—any of them he didn't take care of himself—they would go to jail, for years and years. But regardless, the sordid business continued. It suggested to Venom either that they thought someone in their organization could protect them from prosecution, or they were going to make so much money that a twenty- or thirty-year prison sentence seemed like an equable price to pay. And that thought made Venom boggle.

Or perhaps it meant that they seriously didn't expect to be caught—that they expected prosecution to pass them by. Venom growled, smelling bribery in the air, and the symbiote rippled in response to his anger. *How much money*, Venom thought, *do you have to spend to corrupt a federal grand jury? Or bypass an investigation? Or keep it from ever starting?* Incorruptibility was becoming a rare trait these days. If you greased enough hands, no one would be left who could hold justice's scales. In this case there were doubtless thousands of hands to grease, but if CCRC was making the kind of profits Venom suspected from this tidy little trade, there would be plenty of grease to go around.

The flatboats passed under I-75, where the arching piers of the freeway took it over the canal. Venom shot web at the supports and swung under, attaching more web to a couple of cypresses, then dropped again to the reedy ground as the flatboats roared down the canal, and went on following.

Well, he thought, *we will do some serious work tonight. No more than one of these people will be allowed away to bear the news. Of all the rest of them, we will make a memorable example.* Remembering his own days as a journalist, he added to himself with a smile, *The media will have a field day.*

Now the mercenaries were picking up speed. Venom increased his pace to match. He was unsure of the actual mileage they had covered since he and Spider-Man parted. It might have been twenty, maybe twenty-five. He hadn't run this much in some time, but his anger was giving him energy to spare, and the symbiote, sensitive to that and eager on its own behalf, was doing most of the work for him.

Venom was fairly certain he knew where they were headed. As Spider-Man had said, the Miami Canal went mostly southward and finally to Miami Beach, with connections to various other canals along the way. He thought they would most likely head into Biscayne Bay—possibly trying to lose themselves among the normal night traffic in the water—and from there, make their way down the coast to some quiet beach well south of Miami, avoiding the police attention the nearer beaches were getting at the moment. They might go as far south as Perrine or Goulds, or even Florida City. No matter: he would follow.

But now his problem became somewhat more complicated, for instead of following the Miami Canal all the way down, they turned right, due south, on one of the minor canals near Opa-Locka. Inland again; he swore softly to himself as he followed, and the symbiote caught the anger and started to get hungry for blood. It was a sensation Venom could feel on his skin, strange as it was to be able to taste something there—but ever since he and the symbiote had taken up company, Venom had gotten used to paraesthesias of various kinds, seeing or hearing or feeling things the way the symbiote did. A small price to pay, he always thought, for the advantages it gave him, and the constant sense of wordless companionship. Now, though, its anger fretted on his nerves. No surprise, since its nerves and his were inextricably intertwined.

The route their quarry now took was a more convoluted and twisting thing, always trending southward, but using smaller canals, less direct routes. Once again they had to slow down, and gratefully, Venom slowed down as well. *No telling how long this may last,* Venom told the symbiote. *We must pace ourselves.* He felt it agree, which was good; by his reckoning, they still had at least another forty or fifty miles to go before reaching the southern coast.

He shrugged, kept following, and endured, wondering idly as he went how Spider-Man was doing. Though he might despise him, his strengths were not to be sneered at; of the heroes that Venom knew personally, he was one of the best fitted to handle a chase like this. He wondered, too, whether Spider-Man had been right—whether the target of that northbound group was indeed the Shuttle. If so—despite his preferences— Venom had to wish him well. Like many others, Venom had bitter and painful memories of a morning in the mid-1980s when, at the seventy-fourth second of a seemingly routine Shuttle launch, something had gone very wrong. The memory of *Challenger*'s bizarre, Y-twisted contrail was something that would not go away. At times, when Eddie Brock had watched Shuttle launches since, he would find himself holding his breath until that seventy-fourth second was past. He did not want to see something go wrong with another one. If he can stop some such thing from happening to *Endeavour*, Venom thought, it will have been worth letting Spider-Man go.

The symbiote stirred uneasily. *Oh, you needn't fret,* Venom said silently. *We'll have him yet. But there's no harm in letting him do this job first.*

Southward the mercenaries went, and Venom followed. They plunged into the Chekiko State Recreation Area, another webwork and tangle of canals and reedbed and scrub, another river of grass. From there, they went straight into the Everglades National Park. Here the trees became much fewer, except for low stands of dwarf cypress, more bushes than trees. Great flat wind-wrinkled sheets of water quivered under the

moon, rippling and troubled in the still night where the flatboats' wakes tore through them. Still Venom came after, ex-
ploiting what little dry land was to be found, and leaping from
island to island, staying low and far enough behind not to be
seen, the symbiote changing its coloring to blend with the
background.

On the flatboats went, crossing under Route 27 and making
for Florida Bay. Far off, at the very edge of the horizon to the
east, the lights of Homestead and Homestead Air Force Base
were a soft yellow glow. Venom started to close up the gap
between him and the flatboats, smiling a bit as he went at the
thought of the coastline where they were heading, just north of
the Keys and sheltered by them from the open sea. It had been
one of the great stomping grounds for smugglers of all kinds
for nearly half a millennium. Pirates had used it first, for a
staging area; they had gotten water from the freshwater
streams there, hunted for victuals. Men like Henry Morgan
and Bat the Portuguese and the dreadful L'Ollonois had provi-
sioned their ships there—some apparently by trading with the
Seminoles—bought and sold slaves, and unloaded hot cargoes.
Later, during the Revolutionary War, blockade runners had
sought refuge in the Spanish ports there. Some desperate
traders eager for a fast buck had brought munitions and raw
sugar up the length of Florida from there, helping the southernmost colonies break the chokehold the British had on the
"triangular trade." Then later still, during Prohibition, rum had
been sneaked in from the Caribbean and dropped on these
shores, having run the gauntlet of government vessels in and
around Key West. The running of contraband continued to this
day: little clandestine seaplanes, in the dead of night, would
make landings there in the "river of grass," or just offshore,
drop their cargoes, and go out loaded with cash.

And now these people. Venom was very sure he knew what
they would be picking up—and sure they would treat it as cav-
alierly as any other cargo, as something to be dumped without
a second thought to save their skins. The thought of barrels of

this being tossed overboard to rust—it would be a bad situation even in the open water of the bay, where the delicate coral ecosystem was already under threat from pollution and changes in water temperature, and a concentrated spill of almost any kind of pollution would strain the system to the breaking point. To destroy everything, all that would be required would be a gram or two of plutonium in this water. The sea bottom for miles around would become a sky-blue desert. And if spilled in the 'Glades . . .

It would not happen, he swore. Venom would not let that happen.

The first hint he had that they were coming close to the sea was by the smell of the salt in the air. Looking past the boats he pursued, Venom could see the first thin silver line of moonlit sea to the south. To tell the truth, he was relieved to see it. He was tiring, and the symbiote was fretting against his consciousness in a way that suggested it was getting weary too. He had not often had a chance to push it so close to its limits. *Take it easy*, he said silently.

Venom made a little more speed, to close up the gap between him and his quarry. Then he heard the sound he had been waiting for—the engines slowing down as the flatboats dropped speed, to feel their way through the marsh where the wetlands proper merged with the littoral marsh, the salt marsh that ran down to the dunes, and after them, to the sea.

He grinned. Venom was resolved to let as much of the exchange take place as he could before he acted. One or another of these people might drop information that he would find useful, and he intended to give them the chance. He was particularly interested in any details which might surface about the actual location of this waste-reprocessing plant. Venom was sure that such a thing, which would have to be highly secret, would be hidden away somewhere inaccessible, so there would be no chance of it being found by environmentalists, or politicians, or annoying ordinary people. Venom also suspected that—from the point of view of the people who would build such an unattractive facility—the most sensible thing would be to put it right in the middle of the Everglades. It would not be the little base from which Curt Connors was working. That was much too small, and he would deal with that himself, and with either Connors or the Lizard, in fairly short order. But right now . . . .

He looked down at the shore. The flatboats had slipped into a little tributary stream, which led down among the dunes to the shore. Softly they cruised down it, their engines *putt-putt*ing quietly, and the fans muted to a lawn-mower buzz. The sea grass went sparse around him in the salt water as Venom took to the shallows and followed them, and here and there white sand from the dunes shoaled up in little bars and spits. The flatboats made for one bar that was bigger than the rest.

It was low water now. Later on, by the time any daylight showed, tracks or other traces of their presence would have been washed away by the rising tide. *Very clever,* Venom thought. *But not clever enough.*

There was no cover to be found any closer to the shore. The salt grass grew only a foot or two high. Venom slipped into the water, making his way into the little stream and sinking into it until there was only enough of his head showing to let him breathe. The stream was fairly deep: there was a strong current running in its depths, one strong enough to carve a channel deep in the sand, and right down to the shore. The flatboats came one after the other into the shallows of the bay and edged up to the broad spit of sand off to Venom's right. Very slowly, so as not to ripple the water, Venom caught up with them, instructing the symbiote to blend with the background and got as close as he could to see what was being done.

The bay was quiet. Pseudopodia questing for some distance beneath him told Venom that the bottom here shelved only very gradually, perhaps no more than one foot in a hundred. The shallow water lapped at the boats, but made little other sound. Venom caught the sound of several bursts of static from walkie-talkies as the flatboat crews beached them on the spit and shut down their engines.

"Operation Grab Bag is go," said one voice, tinny, from a good distance away. One of the men on the spit answered on his own walkie-talkie: "That's a roger. Triple Scoop is going ahead."

"Roger," said the other voice. Was it his imagination, Venom wondered, or did he hear, before the burst of static that ended the second message, the crack of gunfire? He wasn't sure. Well, if he had, let Spider-Man handle it himself. Venom had his own priorities just now.

One of the mercenaries, a tall, thin man, said to another, "All right, Joe, give 'em the light."

"Right," a shorter, stocky man said. He came up with a long, thick, police-style MagLite. In the other hand, he held something smaller. A *compass*, Venom thought. Joe began to turn carefully in an arc from southeast to southwest, then paused, taking a bearing, and began flashing the light in that direction, probably in Morse code.

Some of the men sat down to wait then. Joe and his companion stood, looking out southwestward. What with the roil and dazzle of the water under the moonlight, it was hard to make out anything definite. But sound traveled. And faintly, Venom could hear very soft, muffled engine noise approaching from the southwest.

Now, then, he thought. Slowly, dark shapes began to show themselves against the silver of the sea and the indigo-black of the horizon. Shortly Venom could identify two separate sources of engine sound.

Under his "mask," half under the water, Venom smiled. They were boats of the same kind as one he had met off Matheson the other night. That attack had gone awry, much to his annoyance. When he boarded the boat, one of the men who had been there—at the sight of Venom, understanding quite well what was going to happen to him—had shot his companion, and then had defied Venom's questioning to the point where it could no longer be restrained. Blood it had to have, and blood he had given it—sensing clearly that there was nothing further he could do with the man, anyway. He was some kind of fanatic, to have shot the other man out of hand. Now Venom could feel the symbiote's growing excitement. It recognized the boats, too, and knew, in its limited way, who was in it, and what was likely to follow.

Not just yet, Venom thought. *Tonight, my friend, we practice patience.*

The boats approached more slowly. On the spit, one of the men pulled out a spotlight and started to make a quick sweep. Venom ducked hurriedly all the way under the water well before it hit him, so that any ripples would disperse. Under the water, he saw the bloom of the light go over, lingering for a moment, then moving on. Venom stayed under for a few seconds more, then slowly, carefully, put his head up again.

The boats drew in from the bay. One of them now was close enough to make out detail. It had a big, tall man in camouflage standing in its bow holding something blocky and dark: another searchlight. Venom submerged again, waited until the beam swept past, then surfaced once again.

The boat was a thirty-foot speedboat, with significant cargo capacity—made to be able to run fast if it had to. *Probably has a good-sized fuel tank as well. One could run a good way in a boat like that. Cuba? Haiti? Further? He would find out soon enough.*

Meanwhile the first boat drifted up to the edge of the spit. There was a muffled splash as someone softly let down an anchor. The man in the bow of the speedboat said, "Everything all right so far?"

"Dead quiet," said one of the men on the spit. Venom grinned.

"Okay," said the man in the speedboat, and turned to call below deck. "Let's get the stuff up."

The transfer began. Barrels again, as Venom had expected. The second boat came in behind the first, and it too began to unload. *Three men on the first one,* Venom thought, *four on the second, and then four each on each of the flatboats.* He started taking careful notice of who was armed with what. The symbiote was resistant to bullets, but he didn't care to put it in harm's way any more than he had to; that was no way to treat a friend.

One by one the barrels were lowered cautiously from the boats bobbing at anchor, onto the spit. They were rolled across to be stacked up in the flatboats. Venom watched this process with some concern. They were loading both boats at once, which was good, in that it gave him a little more time to consider his options. *There are quite a few of them,* he thought. *If we move too quickly, though, they'll take off in all kinds of directions, and it would not do to let this cargo escape northward. If these people get the sense they're being pursued, they'll dump it. And if it leaks into the 'Glades. . . .* A leak into the bay would be bad, too, but the bay would purge itself far more quickly than the Aquifer. And no one drank the water from the bay.

The loading progressed. The men were talking desultorily but not saying anything that was particularly useful to him. None of them seemed to know the others any too well, and he got the sense that none of them wanted to. Probably wise: the less you know about your co-conspirators, the less you can spill about them if the police or the feds catch you.

This did Venom little good, though. He edged as close as he dared, wishing that the man piloting that first boat would say something. But his speech consisted mainly of "Hurry up!" and "We don't want to get behind schedule, keep it going." But after a few minutes he reached down out of sight, saying, "Here, might as well do this now. One of the hot ones."

"Right," said another of the men, and took charge of a surprisingly small barrel, maybe the size of a one-gallon beer keg, the kind available in grocery stores. Venom looked at it curiously. It didn't seem unusually heavy, and the man carrying it didn't seem at all nervous to be holding it.

The first flatboat was gaining a little on the second in terms of being loaded. Venom started watching it carefully. One man, its pilot, stayed seated where he was, by the boat's control panel and its tiller. The other boat's pilot was not in reach; he was down helping the others load the barrels on.

All right, Venom thought. *Time to move.*

Softly, staying low in the water, he made his way to the first boat, coming at it from behind. The pilot, sitting there, looked thoroughly bored with the whole affair. "Julio?" he said to one of the other men. "You got a light?"

"No smoking!" said the man on the speedboat, quite sharply.

"What're you, allergic or something?" muttered the pilot. But he shrugged, finally, and settled back to watching the others.

He never saw the pseudopod that slipped up behind him. Spasm froze him for the moment where he sat, then he slumped, but not so much that anyone noticed.

Silently, Venom boosted himself up onto the back of the boat to the left of the fan, peered around it. Another tendril rippled away from him, found the ignition key in the boat's control panel, slipped it out, and chucked it overboard.

"Oh, c'mon," said one of the other flatboat crew, "I'm gasping for a smoke, too. If nobody's seen all those spotlights we're using, then no one's going to see a match!"

"Oh, all right," said the man in the speedboat, the apparent commander. "Way out here, the boss won't know. Go ahead."

"Mac?" said the man who was gasping for a smoke. Possibly this was Julio. "Mac, you still wanna light?" A pause. "Mac?"

They looked at him. "No point in sulking," somebody chuckled.

That, however, was the point at which the tension of the spasm started to go out of Mac's muscles, and he began to slump noticeably.

"What the—" said one of the other men loading drums onto the boat. He made his way astern and bent over Mac.

Venom couldn't wait any longer. He boosted himself up onto the second flatboat and paused only long enough to look for its ignition key. It wasn't in the control panel, and which of the other men had it, there was no telling.

A second later he was rolling and diving into the bottom of the boat as the gunfire began from near at hand. He bounced up, sent tendrils rippling at the nearest gunman, tore the machine gun out of his hands, and flung it overboard. More tentacles shot out, one wrapping around the man's neck, the other around his waist.

"Get him!" someone screamed, and someone else yelled, "Get the stuff out of here!" That was what he had been afraid of. A third man came running at Venom, spraying bullets. Pseudopodia ripped his feet out from under him, dumped him on the deck, grabbed his gun and twisted it out of shape, then flung it overboard. The symbiote's excitement ran all through him, a sound/feeling like the purr of an angry tiger, all enjoyment and rage. If it could not have Spider-Man, it would have these miscreants.

Venom was willing enough, but right now a veritable storm of bullets was being fired at him, and a lot of them were hitting. The impact, despite the symbiote's protection, was uncomfortable. He killed the man he had just knocked down, and told the symbiote silently to deal with the remaining man on the flatboat any way it liked.

It did. Screams resounded, and many shots began to go wild.

What Venom wanted to make sure of was that none of the men remaining on this boat had the key for the other's ignition, or at least that none of them could use it. Within a few seconds, that was true.

"Get it out!" the man on the first motorboat was yelling at the men in the other one. "Get it out!" Its engines were stuttering into a roar again. Everyone from the flatboats who remained mobile was clambering over its sides, frantic to escape. And suddenly all the fire of the men who still stood abovedecks on either boat was concentrated on Venom.

The pressure of it was so tremendous that as Venom struggled to stand against it on one of the flatboats, the gunfire actually knocked him back into the water. He stayed under, making his way hurriedly toward the first speedboat under the surface. Spotlights were raking the water, followed by the downward-striking bubble traces of gunfire, and the thick, wet, dull sound of bullets hitting a noncompressible medium at supersonic speed. In the water, the roar of the second speedboat's engine getting started was deafening. To this was added the sound of the first one's engine starting as well. *Too many of them,* he thought to himself, furious. *Just too many.* He *almost* wished, bizarre thought, that Spider-Man were there to help.

He burst up out of the water near the first speedboat, swarmed up its anchor before they could cut the rope, and leapt on board. Venom simply backhanded the first gunman he encountered before he could turn and fire. He felt the skull crunch, and the man toppled overboard, backwards, hitting the water with a fat splash. To the second man, who was machine-gunning him earnestly, Venom strode up, took him by the throat, and let the symbiote throttle him.

A third man, seeing Venom come for him, jumped overboard and began swimming desperately for the other boat. Only the commander was left, and he pulled a high-powered automatic and pumped six very carefully placed bullets straight at Venom's forehead.

The symbiote toughened there, but the bullets still gave Venom a headache. A pseudopod batted the gun out of the man's hand, and another grabbed him around the throat, pushed him up against the bulkhead of the motorboat, and began to tighten.

"Where have you just come from?" Venom said, shaking

the man slightly. The commander shook his head, his face suffusing dark red—

—and then he jumped and jittered in Venom's grip, and slumped dead, riddled with fire from the other speedboat. The boat spun, its engine roaring, and it took off into Florida Bay. As it went, Venom could see the barrels being tossed overboard.

He swore softly again and tossed the commander's body aside. Though he knew the general route these people were taking, it would have been useful to know more about the details, the way-stations. *Oh, well. There are still three boats to examine.* When he was finished with them, he would call the proper authorities and see that the hazardous materials were picked up from the boats, or where they had been dumped, and properly disposed of.

The speedboat that remained was just about empty. Venom noted its name and registration—*Lucky Day,* out of Bermuda. *Not that lucky*, he thought. He could find no trace of other identification in it. There were discarded weapons aplenty, but they could have come from anywhere.

After a few minutes he made his way back to the flatboats. On the way, he picked up the MagLite that one of the men had been using, and with it, examined the bigger barrels. They were all of them very like the barrels from the CCRC caches in New York. Some of them were even painted the same color. Standard fifty-gallon oil drums, nothing special about them— stuff that, if dumped in seawater, would rust quite readily.

More on his mind, though, was that smallest barrel—"the hot one," the commander of the first speedboat had said. Very peculiar, that.

He got onto the first flatboat, found the barrel, picked it up. It was a plain, steel barrel, no distinguishing markings. Venom shook it. It sloshed very slightly. On close examination, the container was actually more like a paint can than a barrel, with a flat tight lid.

Venom put the container down on the floor of the flatboat,

carefully pried it open with one pseudopod, and peered at it thoughtfully. It was full of a dark liquid. He lifted the can, careful not to spill it, and sniffed. A strange flat chemical smell floated up from it; nothing instantly recognizable. It reminded him, though, of the ink and toner scent of the fast copy shops he used to frequent back in his reporter days.

He told the symbiote to bare the flesh on his left hand. Cautiously, he dipped a fingertip of his right hand into the liquid and rubbed it between finger and thumb. Not an oily feeling but slick and then going tacky. Not corrosive, either. He rubbed a little on his skin, looked at it under the MagLite.

Venom's mouth fell open. It was as if he had rubbed on a bit of liquid rainbow. A whole spectrum of colors chased themselves across the wet patch on his hand, becoming brighter as the stuff dried. He turned his hand, and the colors shifted, like oil rainbows on a puddle, never quite the same even when you tried to exactly repeat the motion.

Now what in the world—? he thought, staring at his hand.

Then the memory of a newscast he had seen a couple of months before came back to him, and suddenly it became clear to Venom why this, and not the waste, had been the most important part of the shipment.

The newscast had been a digest produced by one of San Francisco's main news channels with information from the channel's European affiliates. Among stories of folk festivals and the new plays in the West End of London, of troubles in Latverian politics, and the repatriation of Russian sturgeon from polluted lakes to clean ones in Finland, there had been a little feature about the European Union's new paper money.

The European Currency Unit, or ECU, had finally begun to become the multinational currency that the Common Market's architects had intended, even over the protests of some countries who felt that the power of their own currencies would be diminished by this interloper. There were simply too many attractions to a currency that had the same value right across the Union, now one of the three largest trading blocs in the world—a currency which did not have to be exchanged at constantly fluctuating rates. Once the quirks had been worked out of the underlying exchange rate mechanism, most of the EU nations had settled down and allowed paper ECUs to be printed for them.

The main problem, unfortunately, had been counterfeiting. Any currency so popular, and usable anywhere from one side of the continent to the other, was going to attract the attention of the most talented counterfeiters on the planet. The EU security people had been determined to do their best to stop this problem before it became serious by loading the ECU with more anticounterfeiting strategies than any one country's banknotes had even applied before.

They created a counterfeiter's nightmare. Its engraving was courtesy of the Swiss, in cooperation with the most talented stamp engravers from Liechtenstein. Physically, it was a work of art, with the Union's halo of stars and the intertwined national emblems of the member states all rippling and blending into one another across the faces of all the notes in a tangle of impossibly delicate engraving, in nearly a hundred colors. Any given note had embedded in it three discrete watermarks, various zones of microprinting, a band like the embedded silver strip of a British banknote—but this one of metallized plastic, microencoded and programmed with the note's serial number and a one-hundredth-inch-wide data stripe containing other audit information. All these precautions seemed quite sensible in an age when counterfeiting advanced continually on the heels of the technology meant to stop it.

But there was one aspect to the making of these notes which was unique, and that was one for which the Union acquired a license from the French. The French had invented an ink for use in note-printing which changed color on the face of the note, depending on how it was held, what and where the light source was, and how the note was moved—the same way as, say, a hologram would change when moved, in a rainbow shift of color. It was the strongest of all the anticounterfeit measures on the ECU, for it was the one which anyone picking up one of the banknotes could instantly identify as being there or not. The words and pictures printed in that ink shimmered, giving a specious but beautiful illusion of depth.

No counterfeiter had been able to duplicate it. The secret of its manufacture was possibly the most closely held secret in France. As a result, that ink had become the single most sought-after substance in Europe by the criminal fraternity. More was being offered for it on the black market than would be offered for any illicit substance—more, even, than was being offered for plutonium. Several thefts had already been attempted, according to the TV program, but they had all failed.

A keg of this stuff—even a tiny jar, for small amounts of it went a long way—was literally a license to print money in as large a denomination as you liked—and the ECU notes went up as high as ten thousand, equivalent to about five thousand dollars.

Venom crouched there, watching the rainbows chase back and forth across his hand. A nasty scenario was taking shape in his mind. CCRC, he thought, or someone working with them, managed, somehow, to source some of this ink. Possibly someone high up in the EU in Brussels, some bureaucrat with something to hide, perhaps. And one of the major powers in the EU, right now, was certainly Germany. Venom thought of the German merchant bank and wondered if the connection might be there. *Something else to take up with Mr. Gottschalk's connections when we track them down.*

But he could imagine a situation where CCRC or the people they were working with could print their own ECUs, as many as they liked, and use these to buy much more radioactive waste material from both legal and illegal sources—both of whom would accept the currency gladly. And this was only one of the kegs. They had tossed the other one overboard. If they had more, someone at CCRC was most likely this moment trying to analyze the formula. A skilled chemist could do it. It would take time, but it could be done.

Once they had a complete analysis, once they could manufacture as much of this ink as they liked, there would literally be no limit to how many counterfeit ECUs could be printed. The European market could be flooded with them in a matter of a couple months. The whole continent's economy could be permanently damaged. Unless—

Unless someone who liked blackmail could hold its whole economy to ransom, by threatening the EU with just such an action, promising not to take it . . . if the price was right.

Venom carefully sealed the little can up again, and stood, willing the symbiote back down over his hand and shutting the rainbow away. All these possibilities would have to be followed up. But first—first he had business to complete, north of here. There was still the matter of Curt Connors, squatting in his little hideout in the Everglades, doing heaven only knew what—but doubtless up to his neck in this smuggling somehow. If he was . . .

Venom smiled. It was not a nice smile. Connors would find that he was about to be paid for his work, and not in the currency he anticipated.

And then, after that—Spider-Man.

With the little can of ink, Venom turned, and at the best speed he could manage, headed north.

TEN

Three jeeps jostled through rough grass at Cape Canaveral, got back onto the southward-running road, and tore down it, sirens blaring and warning lights flashing. The first and the last ones carried men with guns. The one in the middle carried two NASA security people, an Air Force lieutenant, and a very bemused friendly neighborhood Spider-Man.

"You could have had me thrown in the pokey back there," Spidey said to the lieutenant sitting next to him. "You could have had me shot."

"I could have," she said, smiling a small dry smile, "but it seems a poor way to say 'hello.'"

"Well," Spidey said. "Hello, Lieutenant—"

"Garrett," she said. "I'm a liaison to Kennedy security, based over at Canaveral AFB."

"You're taking all this very calmly," Spider-Man said.

"I assure you, I'm not," she said. "I could have had you shot, yes. And believe me, if the moment comes, I won't bother contracting it out." Her voice was cool and cheerful. Spider-Man gulped.

She was not a big woman—probably about five feet three, with short close-cropped red hair and big round horn-rimmed glasses. She looked a little like an owl. But the thought occurred to Spider-Man that there were some species of owl that he wouldn't like to be locked up with, either.

"Anyway," Lieutenant Garrett said, "if you're asking me why I've given you the benefit of the doubt—I have some colleagues up in the New York offices of the Atomic Energy Commission. I chat with them every now and then. I talked to them a week or so ago, and it seems they think they owe you a favor."

"If you mean the business about New York not leaping in the air and coming down on several other continents as dust," Spider-Man said, "well, yes, I did help with that." It seemed like the wrong moment for false modesty.

"Therefore," Lieutenant Garrett said, "I am more inclined to trust you than not. What I want to know is how you came by the hydrogel. And how you know what it is."

"Am I allowed to take the Fifth?"

"Oh, you can take it," she said, "but maybe I could suggest that it would be less than helpful at the moment. The security of the United States is at stake just now, and I don't have time for jokes." There was something in her eyes, though, a mocking or daring look, even in the darkness, that suggested to Spidey it would be safe enough not to go by the book for the moment.

"Lieutenant," he said, "the least I can do is give you the benefit of the doubt, too." He took a breath, then said, "I found it after someone else had lost it. At least that's how I read the signs. Having found it, I wondered what the heck it was!"

She chuckled. "Understandable. And? What did you find out?"

He thought for a second. "It may not strictly be an indestructible substance," Spider-Man said. "I suppose adamantium has the corner on that market at the moment. But it's close to one."

"That's a fair enough description," Lieutenant Garrett said.

"Then," Spider-Man said, "I found through other sources that it was originally destined for the *Endeavour*. Now, that by itself isn't so extraordinary. Lots of things go up in the Shuttle. Birds, bees."

She smiled. "Yes," Lieutenant Garrett said. "And some of them more controversial than others."

Spidey smiled under the mask. "Like the CHERM. Or should I say the MPAPPS? Or whatever its name was. As far as I can tell, it's some kind of small reactor—and I think maybe it's a breeder."

The jeeps slowed a little; they were coming to a checkpoint. Away off on their right, Spider-Man thought he could hear the sound of gunfire.

"Well," Lieutenant Garrett said, as they stopped and were inspected, "I won't get into that. And what're you all staring at?" she said to several of the security people manning the checkpoint, who stared at her companion. "Haven't you ever had a blind date? Boy, some people . . ."

The jeep tore off again. "It's been days since I had Socratic Method practice," Lieutenant Garrett said. "I can hear the wheels turning in there. You know you can ask me questions, even if I can't answer."

"Well—" Spidey did his best to think through the wind and the noise and the sound of gunfire getting closer "—I confess, I do keep wondering why anyone would want to put a breeder reactor up in space. A lot of people are vague about what reactors are for, but breeders—" He shook his head. "There's no two ways about it: they exist only to make more fissionable material. Specifically, to make plutonium."

"Can't argue with that," Lieutenant Garrett said. "It's common knowledge."

"And the only use *I* know of for plutonium," Spider-Man said, "is for making bombs."

"Common knowledge would seem to bear you out there, too."

"Well," Spidey said, "who would want to make bombs in space anymore? With the new test-ban treaties in place, and the agreement that no one will try to militarize space, we're not going to do anything like that. And it's not like you could do it on the sly, either. All the crews up on *Freedom*, at the moment, are multinational; none of the participants have any secrets from each other. Not that there's any room to, anyway. They're practically living in each other's pockets as it is."

Then he looked at Garrett sidewise, as a thought occurred to him. "Other facilities are being built, though."

Lieutenant Garrett returned the look, and actually batted her eyelashes, a shockingly innocent look. "Go on."

"Yes, well, as I said, why make bombs in space? If you wanted to damage people on Earth, you might as well just drop big rocks on them. Cheaper, safer, and just as destructive, if you're the kind of nasty person who's interested in that. And there's a whole moon full of them, just down the road."

"An interesting approach," Lieutenant Garrett said. "I must make a note of that one." But by her smile Spidey guessed that she had read the idea in the same book that he had and knew that the author of the book, and the name on the space station's new annex, were the same.

"Am I getting warm?" Spidey said.

"You know I can't answer specifically," the lieutenant said. But her expression was getting more wicked. "Hurry up, though. We're getting closer to the hot zone."

"All right," Spider-Man said. "So the spacefaring powers don't want to manufacture bombs in space. Sure, there are others who might want to—various super-villains and nutso dictators and so forth."

"I bow to your superior experience of the first," Lieutenant Garrett said. "But as for the second, it wouldn't make much sense for them to mess with space-based delivery systems, when conventional ones would be so much cheaper, and closer to home. Why bother with space when you can take a Mercedes across Poland and out its east side, and come back with a trunkful of enriched uranium?"

"And a terminal sunburn."

"Only if you're incautious."

"I see what you mean, though," Spidey said. He frowned and thought then, while they passed another roadblock. Between them and the brilliantly lit shapes of 39-A and 39-B lay in their way. It was dark and silent, except for its two big gantries, which shone faintly with red blinking altitude lights: the Fixed Service Structure, recycled from one of the old Saturn V launch umbilical towers and installed here to hold the lifts which serviced the Shuttles; and the Rotating Service Structure beside it, with the midbody umbilical unit that swung in and out to tend the Shuttle's fuel cells and life support, which installed and removed payloads from the main cargo bay.

The jeep started working its way around the huge octagonal pad. Spider-Man stopped, frankly gaping at it as they went by. Seen on television, from the discreet distance of a couple of miles, there was nothing terribly impressive about either of the pads. Seen close, they were another story. The massive gantries, the huge 400-foot flame trench, the big sound-suppression tanks, empty at the moment of the water which protected the gantries from the sound and pressure of launches—it was an extraordinary collection of structures, like a child-giant's Erector set put aside for the night. Spidey felt slightly embarrassed and turned to Lieutenant Garrett to pick up where he'd left off.

"We all do it," she said. "Gape, that is. Someday spacecraft will be smaller, and we won't look twice at them. But right now—it's still pretty neat." She grinned. "Go on."

"I'm not sure where to go," Spidey said. "Somebody's putting reactors up in space to make something. If not bombs, then what? What other use is there for atomic energy?"

He trailed off.

"Yes?" Lieutenant Garrett said.

Spider-Man shook his head at her for a moment. "Oh, my," he said, very softly.

She watched him.

It had to have been ten years ago that he first saw the magazine article. He saw it now, though, as he had seen it last when he had been going through the aging collection of pulps that were still in the basement of his aunt May's house. Both MJ and his aunt had urged him to either seal them up properly in plastic bags and save for another generation, or just throw them out. Their covers were all faded, the pages were yellowed and brittle, and they would flake and come apart in your fingers if you turned them carelessly. He didn't look at them much anymore, just kept them up on their shelf where he knew he could find them: old copies of *Amazing* and *Fantastic* and other magazines. The article he was thinking of was in

Amazing. Someone, way back then, had suggested what they described as the only good use for an A-bomb.

The problem was that to make it work, you first needed a delivery system that would let you get pretty large payloads into low earth orbit, and build things there, like a space station, or a very big spacecraft. The idea in the magazine had involved building that huge spacecraft. At the rear end of it, a huge concave shield or vessel would be built as well.

Then the premise of the article fell apart somewhat, because for that shield you needed an indestructible, or near-indestructible, substance. Once you had built this shield, the idea was that you started exploding atom bombs inside it. The shield, being indestructible, and ideally impermeable as well, would direct the blast away behind the ship, screening it from the radiation at the same time. And Newton's Laws being what they were, in space as well as anywhere else, every action has an equal and opposite reaction: the force would translate itself into a push forward for the payload. Later, when the force from that push gave out, you exploded another bomb, and pushed again. And so you went, gently, slowly, accelerating patiently, on the way to the outer planets.

It was a plan that was both brutal and elegant. It was not pretty. But fission power of this kind was easy to produce and relatively cheap—there was a whole lot of potential propellant for this kind of thrust lying around all over the planet, in the arsenals of countries that claimed they were planning to get rid of it anyway.

Naturally, you would not start the thrust process anywhere near Earth. You would use chemical propulsion to get the ships out well past the moon. But once there, there was no question of pollution. Interplanetary space was already full of radiation as hard as a nuclear explosion. And the explosions would be, by Earth standards, very clean. Most fallout, after all, is dust sucked up by the mushroom cloud from the explosion site. In space there would be none of that. The solar wind would push the particulate matter out to the boundaries of the solar system and beyond the radiopause, where the minute particles could coast harmlessly out and diffuse themselves in the endless vacuum of near space. There was literally no harm they could ever do to anyone.

Spider-Man knew the plan would work. He also knew how it would sound to some people if they heard about it. But the main problem left—now that there was a way to build space stations, and ships, in orbit—was what to make the shield out of.

He thought of the hydrogel.

"I would have thought," Spidey said, "that people would have considered adamantium some time ago for—uh, space-based applications."

"I'm sure they did," Lieutenant Garrett said. "Think of the weight, though."

Spider-Man nodded. Just getting the pieces of an adamantium shield into orbit would use up so much valuable energy that it didn't seem cost-effective. And besides, adamantium was metallic, and repeated atomic explosions near it would render it radioactive itself. *Hydrogel, though* . . . Spidey shook his head. It was just possible that among its weird properties was numbered a resistance to radiation.

He looked at Garrett and said, "It'd be sensible, wouldn't it? To send up hydrogel, and at the same time, to send up the— test material? That way you minimize the danger of sending the stuff up again with every new launch. While locking it in L5 orbit where it can't fall, not for centuries anyway."

Garrett smiled. "It has to be tested," she said. "It's our cheapest way to the outer planets, until the new microwave-driven ships are ready." And he looked at her and blinked at that, but she would say nothing more.

The jeeps roared on into the night. They had come around 39-B now and were heading for A. It was about a mile and a half distant.

"All right," Spider-Man said. "Now all I want to know is, what do these people want? The reactor?"

Garrett shook her head. "They'll have to whistle for them," she said. "The payloads were locked in two nights ago—what we had of them." She looked both grim and resigned. "There's no way to get that stuff out early. Cargo bay is locked for injection and can't be unlocked without a full abort. Even if we could get the bay open, or those people could, it wouldn't help them any, because the entire reactor is sealed in a prelaunch impact shell. We have—" and this time the grim look was completely unrelieved "—learned something about what happens when a Shuttle falls down before it makes orbit. A nasty but useful sidelight of that is that we've learned something about how to build things that don't crack open no matter what you do to them—even if you drop them from a hundred thousand feet to the bottom of the sea. They don't open."

"Even if the whole Shuttle blew—"

"At whatever altitude. That shell would come down safe. Land or water, it wouldn't matter."

Even if it blew . . . And he heard the voice say, earlier, *We've got something to blow.*

Spider-Man's mouth went dry. "Lieutenant," he said, and touched her arm. She glanced at the hand, at him, said nothing. "Whatever you do, don't let them near the Shuttle. Don't." And a horrible thought struck him. "They're not in there, are they?"

"At T minus—" she shook her watch free of her jacket cuff and glanced at it "—T minus two hours? Of course they are. They went up half an hour ago."

"Oh, my gosh." A horrible feeling made itself at home in the pit of Spidey's stomach. "Lieutenant, you don't understand. These people are working with some of the folks who gave some of your New York friends so much trouble. They would have blown all of Manhattan sky high. You think a Shuttle and six astronauts are going to bother them?"

Over the roar of the jeep's engines, he could hear the gunfire much more clearly now, and closer, the incongruous sound of ducks quacking, outraged at the disruption of their quiet night.

As they approached 39-A the sound of sirens got louder—and so did the sound of gunfire. "Looks like we have a problem in that department already," said Lieutenant Garrett softly.

Pad 39-A was seething with activity, like a hornet's nest that had been kicked. Every one of the big Xenon spots was on now, lighting the place up like day. *Endeavour* burned white in the blaze of them, reflecting even more light in the area immediately around the pad. That was a help, except all the light showed was depressing. Jeeps and cars were converging on it from all directions, but once they came within range of the pad they tended to come slowing to a barely controlled stop, hammered by streams of bullets.

"Oh, Lord," Spidey heard someone moan from the next jeep. "The Shuttle tiles." But there were more pressing concerns than the fragile thermal tiles just now. When the people inside the various arriving vehicles came scrambling out, it wasn't to perform their security function but simply to take cover behind their cars. Nobody stood up or moved any closer, for fear of catching a bullet.

Some of the NASA and Air Force security people already had. There were unmoving figures sprawled on the pavement here and there; others crouched behind any protection they could find. Except for their own increasingly battered vehicles, there wasn't much of that in the big empty skirting surrounding the pad proper. They were firing whatever weapons they had at the attackers, but since those weapons were mostly pistols, they were badly outgunned.

Every one of the mercenary assault team seemed to be carrying something fully automatic—submachine gun or assault rifle, the difference was academic when you were on the wrong end of it—and every now and then, to make things even more interesting, one of them would throw a grenade. They were even wearing body armor; presumably it had been stowed aboard the flatboat on the way in. The mercenaries had spread themselves more or less evenly around the circumference of the pad. They weren't bothering with the short, controlled bursts recommended by the manual, preferring simply to hose slugs at anything that moved.

As Garrett's group of jeeps turned up into the pad area, half a dozen of the gunmen turned and began firing at them. The vehicles screeched to a standstill and Spider-Man piled out along with everyone else and hit the dirt. He came down next to the lieutenant, who was unholstering her sidearm and muttering under her breath. Spidey put his head up over the edge of the jeep—then was hit with a warning from his spider-sense at the same time that his eyes caught a red light, and hurriedly ducked again just before a spatter of bullets slammed into the hood of the jeep, making it rock on its springs.

"They've got laser designators on those things," he said, then glanced at the Beretta M9 pistol in Garrett's hand. "Is that all you folks have?"

"This isn't a war zone," she said, then flinched instinctively as another long stream of slugs chewed up the concrete paving behind the jeep. "Isn't *usually* a war zone," she corrected, starting to sound angry for the first time. "Normally we don't need that level of security here." Spidey could hear a hiss and crackle of static from the walkie-talkies of the people in the next jeep. "Jones!" yelled Garrett, "Jonesey—what's their ETA?"

"Three and a half minutes!"

Garrett gave Spider-Man a small, tight smile. "That'll be the choppers from Canaveral AFB. And *they'll* be loaded for bear."

Spidey shook his head. "Three and a half minutes won't be soon enough." He cautiously put his head up again and saw an Air Force man stand up from behind one of the several jeeps spaced around the pad. The man's pistol was braced in both hands and he was crouched low—but not low enough. He got off only two shots before a sparkle of bullet-strikes marched all over the jeep and the rest of the burst punched him backwards to the ground. But Spidey also saw a trio of mercenaries break away from the main group and start sprinting for the hole in the defensive perimeter that the airman's death had opened. The gunfire intensified to cover them as they ran.

"Not soon enough at all," he said grimly. "Lieutenant, one of those guys has a bomb. I'm sure of it."

Without waiting to say anything else, he sprang out from behind the jeep and went after the running mercenaries, feeling horribly exposed out there in the midst of that vast, flat space with all those lights blazing down on him.

A submachine gun chattered and Spidey leaped, rolled, sprang, crouched, then sprang again, changing course once or twice a second as the gunman tried and failed to anticipate his next move—especially since Spider-Man's spider-sense effectively anticipated the gunman's next move.

I'm getting real *tired of this,* he thought, and bounded zigzagging toward one mercenary who seemed to have chosen him as his particular target. Spiders can move very, very fast when they have to, and for the last hundred yards of his approach, Spider-Man exploited that talent to the best of his ability, bouncing across the white concrete like a demented Ping-Pong ball. His final leap took him straight for the mercenary, and on the way in he somersaulted in midair so that he hit the man's chest feet foremost. Spidey had a fleeting glimpse of shocked eyes in a pale, snarling face; then he felt the impact jarring up through his heels and heard the explosive grunt as all the air was jolted from the mercenary's lungs. By the time Spider-Man landed in a half-crouch, the man was already flattened and out for the count, flakvest or not.

Spider-Man scooped up the gun as it went clattering and spinning over the concrete, wrenched the long, curved magazine out of the receiver, threw that and the gun as far as he could in opposite directions—then a vivid red light glowed in the corner of one eye, a blare of his spider-sense, and he leaped and twisted in three directions at once. The concrete where he had been standing exploded in dust and splinters, and his ears were filled with the scream of ricochets. At least one of the mercenaries knew how to handle a gun, and the only thing that had saved him, various superpowers notwithstanding, was that whoever it was had paused for that lingering, laser-lit instant to make sure of his aim.

Spidey decided not to stand in one place for too long anymore.

The next two groups of mercenaries were a good four hundred yards away on either side. At least that increased his chances, laser sights or not. Ahead of him, those three figures were running for the pad. Fire was still being directed at him from somewhere behind, but he let his spider-sense guide him away from the hail as he chased the trio. They, at least, were running too hard to shoot at him, being more intent on making it to the big pedestals at the base of the Mobile Launch Platform; but once among those, they could take shelter and fire as they pleased, while preparing to do whatever it was they had in mind.

Spidey thought he knew. *If I was going to blow up the Space Shuttle,* he thought, his face twisting with disgust at the thought as he jumped and ran and jumped again, *I wouldn't bother with the Shuttle itself. I'd go straight for the main fuel tank.* It would have been full of lox and liquid hydrogen for a couple of hours, and he suspected that was why the attack had been timed for now. Someone knew the timetable by which the Shuttle was fueled and prepped for launch, and why wouldn't they? It was pretty much public knowledge, and had even been included in the press package.

He was beginning to catch up with the running men, and the one farthest behind was just within range of his webbing, if he was careful and shot it just so. Then the trio veered suddenly to the left, and as he caught himself just in time from shooting a web at where the man would have been, he understood why. They were quite close to the six great bells of *Endeavour*'s rocket exhausts, and directly under those bells yawned the huge flame-trench, a concrete chasm some sixty feet wide and another four hundred fifty feet long.

Aha! Spider-Man thought. He took aim once more, and shot web accurately enough that he hit the last mercenary square across the arms and back with it. Spidey braced himself, and pulled. The running man stopped dead in his tracks and jerked backwards, his gun flying. The other two heard his yell and jerked squat black SMGs from clips on the front of their flakvests, blazing wildly behind them as they ran. But they didn't stop, either to help their comrade or even to make sure of their target.

Spidey dove and rolled as the slugs zipped and whined around him, then came up again and made a single huge bound to where the stunned mercenary was lying on his back. Picking him up, Spider-Man tossed him into the trench and broke his fall—with the web that still wrapped his back and arms—a good six feet from the bottom. The man bounced and swung like a mad bungee-jumper as Spidey secured the other end to the edge of the trench and glanced down at him.

"Try getting out of that," he muttered. The sound of repetitive and unimaginative swearing rose like a bad smell from the depths of the trench. *Serves him right,* Spider-Man thought and took off in pursuit of the others.

Both now turned and fired again, as carelessly as before, then kept right on running. Evidently their orders were even more important than taking out the costumed pest pursuing them. But if they were relying on the hail of poorly aimed lead to keep him at bay, they had another thing coming. Then one of the men—a broad-shouldered bald black man—stopped beside the huge wall of the Sound Suppression Water System, smacked a new magazine into his submachine gun and dropped to one knee, while the last man—a tall white man who sported a ponytail—put on an extra spurt of speed.

Spidey noted the one with the ponytail. *That's my boy,* he thought. *I'll deal with you in a minute.* But not this minute; right now he had all his work cut out to get at the bald guy who was shooting, because this one was good. Now there was no wild spraying of gunfire; instead the mercenary was ripping off quick, precise bursts of no more than three or four rounds each, and some of those were coming frighteningly close.

Spider-Man jumped sideways, up onto the wall of the water tank, then scuttled and bounced along it, forcing the man to lean out from his firing position in an attempt to hit him. It spoiled his aim a little, but nothing like enough. Spidey still had to jump around like a fly avoiding a swatter—a nine-millimeter cupronickel-jacketed swatter—as bullets tore chunks out of the concrete all around him.

Damn laser-sights, he thought, and shot a webline to the side of the tank with a slap of one hand, then launched himself outward, spinning more web as he went. The gunfire tracked him, but not accurately enough. That outward kick had given him more momentum than the mercenary had counted on. He swung out from the tank, then back in again in a sweeping parabola, and spinning the extra web had brought him downward as well, almost directly over the gunman's head. Confused by the movement, the man triggered a burst toward where Spidey would have been had he swung in a second arc. Then the burst cut off short as the SMG clicked empty.

That was when Spider-Man hit the wall again and kicked off once more—but this time right on top of him.

The man's reactions were very, very fast in that last instant before impact, because somewhere in the final eight feet of his drop, Spidey was staring down the barrel of the gun. Not that it did the mercenary any good. He was still fumbling to clear the empty magazine when Spider-Man kicked magazine and gun together out of his hands, then hauled off with great satisfaction and no small relief, and knocked him cold.

The gunman had barely hit the ground before Spidey was off again after the mercenary with the ponytail—but he was still just a shade too late. He could see him, too far away to reach, as the man vanished into the gantry elevator of the Mobile Launch Platform. It wasn't one of the open-cage elevators that he was familiar with from news footage of earlier launches. This one was a closed car inside the structure of the platform—and it was going up.

The question is, wondered Spidey, *how many floors will it stop at on the way?* He leapt for the nearest other thing that reached all the way up, the Fixed Service Structure with its big venting arm halfway up. That was his best bet for getting at the external fuel tank.

And that, he figured, was where Ponytail would stop. As he worked his way higher up and became visible from the ground, sporadic gunfire began probing for him as he climbed, the metal girders clanking and humming under his hands as the bullets struck them.

The only good thing about that symbiote, he thought as he worked his way around the structure and out of the line of fire, *was that its black hue made you less of a target. The ol' red and blue does stand out a bit.*

He scuttled up the tower as fast as he could, leaping from one girder to the next. About halfway up, Spidey had a sudden thought, and spared a second, no more, to snatch his camera out, clamp it to a support, make sure it had free traverse, and flick the On switch for the motion-sensitive shutter control. He headed upward, relieved to hear the camera whine and turn and click behind him, reacting to his motion. Just as well; there was no time to fiddle with it now. *Maybe four hundred feet to the top of the gantry,* Spidey thought, looking up, *and three hundred or so to where I'm headed.* But could he get up there before Ponytail did? That elevator was fast. It had been above him the whole time he had been climbing, and was pulling slightly ahead. Spider-Man poured on all the speed he could.

"These people are desperate," he muttered to himself, "and this one's probably the most desperate of the lot." The prospect was unnerving; there were few things more scary than a terrorist who didn't care whether or not he got away, just so long as he did what he was there for. They would blow the Shuttle right where it sat, and not care how many people went up with it. And after the fireball died down, if what Lieutenant Garrett said about the reactor's protective shell was true, then it would be lying somewhere in the half-mile radius of scattered debris, ready to pick up and take away. There was probably another team somewhere out in the darkness, waiting to do just that.

It was a chilling thought, and made him scramble up the gantry even faster. Then the firing from below died away. Spider-Man paused for just a moment to look down, and saw that the other mercenaries, the ones who had surrounded the pad, were pulling out.

Uh-oh, he thought, knowing what that had to mean. They were clearing the blast zone. He started climbing again, and then above him saw the elevator slide to a halt at the level where the vent-arm reached out from the fixed superstructure to *Endeavour*. It was still attached, a convenient, if not exactly safe, bridge between one and the other.

Then he saw Ponytail emerge from the elevator. The man walked straight out onto a wire-grating walkway that led to the venting arm, and Spider-Man practically flew up what remained of the tower. He shot a web at the wire grating, then hauled himself up at top speed, swung onto the walkway, and started running after the man. At the sound of his footfalls, Ponytail turned, pulled a big stainless-steel revolver from a tie-down holster belted around his waist, and opened fire.

There wasn't much room to maneuver on the walkway, and when Spidey flung himself aside he still felt a shock and a stripe of hot pain across his left side as if someone had hit him with a cattle-prod.

Too close! Waaay too close! But he was still grateful that the slug had only grazed him. From the heavy boom of the gun, it had to be firing a Magnum load. Even with an ordinary bullet, that would have left a six-inch hole in his belly—and Spidey had an ugly feeling that to be so casual about firing right beside the Shuttle's main fuel tank, this guy was using something nastier than plain lead slugs. He raised one arm, shot a web at the orange surface of the main tank, and threw himself off the walkway.

The web hit squarely and stuck fast, and he swung right past the mercenary, out and down between him and the tank. He hit the insulated surface and clung to it, then twisted around and shot another line of web at that deadly gun, splatting all over its barrel. That barrel had swung to track him, but not fast enough or far enough to be pointing at him or at the huge cylinder of volatiles on which he crouched. Spidey jerked it out of Ponytail's hand like a pin out of wet paper, then shook it free and let it drop into the flame trench nearly two hundred feet below.

That was when Spider-Man got his first good look at his assailant, and saw, hooked to the other side of his pistol-belt, a package that looked like an ordinary black nylon fanny-pack. The man was unzipping it and reaching inside, feeling for something. Remembering the grenades that the other mercenaries had been using, Spidey leapt from the surface of the fuel tank straight at him, wondering at the back of his mind if he would make it in time, or even make the distance from such an awkward springboard.

He did, and they crashed together, sprawling on the walkway and thrashing to and fro, only prevented from rolling right off by the protective grating to either side—and that was already bulged and sprung in three separate places. Ponytail's hands came up, not wasting time with punches but with both thumbs already stabbing at where Spidey's eyes were hidden by his mask. Spider-Man blocked, snapping his hands out to knock the jabbing thumbs simultaneously sideways, then brought both of them back in again to chop the man hard under both ears. Ponytail went "Urk!" and tried to get up; then he sagged, his eyes closed, and he slumped forward until his lolling head clanked against the metal of the walkway.

Panting, Spidey rolled out from under the unconscious weight and got to his hands and knees, trying to rip the fanny-pack off the mercenary's belt. It wouldn't come free so, very, very carefully, he dipped his hand inside and lifted the contents out.

It was a bomb; very small, very neat, and though its contents were in a sealed plastic casing, he didn't need to lift it to his face to smell that characteristic marzipan aroma of Semtex.

The first thing he noticed was the little LED timer built into the casing. It had no controls that he could see, no buttons to push or wires to cut at the last minute. Just those little numbers, and even as Spidey looked at it, *48* became *47*. And then *46.*

He would never have had time to get off here, Spider-Man thought. *He doesn't care if he dies.* He glanced sideways at Ponytail. *And right now, I'm not one hundred percent sure if I care if he dies. Unfortunately there are other people involved. Including me.*

When the bomb went off it would produce a fair-sized bang, but since it didn't have a metal casing, there would be little more than blast damage. But if it was still too close to the Shuttle and its fuel when it blew, then there would be a really big bang, with enough shrapnel to scythe Kennedy Space Center clean. Spidey glanced about him, discarded the very thought of trying to swing from the tank again with a live bomb in his hand, and looked toward *Endeavour's* wing—and the first thing he saw there was the large, red-lettered stencil that said No Step.

"Oh, no," Spider-Man said with feeling, and bounded up another thirty feet or so to where the body of the Shuttle was mated to the tank. He scrambled up to the side window of the orbiter and banged on it until a startled face inside a space-suit helmet looked out at him.

"Out!" yelled Spidey. "Get out, now!" He gestured emphatically toward the far side of the Shuttle, and the entry/exit doors, and for emphasis held up the bomb with its LED toward the window. *34 . . . 33 . . . 32 . . .*

The angry, surprised expression on the face went shocked,

and the head nodded; a gauntleted hand reached out and slapped a control, and everything started to happen at once. A siren on the Fixed Service Structure began to howl, and as the big access arm began to swing out with smooth, ponderous speed, explosive bolts blew the Shuttle's port door off. There was a jostling inside as people began to pile toward the door, then he heard the booted feet ringing on metal as the astronauts plunged out of the cockpit and into their elevator.

"Good," said Spidey aloud. *26* read the bomb, *25 . . . 24.* "At least I think it's good."

He shot web up higher toward the lightning masts, and swung down past the Shuttle, leapt for the Mobile Launch Platform tower again, barely made it, then clung to it and began to web the bomb up. "Slowly and carefully, slowly and carefully," he kept muttering to himself, a mantra of caution to offset the panicky speed with which his hands really wanted to work. *I can at least confine the blast enough to keep it from setting off the main tank. But not if this isn't done right.*

The bomb was about four pounds of Semtex—enough to make a reasonable hole in a building—and at the back of his mind he started trying to calculate the stresses involved. Then he gave up. Best to just get down off the tower and leap and bound as fast as he could in any other direction.

Not just any other, he thought. *Away from the lox storage tanks would be good too!*

He slapped one palm against the tower and fastened a web there, then began to let himself down, counting under his breath as he went. "Twelve, eleven, ten, nine . . ." Down below him, reflecting the intense light that flooded the whole of pad 39-A, water gleamed and rippled. And then Spidey laughed out loud and yelled "Yes!" He knew exactly what to do.

Of course, this still might not work.

8 . . . 7 . . .

"Well," and he grinned inside his mask, "it's been nice, world. Take your best shot, Spidey." He quickly covered the bomb with as much thick webbing as he could in two seconds. Then he simply opened his hand and let the bomb drop straight down into the water tank of the Sound Suppression System. It hit with a splash and its four-plus pounds of weight cut through the surface as cleanly as a diving fish.

Up, he thought, *or down?* There was no time to calculate the stresses or the trajectories, no time even for an educated guess. Just time for the body's instinctive reaction, which was to get as far away from anything threatening as it possibly could. So he went up almost thirty feet in a single bound, hurled himself behind a girder, webbed himself there with two quick squirts, then closed his eyes and hung on for dear life.

2 . . . 1 . . .

The actual sound of the blast was a muffled *whoomph,* more felt than heard, a giant shock as though the concrete base of the pad had been kicked by some impossibly huge foot. Then there was a vast hissing splash, and an almost solid wall of water came erupting up from the Sound Suppression tank. Spidey had seen old newsreel footage of depth-charge attacks, and the columns of white water bursting skyward in the wake of a destroyer, but he had never dreamed he would ever be on the receiving end of one himself. Everything rattled and shuddered, and the Mobile Launch Platform vibrated like a gong. But as the water—and nothing worse than water—went flying into the sky, Spider-Man began to laugh.

The reinforced concrete tank of the Sound Suppression System contained three hundred thousand gallons of water, designed to protect the launch structures from the protracted sound and blast vibrations of a Shuttle lifting off. Anything that could absorb those millions of pounds of thrust applied for seconds at a time before the Shuttle cleared the pad would have found his tiny pack of Semtex little more than a firecracker.

There was a silence so intense that it seemed to clang in Spidey's ears, and then, out of the clear night sky, it began to rain. It had soaked him on the way up; it soaked him again on the way down. And he didn't care. Unhitching himself from the girder, he crawled back up the structure to where he had left the unconscious mercenary and his camera. Both were still there, though the double drenching with cold water awakened Ponytail enough that he was able to mumble incoherently, and Spidey's webbing and its position under a girder protected the camera from the worst of the deluge. Spider-Man trussed Ponytail up with webbing and lowered him to the ground, then slowly, still being rained on and still chuckling about it, came down after him.

It wasn't over yet, though, not by a long shot. Down by the pedestals, a lot of the Kennedy and Air Force security personnel were waiting. The roar and rotor-beat of the big Blackhawk choppers from Canaveral was deafening as they settled onto the perimeter of 39-A, though several Apache gunships continued overhead to hunt for the mercenaries who had left the area once they thought the bomb was in place.

The security people gathered around him, and there was the backslapping and applause more usually reserved for Mission Control rooms after a successful launch. Lieutenant Garrett came up to Spider-Man and smiled at him.

"I must call the AEC kids in New York," she said, "and let them know that you really are useful to have around in a crisis."

"Always glad to be of service," said Spidey. A man in a space suit approached him. Spidey recognized him, even though the helmet was off now and the expression was no longer shock, but relief and gratitude. It was Commander Luks, from the press conference. He stuck out his heavily gloved hand. Spider-Man took it, shook it, then said, "Er, permission to come aboard, sir?"

"Granted, son, anytime. Anytime at all." Then he shot a thoughtful glance at the sky and looked at one of the NASA people. "Harry," he said, "your weather reports have gone skewed again. Why's it raining?" There was a lot of laughter.

"Never mind," said an older, gray-haired man. "We'll scrub for this morning."

"We couldn't go anyway," said one of the other astronauts. "All the water in the triple-S seems to have jumped out of the tank."

"Just be glad of it," said Spider-Man, and turned to Garrett. "It was Semtex," he told her. "Now, I've a question to ask you. This group was one of two. Another one was going south down a canal when they split from this one."

Lieutenant Garrett turned to one of the other Air Force officers. "Mike, didn't you say that Coast Guard had been alerted about something going on down south?"

The man nodded. "The *James D.* just moved out," he said. "Something about a big dump of radioactive waste, and other contraband. A night-boat job, apparently. Whoever found it stopped it."

"I know who found it," said Spidey. "I'm going to have to go."

"Not before you debrief," said Garrett sharply.

"Lieutenant, believe me, if I stop for a debrief now there's going to be trouble. For me, and for a lot of other people. I'll be back later, tomorrow afternoon maybe, or tomorrow evening. Then I'll give you all the debrief you want. And," he added, "I'll have your hydrogel with me. But right now—" he looked at one of the helicopters that had settled out on the pad "—I came an awful long way to get here tonight. I'd really appreciate it if someone could give me a lift back."

On his mind was the little lab in the Everglades. Venom had clearly found whatever the other group of mercenaries was involved with. With that little matter attended to, he would surely head back up to the 'Glades, to the lab, and to the Lizard, in an attempt to finish his business there as well. And unless Spider-Man was there to stop him . . .

In the small, quiet stuffy room in the little lab building, Curt Connors stood over an apparatus, waiting for its little chime to go off. "This is it," he had said to Fischer about an hour before. "It has to be. It can't be anything else."

Fischer was glad enough to hear it. He had little liking for, or patience with, scientists. They all knew too much. Stuff that might backfire on you somehow—or stuff that they might find a way to use against you, if you didn't watch them all the time. That his boss was a scientist as well made his job no easier. He always had to be careful, when dealing with him, to conceal his basic dislike and distrust of the species. And truly, it was no business of his who employed him, just so long as he got paid. For his own part, Fischer was careful to be conscientious about his work, to deliver what he promised, and to make sure that whatever happened, whether his boss's doing or his own, he didn't get caught at anything.

The subject was on his mind at the moment, since this particular project was rapidly approaching the get-away-and-don't-get-caught-at-anything stage. This place, having served its purpose, was ready to be destroyed so that the project and the organization could move on. Unnecessary personnel would be offloaded, and Fischer would likely go on to another job.

He felt eyes on him and glanced up to see Connors favoring him with an expression that was mostly loathing.

"So?" Fischer said. "Is it ready?"

"A few minutes," Connors said. "One thing, though. Before the insertion, I want this out." He held out his lone arm.

Fischer glanced at the arm, noting the nearly healed scar where the implant chip had gone in. He laughed a little and shook his head. "Oh, no. I haven't had any orders to that effect from upstairs. Besides—" he glanced at the machine "—what if it doesn't work? What if the insertion makes you crazy? What if you get out of control and start trashing the joint? I need some way to manage you. No," Fischer said, "that's my little insurance policy. Just in case you get any—" his eyes narrowed slightly "—funny ideas, when your cure starts to take—*if* it starts to take."

"You," Connors said, "are a lot too fond of control."

Fischer laughed. They had been over this ground before, and he had to admit he enjoyed it. Connors showed his wounds so openly. "It's all about control, in the end," Fischer said. "People are just animals, after all. Some of them more so than others." The pained look on Connors's face amused him; it was amazing, how some people just couldn't bear the truth. "Your little accident just made that side of you more accessible, revealed the truth, whether you like it or not. Like everybody else, you need a hand on the leash."

Connors turned away from the mercenary. "It doesn't matter," Fischer said jovially. "For the first time now, because of the implant, there's a little control over what you do when you change. So if we choose to manage the Lizard a little bit when he makes his appearances, what's it to you? You wouldn't be able to manage what he does at all. At least we've kept you from killing anybody. You should thank us. I'd think your tender humanistic sensibilities would suffer terribly from something like that. And if we can make use of your changes for our cause—a little cash here, a few weapons there, while you're running around the landscape with your scales on, destroying things—what does it matter? It's all going toward your cure, anyway. Without our protection, and our money, you wouldn't be able to afford the facilities you need for all your little experiments. And the Boss wouldn't have been able to offer you that hydrogel. He wouldn't be able to get you any more of it, either, after you lost the last batch. Careless of you."

Connors turned back and scowled at him. "It wasn't exactly my choice," he said. "I was trying to run away. Somebody wanted me to stay and fight Spider-Man, to see what would happen—a little casual entertainment for a slow night, as far as I can tell. You brought it on yourself, and made sure that your lovely Boss thought it was my fault."

"Control," Fischer said, and shrugged, and smiled. "We were still working on the retinal readout, trying to clear the pictures up, for later jobs that'll matter more. If you don't like it, you can leave—or try to. But if you leave, what happens to your cure, if this doesn't work? And we're going to need you for a while yet. The organization has a lot of needs."

"Like threatening Space Shuttles?" Curt said bitterly.

"Oh, what's a shuttle or two? The astronauts won't be hurt—they'll have plenty of time to get out. What's in the Shuttle, our people will probably be able to pick up. A nice bonus, since the real business tonight is further south. If they don't get it, well, they'll still have done their job. Every police, Coast Guard, and Air Force unit in this part of the state will be over there. No one'll have time for something happening out in a swamp when Cape Kennedy is being overrun by 'bad guys.'" He laughed.

He couldn't make anything of the look Connors gave him then, but Fischer had better things to do than psychoanalyze half-sane scientists. The machine made a soft *ding* then, and Connors bent down beside it, opened the little ultrasound compartment, and took out a small cylindrical flask of amber liquid. He looked at it, held it up to the light. The expression on Connors's face shifted to something Fischer could understand: fear. *He's afraid it won't work. Or that it will, and that he'll still be bound to us afterwards.*

His problem . . .

"Where's the medium?" Connors said.

"Just a moment." Fischer went into the next room, tapped in the combination to the lab's small safe, opened its door, and took out the little metal box. He brought it back in to Connors, opened the box. A small piece of hydrogel, a cube maybe half an inch across, lay there. Connors took a pair of tweezers and lifted the hydrogel onto a glass plate, put it into the microwave, and gave it a minute on full.

Fischer looked at him curiously. He knew perfectly well that microwaves couldn't affect this stuff any more than anything else did. "Sterilizing it," Connors said, catching the look. "Be a shame to have the cure work and then get blood poisoning from a chance germ floating by."

"You sure it'll take that?" Fischer nodded at the liquid in the flask. "You haven't tested it before—"

"Oh, it'll absorb it," Connors said absently, peering at the rotating table in the microwave. "The molecular structure of the serum is built to exploit the structure of the hydrogel. It'll lock into it and then disseminate molecule by molecule when it's implanted, and the fluid pressure around it goes positive."

Fischer frowned. "Like one of those time-release nicotine patches, huh?"

"Very like. The problem in the past—" it was surprising how dry Connors's voice went suddenly, when the man himself had so many times been the main subject of the experiment "—has always been with the dosage strategy. Even metered microdosages have been too high. This one, though, will come on demand from serum blood levels."

The microwave chimed. Connors took out the hydrogel on its plate, took a pipette from a rack on his worktable, slipped it into the cylinder of serum, put his thumb over the top, and lifted an inch or so of serum from the container.

Fischer watched with some slight interest. It was odd, the way it looked. The serum didn't so much flow out of the pipette as seem to be abruptly sucked out of it, and the hydrogel went instantly from smoky gray to smoky gold.

Connors looked satisfied, showed just a ghost of a smile. "Now that," he said, "is a good chemical affinity." He looked at Fischer.

"All right," Fischer said, and got ready for his part of this business. He was an able enough battlefield medic, having cut and stitched back together a good number of people under circumstances a lot more adverse than this. Connors took off his lab coat, sat down and pushed up the sleeve of his shirt, then pulled over a bottle of Betadine surgical scrub and wet a cotton pad from it. He spent about thirty seconds rubbing his upper arm with the yellowy stuff, from the point of the shoulder to the middle of the biceps, and used the last stroke of the pad to mark a line about half an inch below the shoulder's point, an inch and a half long, down to the center of the biceps. "Right there," he said to Fischer. "That long. Half an inch deep. Any longer, or deeper, and you might hit the brachial nerve—and mess up another site for your damn implant, if it has to be changed later."

Fischer nodded. From a nearby tray, he laid out a small surgical kit while Connors anesthetized his arm.

Fischer picked up the scalpel. Connors averted his eyes while Fischer worked. Fischer smiled to himself. *Typical, that someone who in his time had caused so much bloodshed and mayhem didn't like looking at his own blood.* With very little ado, Fischer pulled the edges of the wound apart with one hand, and with the other picked up the hydrogel with the sterile tweezers from the suture pack and slipped it into the incision, seating it. A moment later he pushed the wound edges back together again, close enough to start suturing the muscle proper, and began to close. Connors shivered once, hard, as the hydrogel went in, then sat still again as Fischer stitched.

"Anything?" Fischer said.

"No," Connors said, "just reaction to being cut." But there was something in his voice that made Fischer wonder about that. He got busy with the epidermis, meantime looking around the room to see where exactly he had put the control box for the implant chip. He had seen Connors mistime his estimates of change before.

Fischer finished his needlework, knotted the last knot, and cut the last black silk suture off close. Then he got up and went to find the control box.

Connors sat shivering. Fischer was not at all sure about the way he looked. *Could he be having some kind of reaction to the hydrogel?* Fischer wondered.

Connors was ashen. Then the shivering seemed to pass off, and Fischer smiled to himself. *Maybe it's just fear,* he thought, and turned away.

Then he heard the roar . . .

he Blackhawk chopper rode low over the 'Glades, followed by a trail of noise from distraught birds and the occasional bellowing alligator.

Through the front window, leaning between the pilots' seats, Spider-Man watched the moonlit landscape pour by. He said, or rather shouted, to the pilot, "How far does rotor noise travel on a quiet night like this?"

The pilot shouted back, "Oh, in flat terrain like this, maybe a mile and a half, two miles."

"Okay. I'd sooner the people I'm going to meet didn't hear me coming, if it's all the same to you. You suppose you could drop me—" Spidey peered out through the windshield "—oh, about two miles north of here?"

"Mister Spider-Man, sir," the pilot shouted, "my boss told me to drop you on the moon, if you said you wanted to go there. Hoped you wouldn't. I'm due for a lunch break in another hour or so."

"Thanks. You're a pal."

"You could," said the pilot, "tell me one thing before you go."

"Sure."

He eyed Spider-Man's costume. "Don't you find that a mite inappropriate for this climate?"

Spidey laughed. "Brother, you said a mouthful. But I left my tux at home."

The pilot chuckled. Several minutes later, he was lowering the chopper gingerly above a small reed island. "I'm not real eager to set this thing down," he shouted, "on account of I'm not sure I can get her up again. You mind jumping?"

"*No* problem," he said, as another of the chopper's crew pulled the Blackhawk's door open. "Thanks a lot!"

"Our pleasure, sir. You watch yourself out there, now. There's things out there with a lot of teeth."

"You don't know the half of it," Spidey said, waved, and jumped down into the wind-flattened reeds.

The chopper leaned into a turn and headed south again.

Spidey crouched where he landed until the plant life began to stand up around him again; when they did, he did, too, and looked around. He thought he had his landmarks right. He recognized a pattern of smaller hammocks which he had identified as being about two miles south of the main one.

Spider-Man paused a second to put on Murray's little present, then he got moving. It really had been a long night. He was having trouble summoning up the energy he wanted, but there was nothing he could do about the problem except just keep bounding along at his best pace.

Within a matter of a few minutes, he was distracted by the sight, in the viewer, of a bright, swift, man-shaped figure, with pseudopodia streaming off it and helping it along as it made its way from island to island about a quarter-mile ahead of him. He went after it. It would be pleasant, Spidey thought, to be able to surprise Venom for a change, instead of the other way around.

Spider-Man made his way as silently across the uneven terrain as he could. There was, unfortunately, no surprise. As he got within about a hundred yards, he saw Venom's head come up and look toward him suddenly, and his jaws open in a huge, fangy snarl.

Venom paused, crouching, and Spider-Man caught up with him and stopped at a safe distance—if there was any such thing. Spidey would have preferred half a continent or so. Venom opened his mouth to speak.

"Congratulations," Spider-Man interrupted.

This was not what Venom had apparently been expecting. He looked at Spidey and said, "Good news travels fast, we take it."

"I don't think it's all that good for everyone," Spider-Man said, "but I do know what you stopped them from doing. The Coast Guard said to say thank you—off the record, of course."

Did that smile get just a little bit less dreadful? Hard to tell. "They're welcome, we're sure. But we have other business to attend to, now."

"Venom," Spider-Man said, "will you for God's sake listen to me, just this once? Curt Connors is not to blame here. These people have been using him."

Venom started moving again. "Life uses us all," he said, "for its own purposes. If Connors has been used, what better reason to set him free—once and for all."

"And what about his wife?" Spidey said, going along with Venom, matching his pace, though still at a distance. "And his son? His innocent son?"

They made their way along in silence for a few seconds. "It is unfortunate," Venom said finally, "but—"

"It's not just unfortunate," Spider-Man said bitterly. "If you defend the innocent, you have to defend *all* the innocent. You can't pick and choose the ones you like better than the others. What about that young boy, who wants to be a scientist like his dad? What about what his life will become if Curt dies? Think about it. That will be on your conscience, your fault. Not some abstract tragedy. *You* will have caused that."

"The greater good—" Venom began.

"It's an excuse!" Spider-Man shouted angrily, panting a little—the long night was beginning to tell on him. "It's a reason not to think, not to take the responsibility, to say 'I don't care about what's right, I want to do what I feel like!' This is a boy who could do anything, be anything, if his father lives—even if Curt never comes home, that hope will be with William for years. If you kill his father, you snuff that out. You end two lives. Murder, plain and simple. One of them is the victim of an accident that's gone on and on—tragic, yes, but not a criminal. The other is an innocent. Dead at your hands, if not physically, then in essence. And you can't ignore it. Kill Curt, and you betray everything you claim to stand for. What are you going to tell your people back in San Francisco about that?"

Venom said nothing, just kept going.

"I'm not going to let you kill him," Spider-Man said. "I'm going to stop you whatever way I can. I may die doing it, but *you are not going to kill Curt Connors.*"

It took about another ten minutes for them to reach the hammock. They stopped about a hundred yards from it, looked it over. The first words that Venom said, then, were "It seems unusually quiet."

"I don't know for sure that they committed all their people to the two operations tonight," Spidey said. "I saw about seven, maybe eight people total at the Cape tonight."

"Is that device of yours any help?"

Spider-Man was trying to discover just that. He fiddled with controls. "No," he said, "it's going to be hard to tell until we get inside the hammock, and maybe not even then. The whole place is radiating at about a hundred and five degrees—it whites out anything less." He shook his head. "We should go in."

"If we find Connors—" Venom said then, looking at Spider-Man blank-eyed.

"I'm warning you," Spider-Man said.

"If, however, we find the Lizard—"

"Venom, *don't*," Spider-Man said, meaning it.

Venom slipped past him and headed for the hammock.

Spidey went after. One after another they squeezed between the trees and worked cautiously inward. There was the lab, a little prefab building, temporary-looking. It had no windows, but through the viewer Spidey could see cracks where the heat was spilling out, indicating doors. "That way," he said to Venom, indicating the left side of the building, where there was a ground-floor door.

They started for it. And then they heard the roar. It echoed, and the right-hand side of the top of the building shook, shook once more, as something hit it. The roar scaled up to a scream.

Spider-Man and Venom looked at each other. Spidey pushed past Venom and made for the right side of the building, bypassing the stairway that went up the outside by shooting a web at the top of the building and hauling himself up. Venom came after.

Oh, please, Spider-Man said to whatever deity might be

handling the Everglades on the night shift, *please let me save something from this mess!* In his present state, after the night's events, he wasn't sure he could take Venom. But if he didn't, Venom would kill the Lizard, kill Curt, for sure.

Spider-Man pulled open the door at the top of the stairs. Its lock resisted him, so he pulled harder, enraged—yanked it right off its hinges, and flung the thing backward behind him, narrowly missing Venom, who was webbing up after him.

The hallway was empty. The source of the crashing and roaring was farther off to his right, through another door. Spider-Man looked both ways, saw no one, and headed for that closed door, hit it feet first, knocked it open and down.

Beyond it was chaos. He had only a second to take in the scene: scientific equipment smashed and trashed, everywhere shattered glass, twisted metal, the walls of the prefab structure itself deeply dented, here and there punched right through. Splashed liquid, overturned machinery, a slight chemical smell . . . No question but that this was yet another attempted cure for the Lizard gone wrong. And at the far end of the room, there was the Lizard himself, roaring, the desperate roar of a beast which does not want to be a beast, which once again suffers the curse of existence and can find no escape.

The Lizard saw Spider-Man. It flew at him, so fast he couldn't even jump aside. It grabbed him by the throat and flung him headfirst at the wall. Spidey tried to shoot out web and catch something so that he could stop himself, or at least turn. The web caught and adhered, but on a part of wall that had been weakened by blows, and broke loose. He only managed to turn himself enough to take the impact partially on his shoulder and neck, instead of head-on. He slid down the wall, nearly blacking out, trying desperately to stagger to his feet, feeling pseudopodia whip past toward the Lizard, but he could do no more than roll blearily over to at least see what was going on.

The Lizard swatted Venom's tendrils out of the air as fast as they came for him, then grabbed a great clawful of them and yanked Venom toward him. Off balance briefly, Venom stumbled—and the Lizard hit him a huge double-fisted blow in the side of the head. Venom staggered, and the Lizard picked him up as effortlessly as he had picked up Spider-Man, and threw Venom right at Spidey.

Spider-Man rolled over to try to protect his head, still woozy. Venom crashed down on top of him, slamming his head into the floor. The two of them lay there in a heap, while behind them the roaring went on and on, ever more loud and desperate. Spidey tried to rise but couldn't. He wondered whether he had broken something, or whether Venom had broken something of Spidey's on landing, and also bemoaned the Lizard's increased strength. This latest "cure" had apparently served only to make the Lizard more dangerous.

"Curt," he tried to croak, but he couldn't even speak. His vision was going dark around the edges, not that he could see much but a litter of black limbs and limp tendrils, trying and failing to rise. Venom stirred, then sagged, slumped again.

Oh, Curt! Spider-Man thought miserably, as his vision went completely. *Martha. I'm so sorry . . .*

And everything went away.

The sound of moaning intruded. Spider-Man tried to open his eyes and finally managed it.

He still lay on the floor with Venom on top of him. There was no telling how long he had been out. He tried again to push himself up, and this time had more success. Venom rolled partially off him. Unconscious? Dead? No telling.

Spidey managed to make it to his hands and knees. Venom rolled the rest of the way off him, to Spider-Man's right, and Spidey looked at him in concern. He didn't much like the idea of touching the symbiote, but nevertheless he put a hand to Venom's throat, felt for the pulse. It was there.

Just knocked out, then, he thought, and snatched his fingers away.

"Unnnhhh—"

A moan from off to one side. Spidey got to his knees,

looked around. Over there, sprawled against a wall, lay Curt Connors, human again. He looked terrible. He was ashen, and his arm was bleeding. "Curt," Spider-Man said.

Curt opened his eyes and looked at him, registering shock. He glanced up—

—and Spidey's spider-sense went off like someone banging a garbage can lid behind his head. He went straight up, straight for the ceiling—and it was just as well, because as he leapt, machine-gun bullets stitched the floor where he had been.

MJ woke up with terrible suddenness, and sat up in the bed in the hotel room, sweating, eyes wide, breathing hard. It had been an awful dream, involving Venom. That it had also involved the Cookie Monster was no help, though now that she was awake, she could not get rid of the memory of a voice saying, "Ooo, me impressed!" at the sight of Venom's teeth.

MJ found a smile somewhere and plastered it on, more out of reflex than anything else. She had been doing little but smile for the past few days. It was generally accepted that she was no good as the "pouty" sort of model. All the same, smiling was hard. She had not heard from Peter since fairly early yesterday evening, and at the moment that was bad news. He had promised to call her and check in but hadn't done so. She had resisted calling him, last night, as long as she could. Finally she had succumbed to the temptation, but to no avail. Her attempts to call his mobile phone had been rewarded with the sweet recorded Southern voice of the Bell Florida operator repeatedly saying, "I'm sorry, but the mobile you have called is turned off and does not have access to voicemail services. Please try again later."

"Why didn't I get him the voicemail?" she muttered as she got out of bed. It was still dark out. The bedside clock said *5:10*, or rather, *5:1C*, since the zero was missing a piece; it was that kind of hotel. Maurice's indecision had landed them here instead of the Marriott, and this place, the Splendide, was in a state which could best be described as "faded glory."

"Why am I up?" MJ said, fumbling her way into the bathroom. "What color is this wallpaper supposed to be? What's the meaning of life?"

No answers seemed forthcoming, but the shower was good and hot, and she got under it, washed her hair, and came out about ten minutes later, feeling at least human if not particularly beautiful, charitable, or intelligent. *Peter,* MJ thought, *where the heck are you?*

She had never learned to stop asking herself that question when there was likely to be no answer forthcoming. *Useless,* she thought. *And here it is oh-dark-thirty in the morning, and there's no room service in this dump, like there would be in the Marriott, and breakfast won't start for another hour and a half, like it would at the Marriott. Grr. At least there's a TV.*

MJ sat down on the bed in her towel, and flicked the TV on, getting the usual amount of early-morning snow from the local channels. There were numerous Pay-TV channels, but she flatly refused to watch any of the choices, ranging from ill-advised sequels to mindless action flicks. Cable was marginally better: at least there was the Weather Channel, the Landscape Channel, the Irish Channel, the Cuban Channel, the news channel, and the InfoMercial channel.

MJ flipped from the automotive arsonist, to a restful prairie landscape, to an Irish rural soap, to a lady talking very fast and demonstrating how to make a Cuban fried steak, to last night's sports scores. All these were relatively hopeless. Finally she settled on the Weather Channel and settled back to watch one of the nice people who worked one of the most intractable night shifts anywhere in broadcasting getting all excited about a big fat high which had positioned itself over Florida, and promised good weather for the Space Shuttle launch later this morning.

"The Shuttle," she muttered, "I can watch that, anyhow." The news network always watched the Shuttle launches pretty closely—or let you look at the thing standing on its pad, anyway, while it was getting ready to go. The sports update gave way, though not to news, but to a commercial about an exercise machine, being operated by a man who, if anything, needed to stop exercising and go out and get a life of some kind.

"Argh," MJ said, and got up and went to the window, or rather, the door. This was possibly the Splendide's only good point: it not only had windows that opened (relics of a time before air conditioning), but terraces you could go out and stand on to catch a breath of breeze, and the hotel was genuinely on the beach.

MJ went out and stood there, gazing out to sea. There was a three-quarter moon high up, and its light began to be visible out on the waves. The soft restful hiss of the water and its salt smell came up to her, and MJ breathed it in and sighed.

She looked down at the sand—and was surprised to see Maurice down there, walking along toward the waterline.

It was impossible not to recognize him. Maurice had a peculiar stumpy walk for someone who otherwise looked so tall and graceful. Apparently, according to the AD, it was because Maurice had actually had polio as a kid—one of the last cases, apparently, before it was almost completely stamped out. Or so people had thought then. Watching him, MJ breathed out unhappily at the thought that the disease was making a comeback. *Not good,* she thought. *People should do something.*

Meantime, what's Maurice doing out there at this hour of the morning? MJ thought. *He* hates *early. That's why we're not doing the launch, he said.*

He stopped where he stood on the beach. He just stood there for a minute, then there was a soft bloom of light at his feet. And again; and again, repeated.

He's got a flashlight. He's signaling someone.

Far away, in the pale moonlit dazzle of the water, MJ saw something move. A boat?

Suddenly MJ understood. Peter had told her about his own suspicions regarding that mess down south of the city, the other day. That boat out there could very well be tangled up in the same business.

And Maurice?

MJ swallowed hard. She didn't understand what his position was. She didn't know him at all well. Could he willingly be an accomplice of these people? Or had he perhaps been black-mailed into it somehow? He was always so nervous. He had been increasingly nervous about coming here. Like someone who expected something very bad to happen to him.

She heard her own voice suggesting to Peter that she would feed him to sharks, or to Venom. *Well, yes,* she told her accusing mind angrily, *he's a dreadful little overbearing power-mongering loathsome indecisive toad!*

Yeah, another part of her mind said, *so what? If that's something bad out there, do you want it to come ashore without the authorities doing anything? Do you really want Maurice to go to jail for something he might have, say, been blackmailed into?*

You don't know that's the case.

Look, said the back of her mind. *So you hate intuition. Fine. You don't have to take a position on it. Just go out there and stop what's happening. Get Maurice out of it and give him one more chance—a chance never to be stupid again, no matter what's happened to him. And cover for him, while you're at it. If those are bad people out there, make sure there are plenty of witnesses here that whatever happens now, it wasn't his fault.*

MJ slipped back into the hotel room, turned down the TV, and went over to the phone. She rummaged in the drawer of the bedside table for the yellow pages. In the front of the di-rectory, among the numbers for Fire and Police and Ambu-lance, there was also a Coast Guard number, toll-free and confidential, for people who thought they had stumbled into something nasty and wanted to stop it. MJ dialed the number.

"Good morning, confidential help line."

"Uh, yes. I think there are some people about to drop something, uh, questionable, off Cocoa Beach."

"Street address, please?"

"Uh—" She rummaged around the table for the hotel's stationery, and said, so as not to pin herself down, "Fifteen thousand block of Collins."

"Could you—"

"Nope," MJ said cheerfully, and hung up. She then threw clothes on as fast as she could—a T-shirt, shorts, flipflops—took her key, and ran out, locking the door behind her. She never even glimpsed the picture of the Space Shuttle appearing on the TV, or the banner that said "KSC attacked by Terrorists—Shuttle Launch Canceled" which spread itself across the screen. MJ was too busy running downstairs to ground level, out past the half-dozing desk clerk, and out the back of the hotel onto the beach.

Just on reaching the sand, MJ paused for a moment, took a deep breath, thought for a second. Then she took another deep breath and screamed, "*Maurice!*"

It echoed. She had never heard an echo at the beach before; it was impressive. Maurice turned as suddenly as if someone had shot him, and stared at her. *She would just be visible, silhouetted against the hotel doors and the light above them.*

Upstairs, she heard windows and a couple of doors open. This was the moment. "*Maurice!*" she shrieked again. "*I have had it with you, this shoot, this beach, this state, everything! I want to talk to you right now, and you are going to do some serious listening, or else I quit, and I'm going to sue, and then I'm going to the media, and Entertainment Tonight, and anyone else who'll listen, and I'm going to tell them how you've mistreated me and everybody else in this operation!*"

More windows opened. In fact, they started slamming open so fast, it sounded like automatic-weapons fire.

This should definitely be classified under "guilty pleasures," MJ thought. In her TV work, she had seen some world-class tantrums thrown. She had always, herself, felt scornful about the prima donnas who threw them. *Anybody who couldn't get what they wanted by quiet reasoned discussion and negotiation,* MJ thought, *was probably stuck at the mental age of three.* However—now visiting that age for the first time in a while—she had to admit it felt absolutely lovely.

Maurice stood frozen, staring at her. MJ threw her wet hair back, squared her shoulders, and marched over to him like an invading army. He looked completely astonished and very frightened, though MJ suspected that was an effect mostly due to the people out there in the boat.

"MJ—" Maurice said.

"No sweet talk!" MJ shouted, for it was indeed the first time he had called her that since the shoot began, having constantly called "Mary Ja-a-a-ane" in that nasal tone that drove her nuts. "You come inside *right now*, because we're going to have a little chat! Or else I can deck you right here where you stand, you insignificant little—" *Now, now,* said another voice inside her, which MJ suspected was the voice of Damage Control, *don't go overboard* "—little man!" She came down hard on the last word, as if it were insult enough. "Now get your butt in here!"

She turned and marched away.

Maurice stared, openmouthed—threw one glance out at the water, and then came after her.

From the floors above came a patter of applause, and the sound of subdued laughter and shutting windows.

They headed for the doors together. "And for pity's sake," she muttered to Maurice, "shove the flashlight down your pants or something. And afterwards, lose it."

They went in together, Maurice looking at MJ very strangely. So did the desk clerk, as they went by. MJ nodded to him as might a queen passing a minor courtier. She and Maurice got in the elevator together and went upstairs.

As the elevator doors closed, from outside, MJ faintly heard a sound she had heard several times over the past few days: the *whoop! whoop! whoop!* of a Coast Guard cutter out in the water, followed by the two-tone Miami police boat sirens, and the faint crackle of someone using a bullhorn.

There now, MJ thought. *All I have to figure out now is what the heck it is exactly that I'm going to say to Maurice.*

Many miles to the west, Spider-Man dropped from the ceiling again as machine-gun fire raked up toward him. "I don't even know you," he said, leaping for the wall, and clinging there somewhat uncertainly. The wall had buckled when the Lizard hit it last. "Why are you shooting at me?"

The man with the gun laughed nastily. "Breaking and entering?" He swung the gun toward Spidey again.

Spider-Man jumped again, for the other wall this time. Out the corner of his eye he saw Curt roll groaning under a fallen table, and he hoped it was enough protection. "I didn't have anything to do with the breaking," he said. "The entering, yes—"

He kept moving, though there wasn't much room to do it in. On the floor, Venom began to stir. The man with the gun glanced at him. *Guns,* Spidey corrected himself. The camouflage-clad mercenary had a weapon braced against each upper arm—one of them an Uzi, the second with a heavy power pack and an odd bell-like nozzle that Spidey didn't like the look of. The mercenary sprayed Venom with the machine gun, then made an annoyed face and shrugged when it had no effect—conscious or unconscious, the symbiote protected its master, though Spidey found himself wondering how long that condition might last.

Bullets ricocheted in all directions. *Enough of this*, Spider-Man thought, and shot a webline at the machine gun, yanked it out of the mercenary's grip, wrapped it up as useless, and dumped it behind some furniture. "Oh," the man said, and actually grinned as Venom too began to get to hands and knees, glared at him, and the symbiote began to reach out pseudopodia in his direction. The mercenary pulled the trigger of the other gun.

Spider-Man's eyes widened and he froze as a knife of sound went straight through his head, from one ear to the other. He could feel it, a horrifying sensation, as physical as a blade. His muscles stopped working, and he fell off the wall and lay there in excruciating pain, unable even to writhe. Venom fell over sideways too, and a horrible high shrilling filled the air. The symbiote, always susceptible to sonics, stripped itself partially away from Eddie Brock's body in a tangle of blind writhing tendrils, whipping around, desperate to escape and unable to, withering in the screeching torrent of sound.

Another sound began to cut through the racket. For a moment Spider-Man, dazed and blinking, having trouble even seeing, let alone moving, thought it was the weapon again. But it was not. It spoke.

"No," it said, in a low roar. And "No!" again, and furniture rattled and crashed as it was pushed aside at the end of the room, and a figure rose up there. Six feet tall, Spidey thought dazedly. Green. Scales. Tail. But mostly teeth, at the moment. They flashed, and the tongue inside them fought to make words, and the eyes above them narrowed, looking at the mercenary.

"Stop—it—Fischer," the voice said—a terrible tangle of Curt Connors's voice, the Lizard's old voice, and the hiss of something more ancient, more dreadful, the voice of the serpent. Fischer, if that was the man's name, stood still for a moment, staring in surprise at the clawed forearm it held out for him to see. The back of it was terribly torn, perhaps by gunfire, and the edges of what seemed an old scar showed above and below the torn place. Spidey wanted to moan just at the sight of it. But why did the Lizard look—pleased?

"Come on, Connors," he said. "They're helpless. They'll be dead in a minute. Let's get out of here—the Boss has work for us."

"No," the Lizard said, and tossed the furniture aside, and made slowly for Fischer. He may have been suffering from the sonics, but not so much as Spidey and Venom were. *Then again,* Spider-Man thought, still very dazed, *lizards don't depend a lot on hearing, by and large.*

"They came here to kill you!" Fischer yelled, starting slowly to back toward the door. "Finish them and come on!"

Spider-Man tried to get up on hands and knees but couldn't even manage that. His nerves and muscles seemed to be refusing to answer him. The shrieking of the symbiote was getting more deafening all the time, heading for crescendo. Spidey wasn't sure how long it could survive this onslaught.

"They—did not," the Lizard said, struggling to get the words out; he glanced at Spider-Man as he passed, stepped over him, and headed for Fischer. "He—did not."

"But, Venom!" Fischer yelled, still backing up. "He thinks you're an animal, a nut—he's a monster, kill him!"

"I doubt he is—so—simplistic," the Lizard said. Spider-Man tried to roll over again, feeling that he wanted to either cheer or weep. That was certainly Curt's voice showing through there, and Curt's words forcing their way through the saurian throat. "Venom—might kill me for his own reasons—but he would not—think me an—animal, Fischer. As you have. As you—have taunted me—again and again—even when in manshape—with being really the animal, and humanity—just a disguise. As you wear—yours, Fischer. Just—a disguise."

Fischer backed up a couple of feet more. The Lizard reached out claws to him. Fischer ducked back from them but didn't see until too late, and couldn't avoid, the huge sharp tail which came lancing around from the side and knocked the weapon out of his hands, smashing it against the wall. Immediately the horrible shrilling of the symbiote stopped, its many twisting strands fell back toward Brock's body and started to reunite, consolidating once again into the costume. Venom stirred, moaned.

"You're crazy!" Fischer screamed. "They're here to kill you!"

"They—made—no such attempt," the Lizard said, still advancing while Fischer backed away. "You, however—have made—your intentions plain." He glanced over his shoulder, saw Spider-Man getting to his feet again, saw Venom rolling over to get onto hands and knees. "You had better—get out—while there are still only—two of us, who are—prepared to deal with you humanely. The third—will not trouble—"

Venom staggered to his feet, threw a most bemused look at the Lizard, who returned it. Spider-Man swore he saw the two of them nod to each other. Then Venom turned his attention to Fischer. He opened his mouth and grinned with every fang. The symbiote's tongue flicked out.

Fischer turned and fled. Spider-Man, still weak, went after him. As he stumbled through the doorway, he saw Fischer slap a hand down on a control box in the next room, then throw himself out the door and go pounding down the stairs.

His spider-sense stung him hard, and he saw the glimmer of an LED in the next room, saying, *6 . . . 5 . . . 4 . . .*

"Get out," he yelled at the other two, "it's a bomb, come on!" Behind him Spider-Man got a confused image of movement, but he didn't linger to see who went where. In a situation like this it was every man, lizard, or symbiote/human team for him- or theirself. He dove out the door, the way Fischer had gone, and got the briefest glimpse of the man making quite literally for the tall timber, slipping through the trees.

Life went white. The blast caught Spidey in the back and threw him at the trees, but it propagated fast enough to catch the trees, too, and throw them out in front of him. He was dumped headfirst into a morass of moss, mud, and water, and the air whined above him as cypress wood and ripped-up orchids and pieces of prefab architecture went flying by at speeds which would normally have required filing a flight plan. The thunder of the explosion died away after a few seconds, and for the second time that day, it rained on Spider-Man. Not clean water, though, but mud and muck and leaves and more moss and slime and bugs and freshwater leeches, and finally some very surprised frogs.

After a few moments which he spent trying to sort out the

ringing in his ears from the ringing silence that followed the explosion, Spider-Man staggered to his feet again and started back toward where the building had been. There was precious little of it left, or, for that matter, of the rest of the hammock in which it had been secreted. Where it had stood was mostly a large hole, rapidly filling with water.

He cursed silently. *The odds of a normal person surviving that—*

Except that none of us are all that normal.

"Spider-Man," said a voice behind him.

He turned.

"Curt?"

The Lizard dropped his lower jaw in the closest approximation of a grin. "Not—for long," he said painfully. "This—won't last. A temporary effect. The last dose of serum—it was—" The Lizard fought with his breath for a moment, or perhaps with something else.

"Never mind," he said. "The hydrogel—helped a little to slow the release, but—still dosage problems—" He gasped. "Slipping now. Spider-Man—Martha, William."

"I'll take them a message," Spidey said.

"Tell them I—love them, but I—can't come home now. So close, I'm so close—just this lucid moment between states is—such a stride." He struggled for a few breaths during which nothing came out of his throat but growls, and Spider-Man wondered whether the Lizard would go for his throat again. But the Lizard shook his head, gathered his strength again. "But it won't last. There are—probably side effects from the—neural control chip they had implanted in me, when they—sent me out to make—distractions for thefts." He lifted the torn arm. "Atypical hyperstimulation and—paleotrophic myelin regeneration, I'd guess. A—good turn—they didn't mean to do. But it's a once-off effect. Will—have to reconstruct, now, do it all over. Tell them I can't come back. Not until I'm well—"

"Curt," Spider-Man said, "believe me. They wouldn't care

whether you were well or not. Just go home. Let me help you—please."

The Lizard shook his head sadly, wearing an expression like a dinosaur contemplating extinction. "Home. Oh, I want to go home, and just be me, with them—"

His face twisted suddenly out of shape. The eyes went utterly saurian—but flickered back into human expression again. "Not much—time now," the Lizard said, infinitely sad. "I love them—oh, I love them. The most important thing. Never said it enough—now it seems like all I say, all I think, when I can speak—" The sheer pain in the voice choked it, turned it into a moan, then the moan turned into a roar—

Spider-Man ducked as the claw swiped out at him. When he straightened, all there was to be seen was a scaled, shining form, loping away into the paling night, under the declining moon. As it went, it roared, like a wounded thing, and there were tears in the roar.

Spidey stood still and watched him until he was out of sight, his eyes burning.

After a while he moved around the explosion site again and spent half an hour or so looking for any sign of Venom. There was none. *The symbiote is probably recovering from that sonic whammy,* Spider-Man thought. Venom was probably thrown in the other direction and decided to get out and recoup his strength somewhere quiet. *Until he can get at me later,* Spidey thought, *or the Lizard, or both of us.*

But he couldn't quite forget that strange look that Venom and the Lizard had exchanged: the "animal" and the "monster" sharing their humanity for a moment in the face of the inhuman human threatening them both.

Not a bad way to start the day, Spider-Man thought, and sighed. He made his way out past the shattered stumps of the cypresses, into the open Everglades, and looked east, where the false dawn was slowly becoming true. Then, under the mask, he acquired a slow smile, reached into the pouch under his costume, and pulled out his phone to make a call.

TWELVE

He knocked on the door of the hotel room.

It opened. Vreni looked at him, and her eyes widened. She said, "Where have you been?! I've been calling your mobile, but you had it turned off—"

Peter handed her a yellow manila envelope and held up a finger. "Don't say anything," he said, "until you look at them."

Vreni shut her mouth, though plainly it was an effort. She sat down at the table by the window, opened the envelope, and her mouth opened again, and stayed that way, as she started going through the prints.

"My God," she said. "My *God*." And she turned over a couple more of them, and then stopped at the one which Peter considered the prize of the collection, the bomb going off in the Sound Suppression tank, water leaping in the air all over, while in the background Spider-Man looked down from high above, on the gantry. Vreni looked up at him and said, "How did you do this? Do you channel for Eastman's ghost or something? We've got to get these on the wire. Do you know how much the Associated Press is going to pay you for these? How did you *get* these?"

"That Questar," Peter said, in sincere misdirection, "is a terrific piece of equipment."

Vreni looked at him with an expression of profound skepticism. "All right," she said. "I won't ask you how you get these, if you won't ask me about the half-track in Bosnia."

"I thought it was an armored personnel carrier," Peter said.

Vreni snorted. "Never believe the first version of a story."

"So," Peter said "where are you with yours? Did Kate like it?"

"Oh yes," Vreni said, and to Peter's astonishment, she looked sour. "She says she wants to send me to England, to look into the collapse of another merchant bank. Damn overseas assignments! I don't want foreign muck. I want to stay here and rake good old-fashioned star-spangled muck!"

"Yell at her," Peter said mildly. "She likes that."

"I know. Bad habit. She got it from Jameson." Vreni sighed then, and sat down a moment, starting to go through her purse, hunting something. "But we made good connections on this one. The German government has apparently started an inquiry of Gottschalk's bank. I finally caught up with him," she said. "Did I mention that?"

"Not since we talked last."

"Yes. Took me hours and hours to find him, but when we finally met, he seemed most eager to talk. Something to do with someone he'd seen before me. He wouldn't say who."

Peter raised his eyebrows. He had his own ideas about who that might be.

"Meanwhile, the feds are starting a RICO investigation of CCRC's doings down here," Vreni said.

"You don't look pleased."

"They should have done this on their own, six weeks ago," Vreni said, sounding disgusted, "after the New York craziness started to surface. What were they waiting for, an engraved invitation?" She came up with a soft-tip pen from her purse and started indicating crop marks at the edges of the photographs. "They'll go into more depth this time, or they'll look really stupid.

"But, my gosh," Vreni said, sounding more satisfied, "what a haul of stuff, down on the south coast. That ink! Do you know how much that stuff is worth? The story's a bombshell. Ripples are spreading all over, in Europe. Corruption in Brussels! Government collaboration with racketeering in Germany! It's a long way yet to the bottom of this can of worms." Her eyes shone.

"Wait a minute. Don't Brussels and Germany count as 'foreign muck'?"

"Well, yeah, but—" Vreni put aside a print and eyed the next one. "Anyway, the followups on this story alone are going to keep me busy for weeks. The boondoggling in NASA alone is worth a Sunday supplement." She glanced at him, amused. "Still no telling," she added, "what was going on with that reactor."

"Oh?"

Vreni shook her head. "Can't get a straight answer out of them at the moment. They're claiming that the rumors of difficulties with the security, and the supposed change of reactors, was all part of some kind of cover operation, meant to draw these terrorists who hit the place the other night out into the open. Naturally everybody's so horrified by what almost happened on the pad that no one's asking the hard questions. Give it a couple of weeks, though, and once everyone gets over being relieved for the astronauts' sake, the gloves will come off."

Peter nodded, wondering who had manufactured this particular story. He rather suspected that the change in names from CHERM to MPAPPS had had more to do with good old-fashioned misdirection, and a piece of vital "test material" going missing. He had not pressed Garrett very far on the subject, and he had an idea she wouldn't have told him if he had. "What about the Lizard angle?"

Vreni sighed. "We wasted so much time on that," she said. "I wish we hadn't bothered. What he was doing, involved in small-time thefts, I can't imagine. He seems to have vanished again, though. A blind alley. In retrospect, I wish we could have spent that time at Canaveral."

Good, Peter thought. *I'd rather leave Curt out of all of this and spare him—and Martha and William—the grief.*

She finished with the photos. "Well," Vreni said, "these are really nice. Should make you a tidy little fee from AP after the *Bugle* gets its cut. Nobody else has anything so immediate or detailed." She glanced sidewise at him. "Come on, let's get down to the bureau. Then—" She looked closely at him. "Look at those circles under your eyes! Haven't you been sleeping?"

"Well," he said, "last night was a little long."

"I know the feeling. Come on, let's go start getting you rich and me famous."

"Promises, promises."

"If promises are all that life offers you, kid," Vreni said as they headed out, "grab 'em and shake 'em till they squeak. They're better than nothing."

Fairly late that afternoon, as sunset was lengthening the shadows in the Connorses' back yard, a tall shape in red and blue swung down on a web from the nearest telephone pole and landed softly in the well-trampled grass. Quietly he slipped up to the patio doors and knocked.

A head poked around into the living room from the kitchen. "Spider-Man!"

"Hey, William! Is your mom around?"

"Yeah, come on in."

A few minutes later, Spidey was ensconced in the living room again. "No tea, Martha," he said, "thanks. It's a flying visit only."

"You mean swinging," William said, grinning.

Martha was wearing a smile for her guest, but it didn't quite reach her eyes. "You've seen Curt," she said.

"I've seen the Lizard," Spidey said, "and talked with him, yes."

"Talked with him?"

He told them the story, with some discreet editing. "He was very definite," Spider-Man said, "that his condition as the Lizard right now wasn't going to last; it was an accidental conjunction of temporary effects. When the Lizard appears again, it will just be the mindless beast again. But at the same time—he felt he was getting very close to the cure, closer than he'd ever been. He said he just couldn't come home until he was well. I don't think he believes it would be fair to you."

Martha looked at Spider-Man silently. "We don't care about fair," she said. "Either of us."

"I think he knows that. I know he knows you just want him

home. In fact, I told him that. He said to tell you he loves you, he wants to be home with you, just as himself, but right now, he simply can't. He says he has to go back to the work."

Martha sighed and glanced at William, who was intently examining the carpet. "Where will he go now?" she said. "Did he say?"

Spidey shook his head. "I have no idea. Martha, I have nothing concrete to base it on, but I get the feeling that Curt's involved in something much larger than the business of his own cure. I wouldn't know where to start looking, at the moment, but after I have a while to consider, I may be able to think of something. I'll let you know if I find out anything at all."

"You've already done a great deal for us," Martha said. "Don't let it interfere with your proper work."

"This *is* my proper work," Spidey said.

William glanced up at him then. His face was quite calm and composed, but his eyes were too bright and he sounded stuffed up when he spoke. "When he was human," William said, "how did he sound?"

Spider-Man thought of the voice that had so briefly forced its way through the Lizard's throat—dignified, powerful even in such tragic circumstances, and able to see something worthwhile even in Venom—and bent the truth ever so slightly. "He sounded just fine," he said. "Curt Connors is alive and well, never doubt it. And he'll be back."

He looked up to find Martha's eyes on him. They said, *Really?*

All he could do was nod and believe, with Martha and William, that it would be true.

That evening, Peter sat with MJ over the dinner table in his hotel, and listened to her bubble over. It was the best possible salve for his aches and pains, both mental and physical.

"So he offered me a hundred percent raise," MJ said.

"After you spent an hour and a half telling him off," Peter

said, hunting around in his salad for the tomatoes. He always ate them first. "He must have been frightened for his life."

MJ chuckled. "Tiger, I think he was. From me, I mean, as opposed to those other people. I haven't blown up at anybody like that since— Wow, I don't know if I've ever blown up at anybody like that."

"All those years' worth of frustration at once. I'd pay money to see it."

"Be careful," MJ said, smiling sweetly, "or someday you may get a demonstration, free. I found it very liberating."

"I bet. So what about him, then?"

"Well, the cops and the Coast Guard picked up the people who'd made him set up the drop."

"So Murray told me," Peter said, "when I brought him his widget back."

"Yeah. Maurice told me later that he'd been having dealings with the smugglers on and off for a long time, under cover of the agency, and that he was tired of it but didn't dare stop. Now, though, he can take advantage of the city's witness protection plan. They'll get him out of the area and see him set up somewhere else in the country. He'll be okay. He was pretty grateful, actually."

"That's a relief. So where do you go next?"

"Nowhere." She smiled.

"Today was the last day?"

"Uh-huh. And then I'm going home with you—when was it the *Bugle* booked your flight for?"

"Tomorrow. They're pleased, apparently—Kate says she has something else in the pipeline she wants me to work on, which suits me fine. But MJ, if there's more work here for you, you should—"

"No. Honey, this is no kind of life, you running all over the landscape, and me doing the same, and us never being together. The agency down here will refer me to some of their correspondent agencies and former clients up in New York.

We'll see what that brings. But I'd rather starve with you than make tons o' bucks without you."

"We might starve yet," Peter said. "Granted, these AP royalties are nice, and the next couple of months will be okay because of them. But later in the year—"

"Let's see what the future brings," MJ said. "Finish your salad. I want my main course, and the nice lady is waiting for you to stop fiddling. Are you ever going to eat those greens?"

Peter smiled and applied himself to what remained after the tomatoes were gone. After the waitress took their plates, he found MJ looking at him speculatively. "So what did he have to say for himself?" she said.

"Who?"

"That boy with the big teeth. You remember the one."

Peter raised his eyebrows. "He was argumentative," he said, "but we parted friends."

"Oh, I believe *that*!" A steak arrived, which MJ promptly started to demolish. "Tell me another."

Peter shrugged. "He didn't bother trying to kill me after Curt took off," he said, "so either he's decided to let me be for a while longer, or he got killed in that blast."

"I don't believe the second in the slightest," MJ said. "As for the first—I don't trust his reasons."

"I don't know if I trust them either," Peter said, "but I think Curt shamed him into it, somehow. It was an odd moment— but I'm glad I saw it."

"Question is," MJ said, "how long will it last?"

Peter shook his head, then reached out across the table to take her hand. "I don't know. And I have a feeling that whatever Curt's tangled up in is going to resurface eventually, more complicated than ever. But for the moment—"

"For the moment," MJ said, squeezing his hand, "you're here. And I'm here. And tomorrow, we're going to say byebye to Aunt Anna, and catch a plane and go home and get on with our lives in a place with lower humidity. And I will be blessedly relieved! Now eat your pasta before it gets cold, or MJ will be very cross."

Peter looked at her and made an eager face. "Promise?"

Her smile promised a whole lot more.

Peter ate his pasta.

Diane Duane is the author of a score of novels of science fiction and fantasy, among them the *New York Times* hardcover best-sellers *Spock's World* and *Dark Mirror*, as well as the very popular Wizard fantasy series, and the previous Spider-Man novel *The Venom Factor*. *The Philadelphia Inquirer* has called Duane "a skilled master of the genre," and *Publishers Weekly* has raved, "Duane is tops in the high adventure business."

Duane lives with her husband, Peter Morwood—with whom she has written five novels, including the *New York Times* best-seller *The Romulan Way*—in a beautiful valley in rural Ireland. She has a third Spider-Man novel due in late 1996 and is hard at work on an X-Men hardcover.

Darick Robertson started working as a comics professional at the age of seventeen with his self-created and self-published comic *Space Beaver*. Since 1990, he has worked on *New Warriors, X-Factor, Cable, The Incredible Hulk*, and the *Spider-Man: The Final Adventure* miniseries for Marvel and *Superman* and *Justice League* for DC. He also helped design and create Malibu's Ultraverse characters, including *The Nightman, The Strangers*, and his own *Ripfire*.

SPIDER-MAN

__SPIDER-MAN: CARNAGE IN NEW YORK__ by David
    Michelinie & Dean Wesley Smith   1-57297-019-7/$5.99
Spider-Man must go head-to-head with his most dangerous enemy,
Carnage, a homicidal lunatic who revels in chaos. Carnage has been
returned to New York in chains. But a bizarre accident sets Carnage
loose upon the city once again! Now it's up to Spider-Man to stop
his deadliest foe. *A collector's first edition*

__THE ULTIMATE SPIDER-MAN__   0-425-14610-3/$12.00
Beginning with a novella by Spider-Man cocreator Stan Lee and Peter
David, this anthology includes all-new tales from established comics
writers and popular authors of the fantastic, such as: Lawrence Watt-
Evans, David Michelinie, Tom DeHaven, and Craig Shaw Gardner.
An illustration by a well-known Marvel artist accompanies each story.
Trade

__SPIDER-MAN: THE VENOM FACTOR__ by Diane Duane
    1-57297-038-3/$5.99
In a Manhattan warehouse, the death of an innocent man points to
the involvement of Venom—the alien symbiote who is obsessed with
Spider-Man's destruction. Yet Venom has always safeguarded
innocent lives. Either Venom has gone completely around the bend,
or there is another, even more sinister suspect.

® TM and © 1995 Marvel Entertainment Group, Inc. All rights reserved.

Payable in U.S. funds. No cash orders accepted. Postage & handling: $1.75 for one book, 75¢
for each additional. Maximum postage $5.50. Prices, postage and handling charges may
change without notice. Visa, Amex, MasterCard call 1-800-788-6262, ext. 1, refer to ad # 563

Or, check above books **Bill my:** ☐ Visa ☐ MasterCard ☐ Amex	
and send this order form to:	_____ (expires)
The Berkley Publishing Group	Card#_____
390 Murray Hill Pkwy., Dept. B	($15 minimum)
East Rutherford, NJ 07073	Signature_____
Please allow 6 weeks for delivery.	**Or enclosed is my:** ☐ check ☐ money order
Name_____	Book Total $_____
Address_____	Postage & Handling $_____
City_____	Applicable Sales Tax $_____ (NY, NJ, PA, CA, GST Can.)
State/ZIP_____	Total Amount Due $_____

All-New, Original Novels
Starring Marvel Comics'
Most Popular Heroes

__FANTASTIC FOUR: TO FREE ATLANTIS
by Nancy A. Collins   1-57297-054-5/$5.99
Mr. Fantastic, the Thing, the Invisible Woman, and the Human Torch—the Fantastic Four—must come to the aid of Prince Namor before all of Atlantis is destroyed by the fiendish Doctor Doom.

__DAREDEVIL: PREDATOR'S SMILE
by Christopher Golden   1-57297-010-3/$5.99
Caught in the middle of a battle over New York's underworld, Daredevil must combat both Kingpin, his deadliest foe, and Bullseye, a master assassin with a pathological hatred for Daredevil.

__X-MEN: MUTANT EMPIRE: BOOK 1: SIEGE
by Christopher Golden   1-57297-114-2/$5.99
When Magneto takes over a top-secret government installation containing mutant-hunting robots, the X-Men must battle against their oldest foe. But the X-Men are held responsible for the takeover by a more ruthless enemy...the U.S. government.

—COMING IN NOVEMBER 1996—
X-MEN: MUTANT EMPIRE: BOOK 2: SANCTUARY

® ™ and © 1995 Marvel Entertainment Group, Inc. All Rights Reserved.